The
Messenger
of
Magnolia Street

The
Messenger
~ of ~
Magnolia Street

A NOVEL

River Jordan

HarperSanFrancisco

A Division of HarperCollinsPublishers

THE MESSENGER OF MAGNOLIA STREET: *A Novel.* Copyright © 2006 by River Jordan. All rights reserved. Printed in the United States of America. No part of this book may be used or reproduced in any manner whatsoever without written permission except in the case of brief quotations embodied in critical articles and reviews. For information address HarperCollins Publishers, 10 East 53rd Street, New York, NY 10022.

HarperCollins®, 🏛®, and HarperSanFrancisco™ are
trademarks of HarperCollins Publishers.

Designed by Joseph Rutt

ISBN-13: 978—0—06—084176—8
ISBN-10: 0—06—084176—1

For my Aunt Kate—not a work of fiction at all but of flesh and bone and blood. Thanks for the bossin' and the biscuits and for that big bosom of love.

God is walking through Shibboleth, rummaging through the pockets of his memory, the distant past and the near future. The people of Shibboleth are sleeping, unaware of his presence or that he is considering them and their present circumstances.

He turns the corner of Magnolia and Main, observing that time has not passed well here but has come tearing its way along with such deceptive quietness that the people live unaware, tricked into silence. This isn't the way that the story of Shibboleth, keeper of an eternal key, was meant to unfold. Can one simple town be the keeper of something so precious you ask? And can that trust still stand when a hundred years have passed, have rolled their way along into the over and beyond? Well, that's what you're here to discover and what I'm here to write down, because I am the Recorder of all that ever was, is now, or is yet to come. *Tough job,* you say. Well, yes, of course, but then it's my created purpose until the end of—yes, here's that word of elusive comportment—time. But enough about me. Right now you don't know beyond this moment. Only that currently the town of Shibboleth has the smell of rotten eggs. Of secret stealth and things that move along wishing to be left alone. You would notice this if you traveled here. If you were walking down the street in the twilight hours of the evening, you would feel it under your skin, would look over your shoulder twice, possibly even three times, wondering if someone, or *something,* were following. And if you were fast enough on your feet, you might see a dark mist hovering above the ground like the breath of an unseen predator. Watch closely now, it's breathing in and out of the very ground, the very foundation of Shibboleth. An inky blackness that hovers and moves at will. *You* might see it but not the good citizens. As I told you, they are sleeping. In their spirits and in their minds. Some of them have forgotten that the dark passages of their childhood imaginings are relative and real. That their guarded treasure was the Key. The eternal fact that one hope, one dream, one falling wish is worth protecting. Of such simple things the world is made, and kept. In this clear fact, the good people of Shibboleth knew for certain who they were and what was meant to be. In a more distant past, all of Shibboleth knew this. Pilgrimages were made, one by one, or in hand-held groups, down a well-worn path where wild violets bloomed in the grass, to the repository of all their heart's well-worn desires, their spirits best-said prayers, the Well. Coin by coin they cradled wishes and cast them off, dropping them like falling stars into the clear spring water waiting. And in due season, when time passed into time, the dreams and wishes would manifest on the breath of their believing. And the Key was so well protected, so well kept, that the people breathed a heavy sigh of satisfaction, and rested. But their rest fell into a time of rest and then a time of forgetting.

Now look. I stand at the forgotten path, weed-eaten and over-grown. The Well now dry. And my wings tremble with so much loss, while time moves forward full of empty.

On the surface, Shibboleth is still very much the same as many small Southern towns you've driven through on your way to some-where else. There is a town square (more of a circle really) that holds Shibboleth City Hall, Kate's Diner, Zadok's Barbershop, Obie's Salon for Women, a Piggly Wiggly grocery, and on the far reaches of the square, the old PURE station, which has been closed now for many years. The post office is inside City Hall. There are no parking meters, and people can park and take care of business for as long as business takes.

In the middle of this circle is a large Heritage Oak tree. Shibboleth is full of oaks, water oaks and scrub oaks to name a few, but this one is the granddaddy of them all. It has an official plaque that tells how many wars it has survived and that it is so old it was here before America. In the minds of the people of Shibboleth, that's farther back than anyone needs to go.

From a low-flying hawk's eye, depending on the season, you can see fields of cotton and of corn, rows of beans, or rows of collards, mustard greens, and potatoes. But regardless of the season, what will strike you most is the sleepy patchwork pattern fashioned from the living essence of these kindred souls. You will hear people's voices rising on the air, their hands clapping with excitement at the telling of their stories, or the softhearted music of their listening to the stories of another. And on happy occasions, grand occasions, you will catch them buck-dancing until they are red-faced and breathless. I have watched this melody of life for more years than you've been steady on your feet. It is the dance of time.

The people in this small town are busy with the charms of contentedly raising their children, and their children's children, and with the ultimate blessing of divine grace, their children's children's children. One generation after the next gazing over their shoulders at children in the yards or up the trees, calling, "Not too far. Not too high." To the people of Shibboleth, children are the very essence, the future of their faith in everything everlasting and good to the last drop. They memorize the size of their hands, the smell of their sweaty hair, the expressions in their large, trusting eyes, their growing games and funny sayings. And they will tell the stories of their babydom till kingdom come.

The people's lives appear simple because they are, but not because the people are simpleminded. They are not. Not in the derogatory sense that people of prejudice might believe. They are simple out of ritual. Out of generations of placing one thing before the next. Taking things one step at a time. And from passing down the Key.

Do not be mistaken or misunderstand. More so, do not underrate them with any ill-conceived notions of what shape intelligence takes or how it sounds. They are wise, eagle-eyed, and quick. Sure-footed. And they will kill you if they have to. But that would be a hard thing. A terrible thing. Killing is not something they like, and war brings them to their knees in prayer. But they will protect their young and their own with a vengeance. Make no mistake about that.

If you should venture into Shibboleth, either on the road or in your dreams, notice this: when the people first meet you, they watch you very close even when they aren't looking. By instinct, they watch you and what comes out of your mouth. They see whether it falls to the ground and takes root or dances off with the dandelions. If they see that you are true of heart and bold of soul they will mark you *friend*. Then they will fight to protect you, too. To the last breath. It's their way. And their way is grafted in skin to skin, bone to bone, blood to blood, forever and ever and so on. The Protectors know their purpose.

Yes, the people of Shibboleth know their purpose, or more correctly, they once did. Lately, they have become lazy. They are not tuned in to the future but are looking back a long, long way and thinking yesterday is where they're standing. A muffled reality has settled upon them. Can you feel it? It's as if they are being suffocated in cotton candy. Waking and walking in a sticky sweet half-life, a sugar-coated coma. Good Lord, have mercy.

Now God has determined to wake them, one by one, and to call someone in particular to get a job done. This someone is a good boy a long way from home. I say a boy, but by now Nehemiah is all of thirty years, four months, three days, twelve hours, eleven minutes and counting. By all worldly standards a full-grown man, but to the people of Shibboleth, he's their boy. (They have a way of owning what they love.) A charmer he is. Has been since he was two. Has a way of pulling up a chair, straddling it, and holding court on an open porch or the diner floor. And he will tell stories far and wide, or so he once did. And the people would laugh and slap their knees and say, "Tell us another one, Nehemiah, tell us one more for the road." And he would gladly oblige. Grinning his you just gotta love him grin, the one that shows the dimple on the right side of his cheek, he'd rear back and say, "Just let me see," and then pull something from his repertoire as easily as a trick man pulls a rabbit from a hat. If they'd had a football team, he would have been their quarterback. If there had been a crowning, he would've been their prince. But Shibboleth was content for Nehemiah to simply be the apple of their eye, and for a long time so was he.

What a baby boy he was for so on and so long. Not a soul grew up more adored in this good town. Not a soul, I tell you. But then the curtains fell and twisted in such a way that Nehemiah couldn't, or wouldn't, stay, and he turned his back and headed off to a city with enough noise to stop the questions surfacing in the silence. Enough noise maybe to forget. Or at least blanket the remembering.

And so now what we are watching is the unfolding of the beginning. A simple chain of events, of causes and effects, that will render a change in Shibboleth. Just in time. No timetable on trust, you say? Ah yes, but even now I hear the ticking of an eternal Timeclock. It's telling me to move on.

There now. God's feet have reached the end of Magnolia Street, where Magnus lives with her fourteen cats (although she claims only seven). She mumbles in her sleep, stretching out her big feet, lets out a snort of sorts, and two cats move along her side to resettle themselves among their brothers. But it isn't Magnus that God is seeking but Trice (which rhymes with rice) who lives with her in spite of all the good-sense reasons not to. Trice helps Magnus, and for this, well, it's hard to say what she will get, although others say she'll surely get to heaven for caring for the ornery old hen.

God smiles when he hears this, people determining in advance what deeds might usher someone into the Light or what cancels out all possibility of their entry. *Scorekeepers,* he calls them.

God says, "Wake up, Trice," and she does but not as you would suspect. Not as you would suppose. She falls into a deeper dream of things. A dream of images and imaginings. Of visions. Ones that she will not remember in the morning, yet she will remember something. And in that something, a message. She will step outside to see what could be about, could be calling, and there it will be— an unfolding that meets her at the front gate, right next to Magnus's dahlias and tomato plants. *Things have gone wrong. Call Billy.* And that statement will push her into tomorrow. She will see the past laid out before her like a roadmap, the present as it is, and the future, as it will be and will be again in a different way. Where the future is a quick right and a quick left.

Which one is the truth? you ask. The path that time takes, of course.

As quickly as Trice sees this, all the components, the puzzle pieces will evaporate and leave her just a little breathless with a shiver running up her spine. Just like she is, as we see her, shaking her head, running her hand through her uncombed hair. And that's how it happens that things are set into motion when she walks into the house, picks up the phone in the hallway, and begins to dial a number.

Magnus hollers, "Who you calling?" from the other room, her finger in the business.

Trice says, "Billy."

Magnus asks, "What for?"

And Trice replies, "Just 'cause," because she really isn't certain why. Sometimes the answers aren't ready in the making and aren't meant to be.

There are four rings before she gets a gruff "You are interrupting breakfast." Billy has a weakness for fired pig and biscuits. I make no excuses for him. I don't have to.

"You're supposed to say good morning."

"Good morning, Trice." Billy, named William Daniel by his mother, is a lumbering bear of a man who still misses his momma and daddy and tears up when he thinks about them. And he misses his little brother, Nehemiah. He doesn't cry when he thinks of him, just feels an emptiness in his chest like something is missing that ought not to be. He does not miss Trice, who is always interrupting his plans to do nothing. Like right now.

"I just got up and I saw something. Then I thought about you, when just like that"—she snaps her fingers—"I was face-to-face with Nehemiah." She pauses but there is no further response on the line except for the sound of chewing. Billy knows her "saw something" won't be anything that is of the natural. That her "saw something" will shoot right through one dimension into another. A wild place that he can only hear about from her. Afterwards. *You should've seen it, Billy*, she'd exclaim, like he could just click his heels and live in the land of Trice. *You should've seen it. Great white eagles on mountaintops and they were telling me . . .* He has never encouraged her to continue. Not once. But he listens just the same.

"It occurred to me to call you," Trice says and then hushes, waits for his response like always, but as usual Billy doesn't comment on a thing. She stands on her toes and takes little baby dancer steps, a nervous habit since she was two. "Let's take a ride."

Billy reaches for a biscuit from his plate and bites before asking, "Where to?"

Trice cups the phone next to her mouth, sheltering her words from listening ears, and whispers, "Washington."

"You have lost your mind." Butter is dribbling down his chin and he wipes it with the back of his hand.

"Billy, like I said, I've got," her baby steps are full of madness now, heel toe, heel toe, she lowers her voice three octaves and it rumbles across the phone line, "a feeling."

Trice's feelings are not new or news to the people of Shibboleth. They amount to everything from a change in the weather to someone dying and everything in between. Most people find it a bit disconcerting. But they wouldn't use that word. They would say *spooky*. Sometimes something comes of those spooky feelings that people can touch and believe in. Those times will cause them to be amazed in wonder. Sometimes it seems to be nothing at all. Right now he is hoping for the latter because he had hoped to sneak in some fishing and a whole lot of it.

Where did God get off to in the middle of the night? Just out walking around. Taking a bit of inventory. Of the dark and the light. Seemingly not in much of a hurry, considering the encroaching penumbra. Considering that when I look I see an open gate where there should be none. And what longs to enter through it, darkness and devastation. And I can feel that evil longing emptying out the good of Shibboleth, pulling on it with every rancid breath as it stands waiting for the gate to open farther. Waiting to step forward and devour a people. I turn to God and look for answers.

He motions for me to be still. To keep my silence and write the answers as they unfold. So be it.

Now he is standing outside Billy's house drinking a cup of coffee and admiring the oak tree in front, thinking it has fulfilled its promise. It dwarfs the house with roots twenty feet under, branches forty-five feet up. And while he's admiring it, he's also listening to Trice's conversation and Billy's responses. God is known for being a *multitasker.*

He nods his head toward Billy's house, once, twice, and then there is a groan that translates over the telephone wire to this: it is the sound of the words "All right" and boots being pulled on, a truck being gassed up, and a man heading off in a direction he doesn't want to travel for a reason he doesn't understand.

"Good man," says God. And the oak tree smiles.

Old Blue is pointed north, into strange territory. Billy's hands are on the wheel of the '73 F150. The tires on the highway create a steady drone of distance. Sunlight flashes through the pines, shoots across the road. Billy and Trice move forward, vaulting the shadows in quick succession. They are caught in an undertow propelling them onward, beyond the edges of their time.

"I can tell you one thing, Nehemiah is not gonna be happy to see us, that much I know." Billy is anxious, hasn't given in to the present. "And I tell you another thing, I should've called ahead instead of listening to you and us showing up without any warning."

"Maybe he's not gonna be happy to see you but he's dang sure gonna be happy to see me. But you go ahead, blame it all on me if it makes you feel better." Trice is up on her knees rummaging through a bag behind the seat. "Besides, who has to *warn* their brother that they're coming?"

"Sit your butt down, Trice, you are bothering me."

Trice emerges with a pack of crackers. She's a nervous eater but you can't tell by looking at her. Except when she's eating, of course.

"He has business up here. Things we don't know nothin' about." Billy hates being corrected by Trice. Just hates it. "Things we don't want to know nothin' about. What do you think us just showing up is gonna do, Miss Trice? Make him more than happy to see us?"

"I told you. He'll be happy to see *me.* You're on your own now, Billy boy." Trice runs her hands through her hair and tries to untangle what the wind has whipped into a frenzy. She doesn't feel a smidgen of guilt about dragging Billy up to Washington, and she doesn't really care if Nehemiah is happy to see either one of them. His happiness has nothing to do with it. *Serves him right*, she thinks, as she tries to pull through another knot with her fingers. *Old Blue my butt*, she is thinking. *The Chevette has air. Is better on gas. But no, Billy's gotta kick and swear he can't breath in it.*

(Actually, Old Blue was God's idea. He relishes a good ride in the back of a pickup, and the wind doesn't bother him a bit.)

"Nehemiah could've told us not to come." She is yelling out over the wind, holding her hair knotted in one hand. "'Course just let him try that with me. I don't care what a big shot he is now. Besides, I gotta feeling everything is gonna be all right." This is what she is saying, but it's not the way she feels. Her stomach is in knots from leaving Magnus fussing about having to feed the cats (which belong to her in the first place) and her asking Trice questions from the front porch, like "How long you gonna be gone?" and "What are you goin' up there for in the first place?"

"How long's it been since you've seen him?" Trice looks over at Billy, who just shrugs. "Well you should know."

"Now, don't you think you'd know the last time I seen him? Do you think I'd been able to keep that a secret from anybody? And you need to stop bothering me with all this brother business, you hear?"

They ride on in silence for a while. Eventually, unprompted, Billy picks up the thread. "He's just busy, you know how it goes. Got himself this *position*. Got . . . *responsibilities*." Billy slaps the dashboard. "Important things. Better stuff than kickin' around Shibboleth for a hundred years and dying for nothing." Billy says this, but what he believes is that dying in Shibboleth is the best thing a man can do and that Washington doesn't have anything a man needs.

"Does he call you?"

"Naw." Billy pauses, "He writes the longest darn letters you ever read."

"Well, I don't get calls or letters." Trice is quiet, thinking. "He misses you, Billy."

Billy is silent, drives another mile, and then with a slow smile says, "Yeah, he does."

Then she crosses her arms and forgets about her hair, throwing her head back and closing her eyes. "At least you *get* a letter. That's more than some of us."

Billy doesn't answer. Can't speak for his brother. But he catches Trice's hurt out of the corner of his eye.

So here they are, on the road, on a quest, without an exact agenda. They don't know how the story is going to unfold. So after a while they relax, let the road sing them its lullaby, let the sun and the pines and the dogwoods express themselves, while they ride on in the comfort of the familiar. They don't have to talk to each other. No need. They already know what the other one would say. Nothing but time does a thing like that. Sorts it all out in advance.

Most of Billy's life and all of Trice's growing up together in the same place, the same carved out piece of dirt, in the middle of the same magic. And there you have it, Billy and Trice, carrying the same collective memory, the same reference points for the same stories, the same faces from the past. There is no dividing them there. But that's where the tree splits and they head off in different directions. Same tree. Different branches. As different as a muscled-up banjo from a wood flute, but they're making music just the same. There was a time that a soulful fiddle ran with them through the woods, jumped the creeks, collected spiders, caught snakes, and generally reveled in the glory of Summertime, but he has long been gone now. Out of sight. He has moved off into other territory.

If they had been out for one of their regular rides, they might have run over to the Johnsons' to check out the brand-new colt still standing on his shaky legs, or just ridden around avoiding talking about Nehemiah until it was about sunset. They would've decided they were hungry and dropped in at Kate's Diner for the special, with Billy hoping it was pork chops and Trice just craving cornbread. But instead, here they are on some unknown assignment doing such a brave and foolish thing as following it out. They could pretend it was that other kind of drive where they just kick around, but something begins churning.

Trice and Billy are a little jumpy. They take turns snapping on the radio only to turn it off again. They are becoming sensitive to flashes of light and moving shadows. Watch them. They've started glancing over their shoulders with a quirky feeling, as if someone is watching them. They tell themselves it's nothing. Tricks of light. Tired eyes. But they are telling themselves the deceptions of a blind mind. Go ahead, deny the Existence. It doesn't change a thing.

Now they are making their way, hour after hour, their eyes watching the road intently. As if by double necessity. As if at any given moment the road may change shape, alter their direction, lift them off the ground, slinging them into another universe. Unknown to one another, they are each, separately, contemplating gravity. Contemplating the things in life that hold one fast to place. To life. Unknown to each other, they are wondering what happens when those things are erased without a trace. Unknown to each other, they begin to see the past float up before their eyes. For a while, Billy will forget driving. For a while, Trice will forget riding. This is where they'll be.

There is the sound of water from underground springs feeding into secret pools, sliding over the ancient surfaces. Water falling one tiny drop at a time from cavernous rain rooms. Water seeping through the walls all around them. And there is only a little light. Barely enough to make out the shape of two children, one slightly larger but both so small they are almost lost in the space that surrounds them. They stand very still, staring into the darkness. Their tiny light focuses on a small crevice of a hallway between the cave rock. Two things are present with the children: the presence of danger and the pressing need to be quick in the execution of their mission. The girl knows it. She has an awareness of time, feels it the way others feel water. Time runs through her fingers.

"Hurry up, Billy." It's the exasperated whisper of the girl child, urgently pleading. "Hurry up, Billy. Hurry up!" She walks back and forth impatiently on her tiptoes, a flock of wild blond hairs just barely outlined by the faintest of fading flashlights.

"He's coming, Trice." A boy's tanned hand reaches out and cups the girl's shoulder. "Stand still." She calms, places her feet back flat again on the rock floor beneath her. "You have to be still, Trice." He is patient with her, his voice smooth music. "You could tumble off into the darkness. See?" For emphasis he flashes the light to his right, where the path leads downward, then over the edge where there is nothing with one tippytoed wrong step.

The girl turns her eyes on the boy. They appear to capture the light and hold it there so that she looks at him through blue ice, crystals of frozen water, "Why is he so dagburned slow, Nehemiah? Why?"

The boy looks backward to the slow shuffling sound in the distance that will carry his big brother forward into view. "He's just Billy, Trice. That's all."

Nehemiah turns off his flashlight to save what little light is left and they wait in the dark unafraid, determined to carry out their duty. The larger boy appears, his flashlight held between his teeth as he uses his hands to pull himself through the rock crevice. He clears the space, steps into the cavern, and moves the flashlight to his hand, focusing it directly on the girl's face. She doesn't look away. She doesn't shield her eyes. She seems to soak the light up from the inside.

"You know, Trice, one of these days you and me is gonna tussle. I don't care if you are a girl."

"*Time is important, Billy. I know it and Mr. Einstein knows it. Someday you're gonna know it too.*"

"*Einstein is dead, Trice.*"

"*I'll be sure and tell him you said that next time we speak.*" The eyes again. All flash of light.

"*You're a strange girl, Trice.*"

Nehemiah holds up his hand to quiet them. They feel the movement more than see it. Then hear the boy with such an air of authority saying, "*Shhh,*" and they hush. They listen.

"*Wind voices, Nehemiah. That's all,*" the big brother says, but he shines his light to the left and to the right, searching.

Nehemiah smells the air, smells the damp rock, the age-old space, and something else. The wafting smell of sulfur. "*We're not alone down here.*" He says this with bold concern. The three of them lean their backs tight against the cave wall and begin to inch their way along, making the slow, precarious downward descent.

"*Well, we know we're not alone, Nehemiah. If we were alone,*" Trice says while stepping sideways on her tiptoes, "*there'd be no need to guard the treasure.*"

"*I mean, Trice,*" Nehemiah pauses, listens again as an unearthly growl surfaces from the depths below, "*we're not alone right now.*"

The Protectors descend lower and lower into the darkness while something watches, something waits, from somewhere far below.

Billy and Trice shake their heads as if surfacing from miles beneath the earth, opening their eyes to the other world above them. They are still formulating loose cognitive threads, attempting to touch something just beyond their reach. Trice almost palms the pictures, almost puts them in her pocket, where she'll pull them out later over dinner. Then Old Blue enters the District of Columbia, and Trice opens her hand and pulls the directions from her purse. The images begin to fall away and the silver threads of truth dissipate as if they were never there.

Later That Day

Now God is working on another piece of this unfolding puzzle. He is standing in the capitol offices of Senator Honeywell, arms folded, looking over Nehemiah's shoulder.

How can God be riding up Highway 131 in the back of Old Blue, enjoying the new blooms on the dogwoods and simultaneously walking around Nehemiah's desk? Omnipresence. An astounding actuality.

Presently, Nehemiah is discussing appropriation committees and timing. His world is full of negotiations. Compromises. Anticipating everyone's next move. That means seeing through walls. And that means a lot of things.

God leans over Nehemiah, and in a low voice whispers, *"Shibboleth,"* then he sits down on the other side of the desk. Nehemiah appears not to hear, but yet, watch this, he begins to sketch an oak tree in the border of his calendar. You can feel it, can't you? The something happening. The rush of oak leaves in the wind. The sudden sway of its outer branches. Interesting the way that things can surface. Things thought to be long forgotten. See now, Nehemiah sketches the trunk, the branches, a few leaves, before he ends the conversation. Then he looks at the sketch rather strangely because he didn't even realize what he was doing. Can you see him? Sitting at his desk wondering where that tree came from? It's a residue from when he was as much the center of Shibboleth as it was of him. But that was a long time ago. Twelve years, to be exact, since Billy dropped him off in Washington. With first a handshake, then a teary-eyed bear cub of a hug. A lot has happened since then. A man has grown into the skin of what was once mostly boy. Nehemiah has been polished, developed not a roughness but a determined seriousness. And has earned a reputation as a man who will get things done the right way. And, oh yes, there is a right way.

Other than his sketching, it has been an ordinary day. All regular business, nothing unforeseen or unplanned to shatter his created life. Did I mention Nehemiah's suit? It's exquisitely tailored. *Exquisitely.* He is polished perfection, that's what I'm thinking. He doesn't look the least bit like a duck out of water. The fact is, he looks born and bred for what he's doing. But tonight, well, tonight change is about.

Nehemiah turns the corner, and now he is almost home. See the brownstone, the one there with the great green ivy climbing the front brick? He is whistling quietly beneath his breath, which is delightful, considering he doesn't whistle. But God does, and right now God is walking next to him, keeping step and time. They are whistling a brand-new tune, something God just invented. A tune about hidden treasures and things long forgotten. A tune that carries the smell of ages past and of ages yet to come.

Nehemiah spies Old Blue, a dinosaur from another place and time, illegally parked and taking up most of the street. He pauses, considers this apparition, then fights the urge to drop his briefcase and run toward it. Instead, he walks as slowly as he possibly can to the driver's window, where Billy is asleep. Trice is leaning against the passenger door biting her nails. She has been watching him walk toward her. She has been waiting for Nehemiah for a very long time.

"What's going on?" It's a simple question that introduces an explosion of activity from inside the truck. Billy erupts with a stream of choice curse words. Then he pauses long enough to look over at Nehemiah and say, "Hey." Nehemiah grins. It's not his usual Washington smile but a grin from way back when.

"We come to see you," Billy says.

"Well, get on out then." (A man must speak his native language when the natives are about.)

Now you know these two have come a long way. You can see it, can't you? Those tired eyes, bunched-up muscles. Voices hoarse from yelling at one another over the wind and road noise. And now that they are standing here disheveled, in the midst of so many city lights, they feel just a little foolish, just a little country rumpled. And more than a little hungry.

"Is everything all right?" Nehemiah motions to the front door.

"Do we look all right?" Trice has a streak of anger. It's been building for a few years now and she tries to tame it as she speaks, tries to stroke it, to push it back into place like a lock of her unruly hair. "Hello, Nehemiah. It's been a long time."

And then I watch Nehemiah *behold* her. Beholding is better than a long look. Beholding is better than most things. And I watch Nehemiah *remember* her. But this isn't the Trice he left behind. This Trice is all grown up. This Trice rattles his nerves. Nehemiah breaks his eyes away, says, "It has been a long time, Trice," without apology and begins to walk up the steps. He's keeping his facts straight. He's keeping his mind made up.

The three of them settle in at Nehemiah's kitchen table, which doesn't in the least way resemble anything from Shibboleth. It's metropolitan by design. It's amazing how many excellent soul-warming meals have been laid out with little more than an iron skillet, a bowl, and a baking pan. (And, if I might add, the company of angels.) But in spite of all his culinary accoutrements, not because of them, Nehemiah is a surprisingly good cook, so he makes steak and eggs (one of his brother's favorites). And for the second time in a very long day, Billy sits down to breakfast.

This is where they make small talk about the trip, about the people they know, about the precision of Yahoo maps. Then Billy and Trice ask about Senator Honeywell and Nehemiah's work, because it's the polite thing to do. They dance around this man a little with their words. He is not exactly the same person Billy and Trice remember him to be. They keep trying to look at him through old glasses, trying to see the boy of their youth. The one he was right up to the moment he left them. But now, in some ways he is a stranger. They both steal glances when they think he isn't looking. Suddenly, they are compatriots, all their fussing falls by the wayside. After all, they've been together almost every day he's been away. They've held their feet fast to Shibboleth while he has run away. At least that's what they say. But they don't use those words in front of him. Instead they ask, "How is your work?" And what can Nehemiah really tell them that they will understand? Or at least that will not bore them as they smile and nod. He won't waste their time. Won't torture them with the details, for which they have no reference points. He says, "It's just the way you think it is. Takes a lot of paperwork. Every day the same. Every day different." He doesn't mention the closed-door maneuverings that stalk his steps on a daily basis. And they don't pry.

They do ask about the general well-being of Senator Honeywell, one of the South's most prestigious poor boys who's "done good for himself." In their heart of hearts, his constituents believe Senator Honeywell is still one of them, hasn't been eaten up by capitol decay, and they continue to trust him to look out for their better interests. For the most part, this is a mantle that the senator wears responsibly.

All politeness and politics aside, Trice is much more interested in the space of Nehemiah's life than in what he does. About his after-hours and what waits for him (or doesn't) when he comes home. Exactly who is this man who sits before them? The sound of a saxophone filters out from the living room. Trice doesn't recognize

John Coltrane but she likes the sound. She looks at Nehemiah, studies his hands as he tells Billy something, opening his palms and placing them together. *He's learned some things,* she thinks, *he's been some places.* She watches him carefully and purposefully turn up his sleeves, first the right, then the left. Then he slowly pushes the cuffs up over his forearms. And for just a moment their eyes lock. This time, it's Trice who is the first to look away. Her eyes wander over the furnishings and she recognizes the absence of something, a vacancy she cannot identify. She looks for the presence of women but there is none that she can see. Or the presence of *the* woman. The one who would make her presence known even in her absence. Flowers here, a bottle of perfume accidentally left there. Trice considers how road-weary she must look. Considers the possibility of bugs stuck in her hair. She combs it with her fingers as she surveys the living room from her chair. There is a masculine order present, but a different one than she is accustomed to. No guns. No fishing lines or lures. No visible tools. She is pensively puzzling this with one nail in her mouth, when Billy says, "It's all on account of Trice that we're here."

Trice responds by pulling her feet up in the chair and wrapping her arms about her knees. She remembers their reason. "We came to talk to you about something," she says.

Nehemiah looks over at her, raps his knuckles twice on the table as if knocking on a door. "I know you did." He gets up to refill his coffee cup, sits back down and leans back in his chair, hands crossed behind his head. "Why don't you tell me about it."

"Go on, Trice," Billy points at her, "tell him about your *feeling.*"

"Don't get smart, Billy," she says with a hard stare of a dare.

"I didn't say nothing bad. What'd I say bad? You tell me, Nehemiah, did I say something bad?"

"It was your tone." Trice is snappy, red-eyed weary, and not to be toyed with.

"You two have been on the road too long, that's all. Tell me, Trice," Nehemiah offers no smiles, no jokes. "Tell me about your feeling." He says this with the sound of all due patience, moves his arms, crosses them over his chest. He sounds patient but he isn't. Not really. Not right now. He has a lot of work to do and has a strange feeling of his own that there is an interruption coming. An interruption that will try to pull him away from the world that he has worked so hard to create.

Trice unfolds, gets to her feet, and paces the floor, looking down, begins taking those ballerina steps again. Toe, toe, toe, heel, toe, heel, toe. "We didn't see it. Now don't you think that's strange?" She appears to be talking to herself. "I do. I *really* do." She whips around and faces Nehemiah, "and I'll tell you the truth right now, if you don't get *it*—because I'm thinking you getting *it* is very, very important—I get the crazy feeling in my gut that we won't even remember *being* here."

"See what having a feeling will do to someone?" Billy offers this out of the side of his mouth as if he was whispering to his brother but knowing Trice can hear him loud and clear, trying to pull her chain.

"What *it*, Trice, am I supposed to get?" Nehemiah's patience is already cracking. He feels something sucking at his feet. And it frightens him. The selfsame boy who stood impervious and brave facing the unknown darkness now feels a shiver up his spine that he cannot explain. And he wants to tell Trice to stop. He wants to tell her to go away. But instead he says again, "What *it*?"

"The *it* that hit me in pictures."

"Tell it, Trice," Billy's arms fly out over his head. "Tell the whole thing and get it over with."

"The pockets of Time," she says. And stands there as if they understand.

"Just tell him, Trice, just get straight to the story." Billy's exasperation begins filling up the balloon of the room.

"I woke up trying to remember a dream I had but instead I saw all of Shibboleth at once, like from the air. But from the air all at once at different times. As if there were *pockets* of time." She closes her eyes and the times and the timing of Shibboleth open up before her. The what-has-beens and the way things are and the way things will be *or the way things will not be at all* without ... and that's where she stops speaking, because she doesn't know what she hasn't seen.

"I don't know anything more than what I saw." Trice tries to continue, stops. It's difficult to explain a waking dream, a vision of otherworldly things. Trice knows. She's tried for years. "It's as if a storm is coming and no one is ..."—she stops again, searching for a word—"preparing. No, that's not it. Expecting. No, not ... ready. No one is ready. Like inch by inch, something has been stealing ... "

I see Trice struggling with words. Struggling to paint the right image. I look to God. He nods and I exhale, breathe out inspiration. It is the smell of old worlds, of Trice reading words layered upon words, of cornbread and ladybugs, of stubborn patience and understanding, of the soft, green moss hidden on the morning side of Shibboleth, and the scent of bold, pure light. It is the essence of Trice. It lifts on the air, circles her head and shoulders, and settles in her hair. She takes a deep breath in, becomes lucid and literal.

"This is the way I saw it." She stands up and reaches for Nehemiah's fruit bowl, picks up two apples and an orange. "Look." She sets the apple on the table. "This is everything and everyone and all of life in Shibboleth before us, back in the old days, in the early days of Kate and Twila and Magnus and the days before them." She sets another apple on the table. "This is the life we knew. And even in that I saw the smaller pockets. Our times of yesterday when we were kids and all the times of our growing up, including, Nehemiah, the time that we were down at the springs swimming and you kissed me underwater." Trice pauses, wonders why that memory surfaced. Nehemiah arches one eyebrow, but at this living moment he doesn't remember such a kiss. "And the smaller pocket that makes up the very now." She sets down the orange at the end of the line. "Now, this is where it gets interesting. This is the time to come. The future. Get it?" She holds up the orange for both of them to examine the future until they nod their heads and agree they understand. And then she grabs a butcher knife from Nehemiah's knife rack. "But look now!" She slices the orange in half. "Here's one future," she is saying this with one half of a dripping orange held up in her hand then slammed down hard on the table surface, "and this," she turns the other half inside-out and rips the orange out of its shell until the peel is an empty core, "this is the other future." "Still the future," she slams the empty shell down, "but this future is completely empty. Empty, empty, empty. Still time, but time with nothing in it." She pauses, pinches her brows together and lasers her eyes on both of them. They can think anything about her that they want, but they cannot deny what's in her eyes. (*Brilliance* is the word, but they don't use that word in Shibboleth because they think it's too close to crazy.) "Now, after I saw *that*, I thought of Billy and saw your face." She gets up and leans her hands on the table, stares into Nehemiah's eyes. "*Your* face, Nehemiah. And I felt the three of us running. Together. I knew it was six legs, two to a pair, and that they all belonged to us. Now I may not know what we were running to, or from for that matter, but I knew we were *together*." She sits back down in her chair. "And I called Billy because I knew that we were meant to come see you. To tell you that there is trouble.

Serious trouble. That something is being stolen." She points to the empty shell of the orange.

"What is being stolen, Trice?" Nehemiah is taking shallow breaths, trying to ignore that little scent wafting over him from Trice's hair. Try to ignore it as he may, I know what the man can smell. I know what he's made of.

"My guess, Nehemiah, is everything worth keeping." Trice runs her hands through the back of her hair, pulls it in a knot on the top of her head, and closes her eyes before she answers. "Something is trying to steal Shibboleth."

A quiet fills the room with a lot of unasked questions going unanswered. God begins whistling again, hands in pockets. He ambles over to the window and lifts the curtain, looking out. He looks as if he's just waiting, just killing time, and believe me, nobody kills time like God.

Nehemiah is considering all the things in his world worth keeping. But his world and the world of Shibboleth are light-years apart. "This all sounds important, Trice," he waves his arms about, "and it is mysterious as all get-out, but what does it have to do with me?"

"I've told you. Something bad is going to happen. See this?" She picks up the orange peel. "This is Shibboleth," she slowly squeezes it in her fist, "and it is disappearing. I don't have to know the part you play. I'm just the message bearer. What you do, Nehemiah, with the message, that's up to you."

Billy picks up the other half of the orange and begins to eat. He has been very still, very silent, and very seriously listening. To him, if Shibboleth disappears, then there is no hope. Shibboleth is the heart of the planet, and all that is worth keeping is kept there. Only he doesn't remember how. Or where.

"We're trying to tell you you need to come home." Billy surprises Trice by adding this. Shocks her, actually. "Trice is wired a little different. That's her way of telling what she sees. But you *know*, Brother, it's real." He swallows the last bite of the orange. "And you *know* what I mean. We've had proof."

"Like the time Blister almost died except I *dreamed*"—Trice slams the word *dreamed* like a gas pedal to the floor—"about him standing in the middle of those flames screaming."

"That was when he was still just John Robert." Billy adds, "Blister came later." Billy pushes his chair back on its hind legs. "After you got me and Nehemiah to go over there with you at three in the morning, and we pulled his body out of that house."

Nehemiah is remembering the smell of scorched flesh on a hot night. Is remembering staring at the blaze engulfing the house, pacing back and forth. Back and forth. Remembers wishing for, needing, rain. Then clouds, fast, white, powerful, rolling in from the east, a clap of thunder, a sudden downpour dousing the flames. Him crashing through the door and John Robert's identity altered into something, someone else. Remembers looking at Trice with a new respect. A knowledge that her strange dreams were more than crazy hunches. Right then he made a silent vow that no matter how foolish they appeared, he would not deny her their validity. At the time, this vow was not contained in words. At the time, he didn't know one day her dreams would try to rip him from his world.

"All I know is that you have something to do with this entire picture or I wouldn't be here in front of you." Trice crosses her arms over her chest. It's a habit she has picked up from the two brothers.

"I know all about your dreams, Trice. I don't doubt their ... " He starts to say *reality* but he drops the word. Nehemiah rubs his nose, attempts to rub away the smell of remembrance. Now he has a decision before him. Has an unexpected *Y* in the road. One that he wasn't expecting when he rolled out of bed at precisely the same time he does every day, beginning the exact same morning routine. Which choice will he make, you ask. Which road will he take? Time will tell. It always does.

Nehemiah wants to say, "You don't need me." He wants to say, "You have an entire town, take care of the problem." The unidentifiable, nebulous, dark-cloud future of a problem. But he doesn't. He stalls. It only works for a little while, but that may be all he needs. He reaches over and slaps his brother on the shoulder, rocks him a little under his hand. "You look tired, Brother. And Trice," he looks over the table and cocks his head with his dimpled smile, "you look just the same." But he's thinking, *Better actually. Even better. How could that be?* And then he smiles that grin at her, the one with the dimple. And lo and behold, Trice smiles back. I look to Nehemiah, back to Trice, and back to Nehemiah, whose dimpled grin is still held firmly in place. I write down the words *electric* and *current*.

Trice interrupts his thoughts with "You don't have anything living here, Nehemiah." She has put her finger on the absent spot. "No dog, no cat, no bird," she smiles at him, "not even a fish."

"Maybe," the dimple grows deeper, "I have all of them," he points down the hall, "in the bedroom."

"No, you don't." Trice points to her chest, "I would *feel* it. But regardless of what you don't have, I also know you do have hot water and I'm in desperate need of a hot shower."

And these are about the final words of the evening. Billy and Trice deflate into a puddle of road-weary and Nehemiah begins to clean up the dishes. They say goodnight and get settled into proper sleeping arrangements after moving Old Blue to a nontowing location.

Then Nehemiah goes to bed, turns out the light, and just as he is falling asleep gets a feeling he doesn't like. A push from the inside out. Not a physical one, but a push just the same. Let's just say it is a deposit into his soul. One that he'll need should he accept the road ahead of him to the right.

In the following silence, the traffic fades away. The city itself fades away and is replaced with one single solitary image. It is an image of Nehemiah sitting in Old Blue at midnight down at the entrance to the springs. That's what he sees, just as clear as if he were sitting there in person.

He gets out of bed, walks down the hall, and nudges Billy, who is already snoring on the sofa. (Trice has rightfully commandeered the extra bedroom by declaring that she "doesn't care how big or how tired Billy is, that the last time she checked she was a girl and she is getting her privacy.") "Hey, Billy." There is a rattle of rhythm. "Billy?"

"What—what?" His breathing is almost normal again.

"What's going on at the springs?"

"What?"

"I said, what is going on at the springs?"

"Springs ain't there no more." Billy rolls over on his side, speaks into the back cushion. "It's nothing but dust now. The water has left town."

Nehemiah nods, although the water drying up makes no sense. No sense in any natural realm. Doesn't even make any sense the way that Billy rolls it sideways out of his sleeping mouth. As if somehow the water leaving town were an acceptable option.

He walks to his room, and gets back into bed. He lies wide awake now with his arms behind his head, watching the day-glo green numbers on the clock changing by the minute, remembering a place where his memories were once drawn up from cool, clear water.

But now memory has run dry.

Thursday, 5:36 P.M.

Nehemiah is on his way home and into the unknown. Driving south, trailing the two-day-old fumes of Billy's truck, the demands and concerns of Washington occupying his every thought. So much so that he is missing the dogwoods. Missing the sunlight that's left streaming across the road through the pines. Just missing it all.

Before leaving, he had gone to his office, taken off his jacket, rolled up his sleeves, and then sat down, only to stare at his day-old sketch of the Shibboleth Oak. Bam. There it was, waiting to face him straight from his own hand. And if there had ever been a feeling that he was going to have a hard time escaping whatever this call was, it was then. For a second, but only for a second, he thought he had seen the leaves move slightly on the tips of the branches. He had rubbed his eyes and risen from his desk, walked to the window, and looked out past the borders of green hedges, beyond the traffic, until he could almost see Billy's truck beating back the wind.

He had thought about how very long it had been since he saw his brother and how he had let that happen. How he had let that much time get away from him. And how amazingly good Trice had looked. Not good in a hubba-hubba way. Not good in a sleek, city fashionably perfect way. Trice had looked good like, well, good, like for real. Real natural. Or maybe she had just looked familiar. Maybe it was just good to have a slice of his old life invading the new and improved version for the first time. Or maybe she was just the sexiest, most uncontrived woman he had encountered in, well—forever. He was still thinking about this, still stumbling and troubling over it, when Senator Honeywell walked in unannounced. He had to clear his throat twice before Nehemiah heard him.

Let's take a moment to consider the senator, to consider his Southern charms. He looks Texan big, although he's not from Texas. He's from a poor county in a poor part of the country. (It is this fact ultimately that helped win him the election.) He has been on this earth sixty-two years and carries himself like a man of determined accomplishment, which of course he is. Senator Honeywell is also a man with extreme observation skills. Able to spot deception a mile away. Also able to recognize loyalty when he sees it. He knows a thing or two.

Nehemiah had pulled himself away from the window, away from the past, and taken a seat alongside the senator. He has worked for this man for almost a decade. They have become, and there is no other word to describe it, friends in every sense of the word. And the fact that Nehemiah has never, never tried to take advantage of this fact rests well with Senator Honeywell.

They had, at this point in Nehemiah's day, this minute portion of his life, proceeded with business as usual. They had discussed current developments and the upcoming elections. Mind you, these developments are crucial by all means, but not crucial to our story. My assignment is to watch the unfolding path that leads back to the Key. My only purpose at that moment was to watch as Nehemiah made his choices and to record the consequences of those actions.

"I've had a surprise visit." This is how Nehemiah had broached the subject. He had paused then, trying to summon up the words or perhaps the courage to go on. To try to unwrap something that he didn't fully have his finger on. "A visit from my brother." And then Nehemiah had looked up at the senator with an earnestness. "Apparently, there is trouble in Shibboleth."

"What kind of trouble?"

"I wish I knew, Jim, I really do." Nehemiah only calls him by his first name when in private. In public, he refers to him as Senator. Always. "That's part of the problem. They can't seem to articulate it. Just to implore me to 'come home,' as they put it."

"They?" the senator had asked. Ahh, a man that doesn't miss the details.

"Umm." Nehemiah had tried to skip over explaining about Trice because that might open up a door to explain about Magnus, Blister, Covey, Catfish, Shook, Wheezer, and so on and so forth, and it would never end. "A friend came with him," Nehemiah had said and tried to roll it off with such nonchalance that it wouldn't open the door to any further discussion. Nehemiah had tried to explain that although he had no evidence, no exacting evidence, the request had come from a reliable source.

The senator was a good listener. What he had heard between the lines was that a choice had been made, a decision reached, but that Nehemiah would defer to him. Would not leave without his permission. Or his blessing.

The senator had then quietly, quickly steered the conversation back to business. Back to meetings, to votes and to voters. He had covered every necessary topic that a man of his position needed to know from a man who had been his veritable right hand for two terms. Then he had risen to leave. It appeared that the matter of Nehemiah's personal situation had gone unaddressed. But when Senator Jim Honeywell had reached the door, he had turned and said, "Go home, Nehemiah" with a finality that meant no argument. "Take a few days off and just go see for yourself." Then he had added, "But call me," as the door was closing.

It may have been the senator who held the ticket to Nehemiah's trip home. But it's God who is the conductor on these rails of time. There's a lot to be said for divine favor. And it's all good.

And Nehemiah is replaying that moment, and his fast packing, his turning the key in the deadbolt on his door and saying to himself, *Just a few days. I'll be back in just a few days.* And he's still thinking about his return when a red fox runs in front of the car and stops dead in his tracks, forcing Nehemiah to slam on the brakes. The fox turns, locks eyes with Nehemiah, and holds them there, until it finally darts across the asphalt into the afternoon shadows on the other side. This is how it happens that thirty-eight miles from Shibboleth, stopped in the middle of long, empty highway, eyes locked with a red fox, the ties to Washington snap loose. Nehemiah rolls down the window, searches for a fast blur of a tail, a flash of red fur, but there is no sight of him.

Later he will tell Billy about the fox at the kitchen table. He'll say it in wonderment. "Won't believe what I saw," he'll say.

And Billy'll say, "Tell it," the way he does to Trice.

"Saw a red fox run right out in front of me, stop and stare at me, if you can believe that, and then take off like lightning across the road."

"Ain't no foxes around here anymore." Billy will sit down at the table with a hefty sandwich, take a bite, and keep talking with his mouth full. "Ain't been for years, Nehemiah. You know that."

Nehemiah will cross his arms over his chest and say aloud, "I know what I saw."

But that will be later, when it comes back to him, when the flash of red hair brushes against the synapses of his cortex.

Right now, Nehemiah rests his head back against the seat of the rental car, opens up the sunroof, and feels the early evening sun

warm on his bones. Bones that he didn't realize had felt so cold for
so long.

The melt begins, just around the edges, just along the surface.
Nehemiah turns on the radio and the refrain from "Southbound"
by the Allman Brothers kicks in as he says, "What do you know?"
and turns up the volume as the Malibu seems to take to the road
of its own accord. And a thousand important, trivial problems
masquerading as life fly right out that roof, getting lost in the
translation of winter to spring. Our Nehemiah is a glacier moving
south. Ahh, sweet impetus.

Thursday, 6:21 P.M.

Old, white-frame, paint-peeling, sagging porch of a house. Nehemiah loves it all over again. Instantly. The way one loves any
piece of home unchanged and forgotten until you're standing in
the middle of—sinking in the middle of—memory.

Old Blue is not out front. Nehemiah calls out for Billy anyway.
He hasn't heard so much quiet since he can't remember when. He
stands under the oak tree, shadowed in its reach. The sun is setting, the red undercarriage of clouds a moving mirror that says,
One more revolution.

Nehemiah pulls a piece of moss from a tree branch and holds it
up, saying aloud to no one but the tree, "Parasite or poetry, depending on your frame of mind," which sums up his entire thoughts
of Shibboleth in general. But tonight, as the wind picks up, stirs
winter leaves around his feet, Nehemiah is remembering poetry.
And the words are wrapping around his skin, sinking into his being

with every sigh of the earth's groaning. Every smell, every sight, every sound forming an orchestra that takes him back to the beginning.

He climbs the porch steps and opens the door. The last of the sunlight, in its final crash, slants across the wood floor at odd angles, the dust particles becoming a living entity of their own. He walks down the hallway and straight back to the heart of the house, the kitchen, which smells like years of layered grease and fatback and white flour. This is what he remembers most, and he almost expects to see his mother, hands covered in flour, greet him as he steps through the door. Almost. As if, if he wills it hard enough, long enough, it might happen. A circumvent of time. The earth turning backwards.

He turns, walks down the familiar hallway, looks into his mother's room. No mother. But everything else just the same. He reaches the next bedroom on the left, the smallest one, his room. Billy was the oldest. Billy got the larger one at the end of the hall. His mother got the one with the most light. The door to his room is closed, and he stands with his hand on the knob, starts to go in, then backs away, walks out to the porch and steps outside. The screen door slams behind him. It is a comforting *hello* and *good-bye* sound. Then he sits in one of the three old rockers waiting there for a warm body. The cool starts rising up from the ground, and the stars begin appearing high in the sky.

The moon hasn't yet risen when Billy pulls up, gets out grinning with Sonny Boy, who howls at the apparition on the porch. "Oh hush, boy," Billy says, "you can't even see good. That there's your brother."

Nehemiah doesn't feel correcting him on this fact is necessary. "Why didn't you call?"

"I don't know. Figured I didn't need to."

"Reckon you don't." His boots are heavy on the porch steps. "Did you eat yet?"

"No. Just sitting. Waiting on you, I guess."

"Well, let me wash up and we'll head on over to Kate's and get a bite."

Later That Evening

Later, sitting at the diner sawing on T-bones, Billy spends his time chewing and watching Nehemiah. Nehemiah watches everything and everybody. (Public awareness has become an ingrained habit.) Sonny Boy watches through the diner door every bite that Billy cuts and puts into his mouth.

"Trice is gonna be mad that we didn't ask her to come eat."

"Why didn't you?"

"Didn't think about it then. Just thought about it now."

"Well, I'll be doggone! Ed, Ed, look who's here, will you just look?" Catfish has come in and spotted Nehemiah. "Hey, Billy, look who's here." He says this to Billy as if Billy hasn't been sitting with his brother all along.

"Hey, Catfish, good to see you." Nehemiah puts out his hand.

"Doggone," Catfish says again, looking at Nehemiah like he's just been resurrected. "I guess we're gonna hear it now. Ed, you ready to hear a good one?" Ed is nowhere to be seen as Catfish pulls a chair from a table, turns it around, and straddles it at the booth's edge, between Nehemiah and Billy. "Tell us a story, Nehemiah." He looks down at Nehemiah's plate, at the half-eaten steak, the fork and knife in his hand. "Aww shoot, you're eatin'. I got so excited, I didn't even notice. You go ahead and eat, Nehemiah. Get that out of the way, we'll come back over in a minute."

Nehemiah looks down, looks up with an attempt at a smile, trying to find the right words. "Sorry, Catfish, I don't have any stories." Catfish stands, disbelieving. "Well, sure you do. You don't have to tell a new one, just tell us one of the old ones. Hey, tell us the one about John thinking he'd caught a big one when it was Billy under the water holding on to his line." He whoops with the memory. "Tell that one."

Nehemiah looks at him vacantly, and Billy sees what Catfish doesn't. He sees that his brother doesn't even remember the story. Not from being there on that funny fifteen-year-old day. Not from telling it over and over again in the years to come and go. Doesn't remember it at all.

"Catfish, I tell you what, me and Nehemiah's got some catchin' up to do. But he's gonna be around for a few days, so you drop by before he leaves, and one of us will pull a story out of the bag for you." Catfish is as docile as a man can be. Not a mean-spirited bone in his body. He doesn't want to tell Billy that his stories are fine, just fine, but they are not the same. And of course, he doesn't need to. Billy knows this. He's just trying to buy Nehemiah some time. He isn't certain what for. Catfish tries to smile but leaves heavy in the chest, deflated and shaking his head. He is mourning the loss of words that dance. Words that bring life like fire brings warm.

"Billy," Nehemiah puts his fork and knife down, "why isn't Trice married?"

Billy doesn't say anything immediately. He takes a swallow of his tea, tries to sort something out in his mind. Something different that has just come to his attention. "Why ain't you married?"

"You know something," Nehemiah pauses, looks at the dog's eyes through the glass door, "I don't know. Maybe I haven't met the right woman."

"Ain't no woman right when you get her."

"Is that right?"

"Yep, she's not right for about," Billy rolls his eyes up, thinking serious at the ceiling, "'bout nine, ten good years." And he nods as if that settled it. "Then she is just right."

"That's a long time to get things just right, Billy."

"You better get started right away then. Now, I'm a worn-down package, but you, you got some potential."

"When did you start using the word *potential?*"

"Satellite TV will teach you all kinds of things you don't need to know."

Darla is yelling out orders to the kitchen. Dishes are rattling. People are eating, chewing, pointing, yet something isn't quite the same. Nehemiah is trying to pull up files of memory, flip through the cards, tables, and booths, cash register, same smells. But something's missing. A huge slice of empty.

People are watching Nehemiah. One or two occasionally nod a head in his direction. But even the ones who know him don't speak now, after his reception to Catfish, which they find downright peculiar. They are thinking he looks about the same. Richer but about the same. They are waiting to see if the ice will crack and release the man inside. And, as they are waiting, as they are watching, the ice pick appears.

"You got trouble." Billy puts his head down, shovels up a forkful of potatoes.

"How's that?" But the question answers itself as Kate sits down with a vengeance on Nehemiah's side of the booth, the bulk of her pushing him toward the corner. "Well now," she says and pulls her glasses down on her nose, looks him up and down.

"Well now," she says again.

"I know, I know."

"Do you now?"

"Yes, ma'am, I know. Sure is good to see you." She keeps him captured eyeball to eyeball. "Steak sure is good."

"Don't sweet-talk me tonight. I'm too tired for it. Right now, I've laid eyes on you and that's enough. Now get your butt back in here for breakfast, and you and me's gonna have a little catching-up talk."

"Yes, ma'am."

"You go home and get in your momma's bed, you hear, and get some real sleep for a change."

Nehemiah gives her a puzzled look. Starts to tell her that he sleeps fine. Really fine. "I still have an old bed in that house."

"That's not what I said, now is it?"

He starts to add "no, ma'am," but there isn't a chance.

"I said, Go get in your momma's bed. That's not too much for you to do, is it? That's a simple thing, don't you think?" She has risen, cleared the booth, whipped a dishrag over her shoulder, and is moving away, still talking. "I ain't asked anything of you in over ten years. Seems to me you oughta be able to do the least little thing I ask before I drop dead. A person never knows when ... " and she is still talking as she walks through the kitchen, where the rattle of dishes swarms up to eat her words. She is still talking when she says, "Ed, lock up. I'm going to the house. I have had enough for one day."

Kate is still talking to Nehemiah under her breath when she cranks up her big Buick and hits the pedal hard enough to chariot away her heavy body home, where she will take off her shoes, put up her feet, and think about her sister, Twila, who passed on way too soon, and her sister's baby boy, who has finally brought his raggedy butt home where it belongs. "See here, Twila," she says to the air, "I done sent him home to get in your bed and that's the best that I can do. The rest of it is up to you."

Presently, though, Kate has barely made it through the kitchen door and the folks in the diner have watched this occurrence with great amusement, seeing how over seventy-five percent of them know Nehemiah and are busy whispering to the other twenty-five percent the whole story to catch them up to speed. They have watched as Ms. Kate has corralled him, and about half of them make a note to change whatever plans might be necessary so that they can drop in for breakfast in the morning, too. Just to see if he shows up. Or to see what happens if he doesn't. Their lives are far from boring. There is just so much to see and do.

Back at the table, Nehemiah is trying to remember why he had to come down here in the first place. "Tell me again, why am I here, Billy?"

"Looks like right now you are here to get chewed out by Kate Ann."

"I could've come down here and done that any time. I thought there was something going on wrong here according to you and Trice . . . "

"Naw, naw, naw," he holds his hand up in protest, "that was Ms. Trice, and you gonna hafta take that up with her."

"Billy, you said . . . "

"I ain't said nothin'." Billy gets up from the table with his bone (which you will notice he has left a nice amount of meat clinging to) and takes it to the door, passes it out to Sonny Boy, who gives him a wordless but tail-wagging thank you.

He calls over to the waitress before sitting down, "Darla, could you please find me some of that peach cobbler? Nehemiah, you want some cobbler? It'll make you feel better."

Nehemiah looks at Sonny Boy by the door, passes his bone to Billy for the dog later, and says, "Why not? I'm up to my knees in something. I just wish I knew what it was."

"You ain't up to your knees, boy, you just starting to get wet."

And the brothers eat peach cobbler and talk about things that it takes two of them to remember, two of them to get straight. Billy doesn't try to bring up the fishing story. He is testing Nehemiah's memory, checking for holes, searching for leaks. And as this is happening, Nehemiah is thinking, just a few days, I'm going to take just a few days, and then I'm heading home. Then the clock on the diner wall begins to chime, and Nehemiah asks, "When did she put that in here?" His eyes are fastened to the clock over the door, listening to the third chime, the fourth chime, thinking how out of place the clock is.

"What?"

"That chiming clock? When did she put that in?"

For the first time since he dropped him off in Washington, Billy looks at his brother with concern in his eyes. "You're tired, Brother. We need to get you home."

"Well, it's a simple question."

Billy doesn't want to trouble him by actually pointing out there is no chiming clock. That the clock he keeps staring at in a puzzled way runs on batteries. It says *Time To Eat* on the face of it. And it sure as heck don't chime. He should know, he thinks. He gave it to Kate for Christmas five or six years ago.

"Well now, that is the strangest thing I've noticed since I've been back," Nehemiah says as he stares up at the sound of the chiming that follows him out the door.

"I'm sure it is." Billy says, as he cranks up Old Blue, and Sonny Boy, bone in mouth, jumps in the back. Billy watches his brother out of the corner of his eye on the way home. He doesn't know exactly what he's looking for, but he's sure he'll know it when he sees it.

Billy is sitting at the kitchen table the next morning when his brother walks in. He hasn't dropped his guard, is still watching him based on last night's performance.

"Sleep all right?"

"Good as always." Nehemiah says this, but he isn't telling everything. He isn't telling about the smell that came into the room and woke him up. It smelled like gold. It's the only word that comes to his mind, but then how silly is that? How could gold actually smell? he is thinking. And a dream of transparent gold, almost a shower but not beginning from a cloud, not ending on the ground, just floating gold dust and in that smell *power.* He doesn't think he needs to mention this to Billy. Doesn't think he needs to tell him how long he's been awake, remembering what he is certain must have been a dream. Or how long he lay in the comforts of their mother's bed, basking in the lingering traces of her presence. Her still there in the framed faces of their baby pictures on the dresser where they'd always been. Her wedding picture by the bed. The fading face of the father they had barely known.

"Slept just fine," he says again to make it so, give it concrete legs to stand on.

Then he takes down a coffee cup and touches the ages-old pattern on the cup. The familiar is everywhere. It's penetrating his skin. A chunk of ice falls off.

This is when he sits down and sips his coffee and tells Billy

about the fox. This is where they have that conversation, such as it
is. Then they sit, quiet for as long as you can imagine. Drinking
coffee and not saying anything of importance or nonimportance
for me to take down. So I must let them sit there in their silent co-
coon while I record the other things.

The wind has picked up significantly today. Strong enough even
to shake the branches of the oak tree, at least at the edges, to make
the moss sway. The tall grasses try to stand straight but are blown
westward. The wind is coming from the east, as if the sun were
blowing with its rising, breathing heavily over Shibboleth, as if it
were moving things about, clearing all the dead away.

"I love this place," Nehemiah says. He looks to his left and
right as if the words had come in of their own accord, carrying
with them their own agenda.

"You always will," Billy says. Then they are quiet again. It is
the quiet that gives me more words than you can imagine. It is the
quiet that lets me read what's in their hearts, lets me put my finger
on Nehemiah's fear (and he is not a fearful man). On Billy's concern.

"You should paint the house, Billy."

"I was waiting on you." Billy says and spins the lazy Susan in the
center of the table for no reason except to watch it turn.

If we let our eyes wander up and over them, out beyond the
back field where the garden is lying fallow ready to be seeded, and
through the stand of trees, the scrub oaks and big magnolias and a
few firs, they'll carry us straight down the road where we'll run
right into Main Street. There we can easily travel over to Magnolia
to the house of Magnus, and see her feeding and shooing cats, trying to divide their food, making sure the skinny ones get to eat
and the fat ones sit and watch for a while. It is a precarious, de-
manding job.

We can see Trice spooning oatmeal into her mouth at the table, mindlessly eating while she reads from a book. It is a story about traveling to faraway places, a story filled with exotic flavors so pungent that she lifts her feet up off the ground and begins dancing on her toes even while sitting down. She is unaware that Nehemiah is about. She has forgotten about the whole affair. She delivered her message and rode home, sleeping most of the way with Billy listening to the radio because with her asleep he could drive without Trice singing along. You can't get her to shut up. And Trice can sing to beat the band, but sometimes he just wants to hear the music like he is alone. And driving home he could do that.

But now, Trice doesn't look as if she remembers the trip at all. Isn't the least bit concerned about the things that previously had weighed so heavy on her mind and heart. All that revelation has dissipated, as if she had run her portion of the race, had passed the baton, and was now free to sit down, mindlessly spooning oatmeal, at least until page 101, which is where she'll be when Magnus finds something that must be done.

At the wildly manicured yard of Magnus (which provides great hiding places for the cats to slink and pounce), the road takes a sharp curve past the mailbox. We can then turn back and follow it to the center of things and see that Kate is busy in the kitchen making a batch of potato salad that she is going to offer up at lunch. She occasionally wipes her hands on her apron and walks to the front window, looking out between the cafe curtains (which she notices should be washed and ironed again), and looks up at the clock. It is 8:35, and she is thinking Nehemiah is running late. Or might not come. *But that's all right*, she tells herself, *I know where to find him. And if he doesn't walk in here in the next hour, he'll be sorry.* She doesn't even know why she feels this way. Not really. But her sights have been set. She's not backing down.

Billy stretches his legs out under the kitchen table, angles them sideways so as not to kick his brother.

"You know you're not gonna get out of that meeting this morning."

"I know."

"You know she knows you're here now, and she will come looking for you."

"I know."

"If you are gonna let it fall that way, just let me know, 'cause I don't want to be here."

"You want to ride with me down there?"

"Nope."

"I figured as much."

Nehemiah rises from the table like a man wearing a noose. The fact is, he loves his aunt Kate with all his heart. The fact is, his heart jumped a little out of sheer gladness when she elbowed her big way into that seat. Fact is, a tiny part of him wanted to put his head over on that big shoulder like he did when he was five, and fifteen, and might just do when he is fifty if she lives to be eighty.

"So you going on down there?"

"Guess I am."

Billy is chuckling under his breath. "Oh, and Nehemiah, I don't know, it's up to you, but," he rests his hands on the back of the kitchen chair, looking down, then back up at Nehemiah, "I imagine you got a bag with some more clothes in it, but just in case you need 'em, your other clothes are still hanging in your closet." He pauses and the brothers just look at one another for a while, Nehemiah not exactly knowing how to process this information. "I hadn't changed anybody's anything. You know, just in case somebody came walking back through the door one day."

Nehemiah understands the *just in case* scenarios that Billy isn't saying. It's the *just in case* Nehemiah gave up on a different life. The *just in case* their mother resumed hers. Came walking up the front porch steps, her black purse on her arm, calling out, "What are you boys up to?"

Nehemiah got his dimple from his mother, but his is on the opposite side. They smiled at one another like a mirror image. And then smiled even wider.

"I appreciate it" is all Nehemiah says.

Then I wait to see what will happen next.

"Well, I'll just see you later. Me and Sonny Boy's got things to do." Billy says, and heads outside to his truck, calling to Sonny, saying, "You want to take a ride, boy?"

And Nehemiah is left alone in a quiet house with the memories rising up from the floorboards, wrapping around his ankles, beginning to hold him fast to the ground. He goes back to the door to his room, the one he had lived in every remembered day of his life in Shibboleth. And now, he stands before the door as if it's a vortex, as if when he turns that knob, he will have to say good-bye to any future he had imagined because he will not be able to get back across the threshold. Nehemiah is forgetting that the power of choice is just that. And the making of it is all his.

He turns the knob, opens the door, fights the urge to close his eyes. But there is no blinding flash. No irreversible line crossed. There is just the exact same old space. Exactly the way he left it. Exactly the way that he stood, surveyed the room, repositioned that picture on the dresser one last time, thought about taking it, and for reasons he still doesn't understand, left it sitting there. It's the one taken of him and Trice and Billy. When they were seventeen, sixteen, and nineteen and in that order to be exact. Their faces are still water wet, smiling, hair dripping around their faces. Trice is standing between the two of them, her arms hooked inside their elbows. It had been a perfect picture. Somehow capturing all their summers. All the green, and the wildness, and the freedom. But then, to capture it fully, you have to have Billy's fingers behind Trice's head because that's the way it was. And you'd have to see what you can't. The fact that Trice was pinching the inside of Billy's forearm—hard. And you'd have to know about the warm place her hand had left on Nehemiah's arm long after it was gone. What I can see is that Nehemiah can't help but soften when he looks at it. He picks the picture up in his hand, studies the image, wipes the dust from the glass before he puts it down.

He opens the closet door. It squeaks on the hinges. Billy is true to his word, not a thing has changed. There is the slightest smell of mothballs, placed there forever ago. Nehemiah runs his fingers down the arm of his old jacket. But then something on the closet shelf catches his eye.

"Hey," he says aloud. "I'd forgotten all about this."

Trice looks up from her reading and pulls her eyebrows together. She listens, but there is no sound except the wind and Magnus saying, "No, no, you are too fat already." She knows this must be directed toward General, the gray tomcat with the yellow eyes. He's a pushy one. She listens a little longer and puts her nose back in the book. She is up to page 99.

At this precise moment, between the written lines a solar eclipse is taking place. The world is falling into shadow and the people are perplexed. They do not understand the word *orbit* and are full of fear and trembling. They believe that something catastrophic is about to happen. And that following this event nothing will ever be the same.

Friday, 9:28 A.M.

It's almost 9:30 when Nehemiah walks through the front door of Kate's Diner. A few die-hard stragglers have been holding on, wanting to see the hornet's nest in full fury, but they are forgetting something as Kate steps through the kitchen door. She looks up and fills her eyes with Twila's boy. Not the one that had smelled— now how would she put that—*good but foreign*. Not the one with the manicured nails and all that slickness hanging about him like so much strange air. But the one that had just walked through her door. The one that was standing before her in his old, faded, threadbare jean jacket and blue jeans. And she thinks, *By God, if he doesn't even have his boots on.*

Her wrath spills from her shoulders until it is only a puddle at her feet. A puddle she easily steps over on her way to wrap some fleshy arms around *the boy*. And with that enormous hug, with Nehemiah's head disappearing into the body parts of Kate Ann, the audience members shake their heads and start to count their change. Doggone if the show isn't over before it had good begun.

Kate pulls Nehemiah to a booth in the corner, one situated where other people can't be tending to their business.

"Did you eat?"

Nehemiah says no, but he is looking at the clock. "You changed that clock out."

"Well, I reckon so, it's been over ten years since you stepped foot in here."

"Wrong. I was in here last night."

"How 'bout some biscuits and gravy?"

"Sounds good."

"And some bacon, or a pork chop, would you rather have a pork chop? And I've got some . . . "

Now he knows she is talking about food. See him nod. See him plaster on a smile, lock it into place. Nehemiah is no fool. Not by a long shot. He knows that clock hasn't been moved since it was hung there. He now knows what he saw, what he heard last night, was either a delusional apparition or something much more interesting. He starts to look around with a heightened sensitivity. *What's going on?* he wonders. His eyes are still fastened on the clock when Kate begins to deliver a breakfast of sausage links and grits, scrambled eggs, fried potatoes on the side, biscuits and gravy, and homemade blackberry jelly saved from two years ago.

"We didn't get enough rain last year to count for nothin'. Blackberries dried up on the vine."

"Aunt Kate, is anything strange going on around here?" Nehemiah doesn't call her Aunt unless he's serious. And he's serious. He's thinking about Trice's dream, and the gold rain and the clock.

"Well, I guess so, I'm sitting here looking at your face."

He stops thinking about clocks and looks into the familiar face across the booth from him. The hair is curled up from the kitchen heat, the blue eyes are still full of spark. "How's it look?"

She cocks her head, "I'd say, just about like it did when you were about five years old. Just about exactly the same."

"I have a few more wrinkles."

"I'm looking in between 'em." She would like to reach over, put the back side of her hand on his face like she did when he was a boy, but he is so new. So new all over again, and she doesn't want to scare him away. "So now, Nephew, tell me, what is going on up there in the high and mighty business of the capitol?"

"Well," Nehemiah begins a truly serious attempt to answer when he suddenly remembers he is hungry. Then the hunger turns into something else, as if he is growling from his toes, his arches, his ankles. He is voracious. He thinks that he hasn't eaten in, well, *only a few hours, only since last night,* comes to him as a surprise. But his hunger feels much older than that. Hunger that winds and growls around the empty places of his soul. Before he knows it, he isn't eating. He is diving, rolling, wading through food. Rejoicing in food. Passionate all over again, in a brand-new way, about food. About each dish laid out before him. His knife is the conductor, his fork the first string, and he is performing for a private, delighted audience of one. He has wandered right into being love-drunk on gravy, and just another bite of that jelly on just one more biscuit. He is full of so much love, so much flour, and pinches of this and that, that his eyes water. And he can't say a thing about the capitol. Right now it is a far, distant, disembodied land. He is living on the isle of warm comfort. He is swimming in its languid spell.

"Well, then, if you don't have anything to say about your work, what about the women?"

And again Nehemiah can't answer. He tries. He tries to conjure up a face of the adjunct professor he had dated for almost but not quite seven months. But instead he bites a link sausage and forks up the home fries. Says something about a "nice girl once. Went to Europe. Didn't come back."

"She was probably testing you and you failed."

Nehemiah nods but he doesn't understand what he failed at. Doesn't remember a test. Just a blue dress at the airport when he told her good-bye. And now that is what surfaces, a blue dress. The blue dress is wearing brown hair with sorrowful eyes and the scent of lavender.

"She was wearing blue last time I saw her."

"See, it was a test."

"I must've needed you there to sort it out for me." He gives her a wink.

"You don't need me up there, honey. There'd be trouble in that move. Washington would never be the same."

While he eats, and butters, and dips, and dives, Kate fills him in on the remember-when's. She paints pictures of his mother, tells stories of Billy and Trice and him running around swearing they had discovered treasure. "Made up a treasure map so you could find your way back. Knocked right there at that back door to the kitchen," she points through the kitchen in the direction of the door, "and asked me for tools, for *knives* to guard the treasure! Can you just imagine? I gave you spoons, said, 'Guard it with these.'"

For the slightest second, Nehemiah hears, "Hurry up, Billy. Hurry up!" But it's an echo and it fades before he swallows the next bite. "Then you took off again. Down to the springs. It's a wonder you didn't all drown. Mercy me."

Nehemiah's cheeks are red, flushed. The warmth is spreading through every region. Even the ends of his fingers feel flushed. But he hears the word *springs*, knows it is important, and tries to lash onto it. Tries with all his might to use the word for leverage to pull himself up from the plate of gravy, pull his face up from the bite he is about to take. And he does, but by the time he focuses on Kate's eyes, he has forgotten the word. He couldn't carry on an intelligent conversation if he had to.

"Guess you'll be ready for a nap soon."

"I don't nap," Nehemiah says, suppressing a yawn. "Besides, I just got up."

"Is that a fact?"

He looks at the clock, the regular diner clock, but the time says 12:04. He prairie-dogs his head up above the booth. The restaurant is almost full of people. The noise carries up where he can hear everything that he was missing. "I've been eating for two and a half hours?" He looks at the plates, realizing some have been emptied, taken away, others refilled.

Kate gets up from the booth; she does this by pulling on the edge of the table until she has enough leverage to hoist herself up and out. "I couldn't say exactly. Just that right now, you look well fed. And like you need to go to bed."

Caught in some strange tide, Nehemiah gets up from the booth and makes his way out the front door. He forgets if he said good-bye or not. He forgets if he offered to pay (knowing Kate would say no but offering just the same). And later, when the sun is much lower in the sky, he will forget exactly how he got back to the house, passed Billy on the porch steps, and went straight inside to his mother's bed and lay across the top quilt. If he had been a little more aware, he would have noticed the residue of gold dust pressed between the pattern, but he has placed his face in the middle of the threads and gone deeply, dreamlessly to sleep.

The glacier has met his match. There is the slightest scent of hope in the air, the barest whisper of a whistle on the wind.

Friday, 4:44 P.M.

When Nehemiah wakes for the first time, he realizes the magnitude of something peculiar enveloping him. He sits on the side of the bed, looks out the window at the low glow in the west, the shadows being cast across the yard. He pats the quilt next to him and raises his hands to run them through his hair, and stops, holds his palms out before him, bends his head down, rises, and walks to the window. He holds both palms up, turns them to the light, and there, unmistakably, is the glow of gold. He returns to the bed, kneels down, and peers carefully and closely at every thread, every pattern's curve. Then he rises very slowly, his hands still in the air, and moves toward the door. He is calling Billy. He is trying to turn the doorknob with his elbows. He is calling again and again, trying to call out while looking away, to call without breathing on his palms. He is looking for, longing for, validation, proof, confirmation of this incredulous occurrence when the dust begins to dissipate. He watches, no longer calling but quietly watching. The gold appears to shimmer, rises in the air, then falls back into his palms, sinks below the surface. He doesn't need to turn around, doesn't need to examine the bed to know there is nothing there.

Billy is driving around thinking about his brother, who passed him hours ago with not much more than a grunt then fell into some sort of unnatural sleep on the their mother's bed. He had watched him long enough to make certain that he wasn't sick or drunk. Nehemiah wasn't a major drinker when he left town, but a lot could happen, obviously had happened, since he'd been gone. No smell of alcohol. No sign of fever. He had quietly pulled the door to and said, "Come on, Sonny Boy, looks like we got some sniffing around to do."

Billy is looking for pieces of something, but the question he asks himself is, *to what?* He drives over to see Trice. This is one time he's hoping she's seen something, anything out of the ordinary, or had any strange feelings at all, particularly where Nehemiah is concerned. Then he realizes that he hasn't even told her about Nehemiah being home, so he drives on past the house, down to the river, just to think for a while. And maybe, while he's at it, he'll drop a line.

Back on Magnolia, Magnus is sitting in her porch rocker, rocking fast and clippity, her feet touching the floor then pushing off quick and hard again. *Was that Billy that just drove past too darn fast?* She thinks it was and makes a mental note to tell him he better slow down. Did I mention that Magnus dips snuff? Right now her bottom lip is full, jutting out below her top one. She is rocking and dipping too fast for the cats to ride along in her lap, but they are keeping an eye on her just the same.

Occasionally, her feet come to a solid stop, then she looks hard off into the distance until she nods to herself and takes off again. She is sorting through some business. She is making up her mind.

In the midst of this decision-making, Trice opens the screen door, sits absently on the porch swing. Her swinging is slow, rhythmic, her toe barely touching the porch to push off again. This has an effect on Magnus. Without her realizing, she begins to slow, to rock more comfortably, to keep a steady beat. General jumps up in her lap, stretching his paws out almost to her knees. Magnus spits off the porch, her fingers forming a *V* beside her lips.

"It's gettin' dark," Trice says.

"Yep."

"Looks like those dahlias could use some water. I'll get them in the morning."

"Well, then, while you're at it, check those tomato plants for weevils, Mr. Daffin said the other day his were *ate up* with 'em."

"All right."

They are still swinging and rocking when Billy pulls up in the front yard.

"Hey, don't you bring that dog up in here." Magnus is saying it like she always does, but as usual it's too late. Sonny Boy is out of the truck, down to the ground sniffing around.

"He ain't gonna chase no cats, Magnus."

General puts out his claws, stiffens his fur, growls low under his breath.

"Tell General that before he claws me to death."

Magnus spits again through her fingers. She is aiming for the dog but falls an inch short of the target.

"Whatcha up to, Trice?"

"You're lookin' at it." Trice is running her fingers through her hair; she is thinking about eclipses. She is picturing the one that she saw when she was little. How Kate had told her not to watch it or she would go blind.

"You up for taking a short ride?"

"What for?"

"I got something at the house that I want to show you."

"Can't it wait till morning?"

Magnus snorts under her breath. "Oh get up and go on. You ain't doing nothin'."

Trice is hard to get moving, but once she does, it's as if all the lazy energy in the world comes out in one spurt. Then she can't be still. If Magnus let it, this would drive her crazy. She wants Billy to get that hound dog out of here because all the cats have run up the trees and under the house, where he is nosing and sniffing. She can just picture them under there, crouched down, furred-up, shaking, ready to run or to fight to the last breath. She has tried to explain this to Billy to no end. It's not that the dog will hurt the cats, it's that they *think* he will and that's enough for her. They are at home minding their own business. On top of this, she knows in an hour or two Trice will get wound up (for no apparent reason), and she will begin to talk to her about whatever foolish book she is reading and follow her around, try to get her to sit down and listen to her talk about Mr. Einstein like he were still alive as if she doesn't have better things to do with herself with Wheel of Fortune coming on. Trice has been known to wander in and start reading right in the middle of a spin and that's just about a sin. Not quite, but just about. Magnus starts mulling over what exact types of sins there are that may not be listed in the Bible. She is thinking if she was God, she'd make everybody sit down and be quiet during Wheel of Fortune.

"Trice, I need to get going if you're coming."

"All right, all right," Trice says and gets up, releasing a tense ball of orange named Stella to the ground. Magnus names the cats. Trice buries them. Heavy work for her graceful hands, the very same ones that can go shooting off into the clouds and across the horizon when she needs to express her latest passion, but those dancer hands can grasp a shovel and hit the solid dirt with an iron will. Those hands will not back down. When the problem meets Trice, the outcome is really very simple, Trice wins. It is an unsuspecting advantage. One we might just be counting on.

Friday, 5:57 P.M.

Nehemiah is sitting at the kitchen table, holding a cup of coffee in both hands. He is staring into the cup so intensely that his eyes reflect back in the dark pool. He is still staring when Billy pulls up, still staring when he hears voices spilling up the porch steps. The screen door opens and Billy and Trice make their way into the house as Billy calls out, "Nehemiah?"

Finally he hears "Back here" in response. From the hallway the only thing evident is Billy's bulk on all sides, but when he steps into the kitchen there is Trice behind him in a white T-shirt, a blue jacket, and jeans. The sight of her brings him an unexpected comfort.

"Well now," she says, puts her hands in her back jeans pockets, leans against the kitchen doorframe.

"Yeah, I seem to have that effect on people."

"You look like your old self." Trice says, and I look from Nehemiah to Trice and back to Nehemiah. I write down *electric current squared.*

Nehemiah opens his palms, looks at the empty skin. "We need to talk, Trice. We need to go over your dream again."

Billy walks to the counter, pours a cup of coffee. Gets the milk and sugar out. "Trice, you want coffee?"

"Might as well, I have the feeling it's gonna be a very long night. And it wasn't as much a dream, Nehemiah, as an awakening."

Now they are where they are meant to be. Circled. Listening. Touching the very fringes of the truth. I want to shout, to encourage them, to say, "Yes, yes, now you're moving. Hurry. Hurry." But that's not my job. My fingers stay wrapped around the liquid, my eyes focused on the fire.

Nehemiah is contemplating how much to say, which stories to tell and which ones to hold at bay. He decides one piece will connect to the other. There will be no telling without all the details.

Billy figures they need a starting point. Figures he should be good for something, so he offers to break the ice. "Nehemiah, why don't you tell Trice about you knocking me down to get right back in that bed today and sleep like you were a dead man."

"Trice, have you ever heard a chiming clock down at the diner?" Nehemiah ignores Billy's prompting, tries to assimilate. To figure everything out. And hopes, so very much, that he is not trapped all alone in some strange hallucinogenic psychosis. He thinks if anyone is going to be in the river of strange with him, it will be Trice.

"No." She narrows her eyes, says in a hushed voice, "but I am hearing one right now."

Nehemiah and Billy freeze their positions, hold their breath, strain to hear the chimes.

"Guys, I'm just kidding."

"Look here, Trice, I am serious, and I came down here on the hem of your dream, so the best thing you can do is help me out here."

Oh, just look at those righteous ruffled feathers. A man holding doing the right thing out before him like a martyr's trophy.

"Look, excuse me if I get a kick out of the possibility, just the slight possibility, that I'm not the only one swimming in the river of strange."

Nehemiah raises his brows. "Did I just say that?"

"What?" This comes from Billy and Trice both.

"The river of strange, did I just say that aloud?"

"All right, Nehemiah, let's start with the clock then." Billy is trying to corral their words. "Let's talk about the clock, because I wasn't really gonna bring it up. I guess you figured out that there ain't no chiming clock in the diner. Never has been."

I wish I could tell you that they were making sense. That they were finally getting somewhere. That the clock I always hear was on their side, in their favor. But they are struggling so hard to make *sense* of things that they are missing the things that make sense. They are looking in the hard-to-reach places when they should be looking at what's right before them. Right before them at the center of the table. Right where it's always been. But they don't see it.

Nehemiah tries to build logical bricks, tries his very best to lay the skills of Washington, the skills he has worked so long to perfect, on the table. To dissect the problem and develop a program, a plan to get to the other side. He is still trying to do this when Billy gets up and rummages through the refrigerator. (His stomach is always the first to growl.) He pulls bologna, mayonnaise, cheese from the refrigerator and puts a loaf of white bread on the table. It's a self-serve dinner. Trice picks up potato chips from the kitchen counter, opens them, and walks around with her hand inside the bag. Before the night is over, she will eat them all. Nehemiah will eat nothing.

Billy wants to voice that he's just along for the ride, but what he really wants to say is that he sure is concerned about his brother acting peculiar. He is used to the peculiar antics of Trice. Everything from a cat sleeping on the motor and her *knowing* it before the car cranks to showing up saying, we got to drive over to Troy and pick up somebody from the bus station right *now*. Never mind what he was fixin' to do. Never mind that she doesn't know who or why or what for. But off he goes to satisfy her every whim, again, and lo and behold if Joshua Johnson wasn't standing there fresh out of boot camp and ready to surprise his momma but had forgotten all about how he was gonna get from the bus station in Troy to Shibboleth except to walk it out. (Boot camp had done him some good but in some ways he was still the same old Joshua. Nothing another decade wouldn't fix.) Billy had just looked at Trice (who never rubbed it in when she was right) and shook his head and said, "Hey, boy, you looking for a ride home?"

So all the antics of Trice were buried under his skin until they had become, well, just about normal for *her*. But with Nehemiah, well there was just that one great episode (and even now he can see Nehemiah walking through the flames carrying Blister in his arms). But besides that time, Nehemiah had been as normal as a life can seem to be. He is beginning to wonder if bringing Nehemiah down here was such a good idea.

"About this awakening," Billy waves a sandwich, his cheese falling out of the edges of the bread, "stop crunching, Trice, and just tell it."

"Already told it." She glares at him as she shoves more chips into her mouth.

"Well, tell it *again*."

Trice tries to recapture the pictures and to put words to the images of what she sees. "Black wings," she says. And the word *darkness*. And it occurs to her to use the word *eclipse*. It occurs to her strongly that this is the *right* word. The word she has unknowingly been searching for for days. "People are not expecting the eclipse," she says. "And it isn't a natural one. Not this one. It is brought in on black wings." She closes her eyes. "On dark desire."

"Black wings and dark desire my rear end," Billy says. "Trice, you been reading too many dang books."

Now can you imagine the human right-thinking mind trying to fashion sense out of Trice's description? Can you imagine trying to figure out your purpose in a plan that has no boundary lines? No noticeable rule book? But that is exactly what Nehemiah is struggling with. He is trying to figure it out when all he has to do is remember. *Remember.* I want to say the word with all my might. But I am willing what isn't mine to give. I am thinking of the liquid between my fingers, tracing the word *remember* in the air, but they don't see the word any more than they see me. It's not my purpose. I can't reach them. Not that way.

I am contemplating this, watching their blundering attempts, when suddenly there is a crash outside, the sound of something heavy falling, which brings quizzical eyes all around and a howl from Sonny Boy beneath the porch. The three rise from the table, move down the hallway single-file in quick succession. First Nehemiah, then Trice, then Billy in the rear. A childhood band of three, they marched this way together all their lives before Nehemiah left. Now they march that way again. Have taken up the rhythm of their lives in unison.

They step out onto the porch. There is a slight breeze but not a wind strong enough to push that hard. The moon is hanging, almost but not quite full. The moss on the trees is swaying slightly. Billy reaches back inside the door, flips on the porch light with his right hand, his eyes still fastened in front of him. Beyond the porch railing, leaning against Old Blue, lies a branch of the oak. It is a large branch, not a loose limb dangling but a strong arm of the north face of the tree. Billy says, "Hold on," and goes to retrieve a flashlight. He returns and the three walk toward the limb now lying partially on the ground, partially against the side of the truck, its smaller limbs falling forlornly into the truck bed. Sonny Boy sits at the foot of the limb, howls as if he is voicing its pain. The flashlight beam runs up and down the branch, around the yard, for a sign of a reason. The light is cast up to the tree, where the white, splintered shoulder is visible, raw and naked.

"That tree have dry rot?" Nehemiah asks. He asks this even though the flashlight tells the story. He can still see the green life pumping.

"Nope."

Billy runs his hands along the tree branch as if in apology, before he lifts it up with a grunt, pulls it over to the foot of the tree, and gently lowers it to the ground.

It's Trice then who says, "Why don't we go back inside and start over?"

And they nod in the solemn darkness as Billy says, "Come on, Sonny, it's all over now." But what he senses, what I'm privy to know for certain, is the fact that it has just begun.

They return to their chairs, sit in the same seats, but they're wearing different faces. If any of them had any lingering doubts that something peculiar was about that was going to be neatly squared away on Nehemiah's long weekend home, those thoughts are put to rest. They don't spend time wondering about the tree. They don't try to figure out if it was a freak streak of lightning or an odd break waiting to happen. They don't talk about the tree at all. They're beyond that. They pick up where they left off. At the word *eclipse*.

Trice asks for a piece of paper and a pen. She begins to write down the words they are saying, to take notes. She doesn't write their thoughts down in linear arrangement, as in one-two-three, the way that Nehemiah or Billy would. She simply writes the words in loose arrangement. She draws circles around them. Arrows pointing from one to another or tiny interrupted dotted lines from circle to circle. She writes the word *clock*. The word *eclipse*. The word *path*. She writes down *dreams*. When Nehemiah talks about eating for hours at the diner and how the time had disappeared, she writes the word *TIME* in big, bold letters, and in another, much smaller space the word *memory*. And after Nehemiah has told the hardest part for him to tell, the part about the gold dust on his hands, between his fingers, in the curves of the quilt threads, she writes down *gold* and *dust* and links them together with a heart, and never once questions the validity of Nehemiah's story.

Billy says simply, "Momma would like gold dust on her bed."

Now if only Kate could see their heads bent and determined, could see Billy's huge hands pawing at the table cloth, pinching it into wrinkles and then flattening it out again. If Twila could see Nehemiah's big brown eyes thinking their hardest. If Magnus could just peek over Trice's shoulders and see the pattern she is making, the weaving and the winding, she would recognize something from a long time ago. They all would. But right now, these grown-up children are on their own. The guiding eyes and voices of the past have all gone to bed, or beyond. And there is no one near to guide them into clear air. At least, not yet.

They alternately sigh under their breath. Nehemiah no longer wonders if his coming home to Shibboleth was a wild goose chase. He makes a mental note to call the office in the morning. To ask for a few more days and hope the senator understands. Trice is hoping that Magnus isn't waiting up near the door, her housecoat bunched up around her knees; she doesn't want to field the questions. She is too tired. She folds her note paper and slides it into her back pocket.

It's just before midnight when Nehemiah and Billy drop Trice off at the front door and wait for her to go inside. They are both too tired to talk and too wound up not to.

"Do you remember when Trice first showed up?" Billy asks him, as he watches her opening the door, turning around to raise her hand in the headlights, her lips mouthing, "Good-bye."

"No."

"I guess not. You were not quite two. Still," he puts the truck in reverse, reaches across the seat to look behind him, "it's the kind of thing that would stick in your mind. Not every day a baby comes to town, you know, by itself."

"That's what the stories are for, Billy. To fill in all the unknown spaces." These are some of the first great words that have come out of Nehemiah's mouth. The first words that are good medicine. I smile as I write them down. Liquid on Fire.

Nehemiah is quiet for moment. "You know, now they have all kinds of tests, and computers, and ways to track things. I guess if somebody tried hard enough, they could get to the truth about it. Track something down. I could ask around in Washington."

"Trice might not want that. She seems content to be who she is. You know?"

"Yeah, I guess you're right." Nehemiah squints in the dark, looks into the distance down the road. "Hey, turn right and head down Main, will you?"

"What for?"

"Just want to drive around a little. Check some things out."

And so they do. Billy drives down Main, circles the Heritage Oak, and they both picture the oak tree at home with the severed limb. He drives around the square twice, passing the oak, the Piggly Wiggly, and Kate's. It's locked up tight, all lights out. They drive on aimlessly, through the emptied streets. Nehemiah cranks the window down, and the sweet smell of spring gets thicker. The promise of wondrous, blooming things, but peculiarly mixed in is the scent of their already dying before they have begun. It is the smell of flowers in a funeral home, overpoweringly sweet, carrying the scent of death in every seed, on every petal. Occasionally, a dog barks over the transom of the small city streets. Sonny Boy is not inclined to answer. Nehemiah thinks about him in the back. "You want to put that dog up here with us?"

"He's got a name."

"I'm just asking."

Everything appears to be in order. Every sleeping thing. Then something crawls up Nehemiah's back. Nothing he can put his finger on, but a creeping sensation that climbs up the back of his spine. A low whistle escapes through his teeth.

"What?" Billy asks plain and simple.

"Something's not right here." Nehemiah leans forward, peers to the left and to the right out the front windshield. "Something's changed."

"Been a long time, Nehemiah, something's bound to change."

"Not this kind. This is dark, definitely dark." Nehemiah has a sudden parched feeling, an I can't swallow, can't get enough water feeling. "And it's coming from somewhere. Actually *coming* from somewhere." He looks up and down the streets again, rubs his throat. "Let's take a ride down to the springs, Billy."

"I told you. The springs are gone. Sucked dry."

"What are you talking about?"

"I told you the first night I saw you. You woke me up asking." Then he repeats himself for emphasis, "The springs are gone."

Hot summers. Cold, green waters. Secret caves. Billy and Trice. "Why would that happen?"

"Nobody knows, Nehemiah."

"Let's go down there and check it out anyway."

Is it premonition in Billy's heart that makes him hover, pull back? "It's dark," he says.

"Look, the moon's almost full. We'll be able to see enough to get by."

"What are you expecting to find this time of night?"

"I don't know. Just searching for some clues, Billy." He looks over at his big brother and places his hand on his shoulder. Billy turns and looks him in the eyes. "Something strange is going on around here, just like Trice said. It's not anything we can touch, Billy, but we've been through some odd places in this world before. Like the night of Blister's fire. Downright supernatural weirdness.

"You got that right."

"And some other things that for the life of me I'm having a hard time remembering. It's like they're almost there," he reaches his hand out, brushes the air, "and then, poof, just as fast as I felt them, they're gone."

"Like when you wake up and try to remember a dream but it's missing and you can't pull it back."

"Exactly."

"Been happening to me some, too." Billy leans his face out the window and breathes in deep. "But not like you. You've been downright spooky yourself, Brother."

"Yeah, well . . ."

"And you didn't even remember the time we tricked John when he was fishing."

"Billy, I think what happened tonight is more important than a fish."

"That's just it. There was no fish. It was all a trick you schemed up." He waits for Nehemiah to respond, to tell him that he remembers now, but he doesn't. "And something smells funny."

"You smell it?" Nehemiah thought it was another one of his imaginings. That he was having some sort of home, again, home again, hallucinations.

"Like something burning, maybe? Sometimes I get a whiff of something that doesn't smell like, well, like Shibboleth."

"Like tar?"

"Like hair burning."

"Well, now, this may be one of those times where we have to stop thinking and, you know, just walk it on out."

Billy nods but still wants to turn the truck toward the house. He's thinking tomorrow morning is plenty early enough for walking through whatever is waiting. He's also thinking if they're gonna be *feeling* things out it might be better to have Trice with them. He thinks this so much that he says so. "But we have never *feeled* anything out without Trice. Maybe we should go back and get her."

"Sure, and wake up Magnus and the cats—I'll pass."

So Billy concedes to Nehemiah, and they drive east off of Main and farther away from town until they crest a hill, then turn to the right again. The turnoff they are searching for is so overgrown they barely recognize it, pass it by at least ten feet, then Billy slams on the brakes and throws it into reverse. Wild kudzu forms gigantic canopies from treetop to treetop over the small slice of remaining dirt road. It is barely navigable, and the overgrowth tears its way along the sides of the truck like old claws ripping into flesh. Billy shakes his head, pats the dashboard as if to say, "There, there, Old Blue. Steady, old boy." They stop where the nearest lagoon used to be. Nehemiah opens his door slowly. Wonders how the light of the moon can be so weak and strangled out.

The other door opens and Billy steps out, large and on guard. Without any enthusiasm, Sonny jumps down out of the truck bed. The dog keeps his nose up, no sniffing around, no interest in the decay.

Billy and Nehemiah walk forward in the sparse moonlight, toward the water that they should have heard by now. Bubbling up and moving softly within its boundaries. But every step is taken with a hard labor of will. They reach the dry ground of what was once their favorite pool. There is a dry, bitter scent in the air, and Nehemiah is trying to place it, identify it, as their walking grows heavy. Sleepwalk-heavy. The ground has become dry, cracked, not even the residue of mud. Nothing but bones, lost rings, bottom things, skeletons of other life forms. Completely lifeless with the exception of scurryings of unseen scavengers. Large webs are strung out between every empty, open space. Nothing appears to remain but the invitation to die.

Nehemiah looks just to his left, stares hard into the darkness, begins to walk forward, begins to take the old path to the Well. Even with the undergrowth tearing at his legs, he continues.

"Where are you going?" Billy is standing where they used to swim, in a natural pool surrounded by low bluffs with shade trees. He searches for an old tire swing, or even a rotting rope, but there is no sign of anything familiar.

"I don't know, Billy, but something important is . . . over here. It's right this way, or maybe," he takes two steps to the right, "or maybe over this way."

"Sonny Boy," Billy calls out, but his voice is a strained whisper. The dog shuffles silently to his heels. "Just checking on you, boy." And Nehemiah understands the feeling, because there is a real threat of danger surrounding them. As if he could turn his back and Billy would be gone, eaten up in the suffocating dark. He starts to apologize, to say, *You were right, we shouldn't have come,* but the words are blocked, can't come out.

Nehemiah pulls at his collar, pulls harder, but his collar isn't tight, it's the air that is tight and growing tighter. His neck feels hot. Swollen. "I can't breathe, Billy," he says finally, but when he looks, Billy is bent over, his hands on his knees, and as Nehemiah tries to reach him, Billy's knees crumble to the ground. Nehemiah hears the scurryings growing louder as he attempts to push through the solid wall that was once air, the smell, the taste of sulfur, dry and bitter. He tries to reach Billy, but the ground itself seems to be rotting out from beneath his feet, opening up to swallow him. Sonny Boy falls down next to Billy's feet, gasping for breath.

I am tracing the truth, but with all my might I am hoping the truth will turn around. I am hoping what I am recording will not be the road truth takes. And as I watch the scene before me, I see a familiar glow in the distance between the trees. It is no larger than Trice's small orange, and I am hoping for Nehemiah and Billy, and Sonny Boy too, to look, to have hope, but they are beyond seeing.

The ball moves toward them, dances over them, between them, then it releases its light and the light surrounds them, throws itself over them like a net, and in that light there is breath. In that light there is life. It's the light of old prayers—long said but not forgotten. The prayers of a mother on her knees from years and ages past. Prayers for protection. Divine protection. All the days of their lives. But they don't know this. They don't know that power.

Not yet. They don't know that every good prayer spoken takes root and substance. They don't know the layers of prayer that Twila has covered them with like quilted blankets as they lay sleeping. Or that her prayers have taken on significance, a manifested presence. All they know is that they can breathe. They slowly stand, Billy scooping Sonny up in one arm in a single move. Wordlessly they back away, toward the truck, keeping their faces toward the menace, staying within the diameter of the light that surrounds them.

Billy has the truck back on the road, out and away from the arid hole, before the last particles of light have dissipated. They are back on Main Street before the edges of the magnitude of what just happened hits them. They are home, all the way home, before they say a word. But now, the words will not stop.

They stay right where they are, in the truck cab, with Sonny parked between them and the windows rolled down, and talk about the light that saved them, wondering where it came from and where it went. They talk about the attack by an unseen but real and formidable enemy. They talk about Trice, about her gifts, and about her strange delivery to Shibboleth. And in the quiet, in the honesty of thankfulness and rescue, Nehemiah confesses to the new comfort that he has discovered in her presence.

Billy says, "It's just that old thing."

"What old thing?" Nehemiah asks, and Billy looks over at him like he has lost his mind.

"That old *thing* between you two," he says again and leaves it at that.

They talk about their mother and then scratch, hunt, and peck, yet again, at the memory of their father, and they try their very best to formulate some type of plan. They talk about Blister, about that supernatural night from so long ago. About needing to have some trusting eyes and ears. About whom they might go to for some type of advice. And they agree that Kate fits the bill first and foremost. They talk until the earliest shades of sunrise lighten up the sky. Then they walk, bone-weary, both chilled and sweating, up the porch steps and into the house, where they fall completely, totally exhausted into their beds. But their sleep will be short, because in only a few hours something will call them up, on their feet and into action. I know this because every variation of tomorrow shows these next hours to be identical. Regardless of the outcome, the immediate future will be the same. And there will be no turning back.

The phone is ringing insistently. It is ringing with the question of Magnus. "Where's Trice at?" she asks. It is Nehemiah who has answered, still trying to remember that he has come to Shibboleth on the dare of a dream, has gone through some strange imaginings. Magnus's voice is trailing acid as she repeats for the third time, "I said, where's Trice at?"

"Home," Nehemiah says, wondering why she has called to torture him.

"She was with you."

Nehemiah walks with the phone, cord stretched to its limit, so that he can kick Billy's door.

"Get up, Billy," he says, holding the phone out. "Have you looked in her room?" he says back into the receiver.

"Well, of course I looked in her room."

"Did you look around? Maybe outside. She likes to be outside." Funny how he remembers this now. Remembers in a flash Trice spending most of her life in the water, under a tree, on a porch.

"She was with Billy." Magnus is not so big now; she is perplexed, getting smaller by the moment.

"I know, Magnus, Billy brought her here. We took her home last night."

"Well, she's not here."

"Billy!" he yells again, in the other direction, but there is no response. "She could have gone for a walk. Just admit it. It's possible."

"No. It's her day to feed the cats, all the cats, before she goes anywhere. But the cats haven't been fed."

"Let me call you back, Magnus."

"Somebody needs to call the police."

"Fine. Call the police."

"No, you need to call the police."

"Why me?"

"When did you get home anyway?"

"Hold on, Magnus, now hold on." Nehemiah is trying, after a very strange night, to comprehend the morning on too little sleep. "Listen, I'll get Billy up, and we'll come over there. Then we'll all decide what to do next."

Nehemiah hangs up the phone. Opens Billy's door, expecting to be overwhelmed with the snores, the heavy-lidded eyes of the stone-cold sleeper. But the bed is empty. The room is cold, chilled from the night, even with Spring sitting on top of them.

"Hey, Billy." Nehemiah walks through the house, opens the front door. Old Blue is parked sideways in the front yard. The missing oak limb lies beneath the tree as a not so subtle reminder of last night's realities. "Billy," he calls again. Then he sees him. Standing off to the side of the house, looking out to the west, his big arms folded like planks across his chest. As Nehemiah approaches, Billy never removes his eyes from what he is staring down.

"What do you see?"

"We got to go back out there." Billy never turns. "And I don't know exactly what to carry with us. So I'm wondering, what do we take to the fight when we can't see what we're fighting? Don't imagine guns are gonna make much of a difference. That'd be simple. But bare-handed or not, we gotta go back." He looks at Nehemiah for the first time. "You know that, don't you?"

"Yeah, Billy, I do, but first we've got another problem."

And Nehemiah explains about the phone call. About the supposed disappearance. Then they both agree that they will find her. That this must be a simple misunderstanding.

This is the way that they will struggle through the first missing moments of Trice. Imagining her out for a walk, absently forgetting to feed the cats. They make very strong coffee, wash faces, forgo showers, and dress quickly to drive over and appease Magnus and to find Trice somewhere obvious. Or so they believe. She'll be curled up with a good book in some crack or cranny where Magnus with her perpetual things-need-to-be-done list will not find her.

Now the amazing thing, quite remarkable really, is that the morning doesn't appear to hold the dust of last night's wanderings into the unexplained. It is one of the most beautiful spring mornings anyone will remember. The temperature is just right. It's the kind of weather that makes people around Shibboleth say, "Oh, if only it would stay this way all year!" and mean it. The magnolia trees are just about to blossom, the huge new heads of buds swearing they'll pop open at any moment. The azalea buds are promising a profusion of color, and even the pecan trees are bringing forth the tiniest of new leaves. How in the midst of so much promise, so much life, can there be darkness? Surely not. Surely, surely not. Just look around and see. All is well, yes? Well, it appears to be. So, on this promising, delightful spring morning, the brothers set off in Old Blue with Sonny Boy to find Trice and formulate some type of understanding of the night's events, and then a plan.

They begin *officially* looking before the twenty-four-hour window has passed because Duane is the county deputy and Blister is his first cousin, says he owes her for his life and that's that. They drive up and down the roads, they search the woods, drive down by the river. By 2:00 P.M., when Trice hasn't wandered back home again to eat or check on Magnus or generally be busy with the business of being Trice, Nehemiah and Billy no longer wonder. They know that something bad has happened. What they are hoping for now is that the only bad thing is that they don't know where she is yet

"Good Lord, boys," Kate is once again shoved up against Nehemiah in a booth, with Billy centered across the table on the other side. She has been listening to their story. All of it. Nehemiah has told her everything (with the exception of a tiny part that he has truly forgotten to mention), including the gold dust, the oak tree, the dry smell of sulfur and them choking, convinced that they both were going to die, and then the light. And now this. "Seems you've been through a lot in twenty-four hours. Reckon you need to eat something."

"Aunt Kate, we don't need to eat, we need to find Trice." This comes from Billy, who has never passed up a meal in his life.

"I reckon I know what I know." She has already leveraged her way to the end of the booth, is in the process of standing. "I reckon I don't need somebody tellin' me what I don't know when I know what I know. And you both need to get over to Zadok's and get shaved and, Billy, you need a haircut. Y'all are starting to look walleyed crazy." And now she has cleared the booth, is walking to the kitchen.

"Why does she do that? Why is food her answer to everything?" Billy is asking a question that he has never asked before.

"I don't know, but she's got some strange magic in that cooking." Nehemiah runs his hand over his chin. "And I look good without a shave, but she's right about one thing. You sure do need a haircut." Nehemiah is turning his coffee cup in complete circles. One circle. Two circles. Three circles. "Besides, maybe we'll eat the food and suddenly know right where Trice is. Maybe we'll eat and walk right to her, find her sleeping under a tree, then we'll hold one of Kate's biscuits under her nose and she'll wake up."

Billy starts laughing, which might be from exhaustion or because Nehemiah's story seems plausible.

Then a clock chimes. Nehemiah doesn't appear to hear it. Doesn't even look up. Doesn't even wonder anymore. He has crossed over into a world where the unbelievable can happen, where spring is still indescribably beautiful in the middle of what he now knows to be an encroaching darkness. Trice's eclipse. He is no longer banking on the plausible. Not putting stock in tangible evidence or *logic* or *reason*. *All well and good,* he thinks, *all well and good but not enough. Not good enough to win this fight.* And still he doesn't know what the fight is about. He still doesn't remember. Doesn't remember the Key, or the Treasure, or the Promise. But he is beginning to forget the things that block their remembrance. He is forgetting the word *Cuisinart.* He is forgetting that today the senator is stepping into a meeting about his upcoming reelection. Or that his job in Washington is only a breath between votes.

Because what he is thinking about, what he is toying with at the fringes of memory, is something he heard last night. Something he can barely remember, but it is there and haunting him. Something he heard as the air was being choked from his windpipe and his nose filled with sulfur. As the clock chimes, as Billy looks above the door, as Kate puts dumplings and fried chicken and fried okra and sliced tomatoes and sweet iced tea on the table, he knows without looking that time is running out. That now time is of the essence. That there was something last night that he must remember, and that in it is a catalyst that will carry him back. Farther back than the fire. Farther back than Blister in his arms and Trice's big blue eyes full of tears, full of wonder.

"Now, boys," Kate sits herself down, "you're going to eat, and I'm going to tell you a story. Something to set your mind at ease." And once again Nehemiah wasn't hungry until the food was before him, but now the eating of it consumes him as much as he consumes the food. The boys, such as they are in their grown-men states, begin to eat, and Kate begins to tell them a story. The story is the book of Trice. It is of her beginning, of how she came to Shibboleth, of how she was left in a bucket, not a basket as the story has been told by those not paying correct attention to the story. And that she also wasn't left on Kate's porch.

She tells them about going to the Well. It was her "remembering place," she tells them. And when people died, it was her grieving place. After all the work of burying her mother was done and everyone had gone home, Kate had gone down to the Well to remember that she had to keep believing. And while she sat, she told them (and they have heard this story before but now they are hearing it again), she heard a noise echoing up from the Well. An echoing sound from a long way down. Not a cry, not a whimper, but a sound that spoke, *precious*. A sound that whispered, *soft jewel*. And when Kate pulled the bucket up, very slowly, very carefully, one rotation at a time, turn upon turn, what came up out of the dark, watery depths to the surface of the earth was a baby. And the baby was Trice. Nehemiah and Billy have stopped eating, looking into Kate's clear eyes. When the baby emerges, they always stop. They are compelled.

"Can you imagine me there holding this tiny infant in my arms, naked as the day she was born? Not a mark on her, not a bruise, not a brushstroke."

"And now she's gone," Billy says, and his eyes are getting watery. He looks away.

"You'll find her." Kate says it with such finality, such fearless knowledge that at once they believe her. "A child comes to me in such a way," she shakes her head. "No, don't worry, you'll find her. That baby had angels watching over her. And wherever she is, whatever has tried to get ahold of her, she has angels watching over her still."

Kate pulls herself up, turns, hands on hips. "What I'm trying to tell you is that she's got more of a purpose than feeding Magnus's blame cats, I can tell you that much." She starts to walk off, turns back, and leans in to the boys, her hands propped on the table. "And let me tell you this much: when you find her, and if you re-trace your steps you will, you better listen to her." She picks up the dishes and she is gone.

The clock is chiming again. Billy is looking over the door, look-ing at Nehemiah.

"You see it, don't you?" Nehemiah glances up at Billy, who has a peculiar look on his face.

"What's going on, Nehemiah? Can you tell me?"

"No, I can't, Billy. But I have a feeling that we're going to find out. Now." He turns around, looks at the clock above the door, where *Time To Eat* is nowhere to be found. This clock has no hands. And now that he's looking at it more closely, the face has no num-bers at all. He rises slowly and goes to stand under the chiming, staring above the doorway, trying to examine the face of it. The numbers are not numbers. They are dots and dashes. They are tri-angles and geometric patterns. And somehow, they are vaguely fa-miliar.

"Did we ask Kate what we came to ask her?" Billy is standing by his side, both of them now with arms crossed over their chests, looking above the door.

"What did we come to ask her?" Nehemiah considers climbing up there, taking the clock down, but he already knows it won't be there when he does. His hands won't touch anything tangible. Not in this world anyway.

"What we're supposed to do next."

"She told us."

"Remind me."

"She said to retrace our steps."

"You know what that means."

"I think I do, Billy. I think I do."

They are still frozen in place, staring at the clock, which contin- ues chiming, as if time itself was a slow-motion carousel. One large, eternal revolution.

Saturday, 3:46 P.M.

Nehemiah and Billy make mention to go round up Blister and Cat- fish and John Summer with all his hunting dogs but decide against it. Or more so, they decide in favor of Kate's suggestion that they re- trace their steps. Decide that's at least the starting place.

Sheriff's Deputy Dewey, with his cousin Blister in the front seat beside him, is already out covering the south side of the county, knocking at doors along the way, riding all the back roads. They're looking for anything unusual when Blister tells him for the four- teenth time that day how he owes Trice his life. Then he'll ride along quiet awhile and then say, "Well, I reckon I owe Nehemiah most or second most, depending on how you look at it." Then, after some more quiet, he'll add, "And Billy too. I reckon they were a team." And while all this is going on, news of Trice's disappear- ance is being passed from mouth to mouth.

Nehemiah and Billy slowly make their way back to Magnus. She is on the front porch when they pull up. She gets to her feet, peers hard into the truck from the porch railing, hoping for sight of that mop of blond hair.

"What you doing here where she ain't?"

Isn't she a pistol? Magnus is a special piece of work and if the day ever comes that I'm on relief of my duties, I'll catch up to God when he's in a whistling mood and find out just what type of inspired moment she was in the making.

"We didn't know, Magnus, that she wasn't here till we came back." Billy slams the truck door. He is too tired to tussle with Her Majesty.

"No word from anybody? No call from Dwayne?"

"Not a word. See, just like I said this morning, something's wrong."

"We believe you, Magnus."

"Well, if ya'll believed me sooner, you might've found her by now." She spits, full of sour.

"Magnus, I know you want us to stay right here and visit with you all day, but could you just go find something of Trice's, some shirt or something for me to give Sonny Boy here to go on."

Magnus snorts. Actually snorts, which is rather insulting to the dog, but he pretends not to notice, to be absently occupied with the cats hiding up under the porch. Snort or not, though, she gets up from her chair and goes inside.

"Billy, don't take it personal, but can that dog actually track anything?"

"He can track, Brother."

"But can he find?"

"Sonny's not only got a nose, Nehemiah, he happens to have a heart."

Magnus returns carrying a sweatshirt in her hands. "She's not the tidiest person in the world. She's a clothes strower. I just close the door and let her go. Long as I don't have to look at it, I tell her ..." Then Magnus stops because she can't go on. She starts winding her hands together, one over the other. "It's gonna be dark soon."

"She's right, Nehemiah, let's get on while we still have some daylight."

"Don't worry, Magnus, we'll bring her home." Nehemiah turns toward the truck, opens the door, then turns back. "Magnus," he pauses, looks at the ground, then back at her over the door frame, "you still pray like you used to?"

"Don't know what you mean."

"I think it might be time for some of those prayers."

"Your momma was the prayer glue, didn't fall to me none." She spits again. "You should ask that old, sassy Kate to pray, that's who orta be praying."

"Magnus, Kate hasn't stopped praying since the day she was born." Billy slams his door shut. "Guess that means you are what you might call the second string."

Nehemiah whispers hard under his breath as he gets in and shuts the door, "I'm trying to give her something to occupy her mind. Don't make it worse by making her angry."

"Shoot, boy, don't you know nothing, that's just what she needs." And Billy stirs up the ant bed as he backs out of the driveway by yelling out the window, "God probably don't listen to your prayers anyway, so don't even bother."

They are pulling away as I record Nehemiah saying, "That was just downright mean."

"Wrong. That old snuff dipper will be in there praying heaven down to earth. You think Magnus is gonna stand for somebody not listening to her? Specially God."

And with Billy's diplomacy, Sonny's nose, and Trice's sweatshirt, they set out to make just one more stop before they return to what once was but is no more.

Nehemiah wanders through the house thinking that there is something he should be taking with him, some tool of defense that is just within his reach but that he can't see. He walks into his mother's room, opens the closet still filled with her clothes and shoes. *Guess we should clear this stuff out,* he thinks, knowing they never will. Somebody might, but it won't be them. Nehemiah closes the door just as something catches his eye, and he turns and reopens the closet. There, on the floor, between two pairs of practical shoes (one black, one brown) lies a silver thread. The silver is luminous. Puzzling. There is nothing this color in the closet. Nothing even close. Nehemiah picks it up, fingers the silky feel of it, is holding it up before the window studying the texture and the light when he hears Billy calling, and shoves it into his right jeans pocket.

He finds Billy standing by the door with the shotgun. "Don't reckon it'll help."

"Nope. But don't reckon it can hurt." Then Nehemiah turns back down the hall, calling over his shoulder, "Hold on."

He goes back into his old room, opens the closet door, and takes down a green duffle bag. Then he closes the door and walks back to the front door to meet Billy.

"Hey, good idea." Billy says.

"Yeah, I thought it just might come in handy."

And suddenly, it is I who am surprised. I am the one who knows most all things, sees the future in all its configurations, has the past recorded down to the detail of a heartbeat, and yet, on occasion, I am surprised by the human heart, by its capability to know and yet have the courage to continue. What has caught me unaware is the knowledge that Nehemiah and Billy aren't searching anymore. They know where they will find Trice. And they are going to get her.

An Hour Before Sundown

The sky is disappearing, the blue fading into dusk. There is the promise of an hour of sunlight, but nothing more than a promise, as Billy parks the truck on the side of the road. They appear to be walking by instinct, picking up the remains of some long-forgotten trail. Billy carries the shotgun, his pockets full of extra shells. Their faces are serious, locked up tight. They're now-or-never faces.

Billy takes Trice's sweatshirt in one hand, kneels down next to Sonny Boy and whispers in the dog's ear, then he holds the shirt before the dog's nose and mouth, rubs it on his long ears, and slaps him lightly on the rump. Nehemiah stands waiting to the side, pacing slightly back and forth along the edge of the road. Pacing the same worn spot.

When Sonny Boy begins to move, so do they. Wordlessly. The dog plows out the path, but the two men walk as if they knew he'd turn in that direction. He is not retracing last night's journey. He travels farther, much farther along the road before he turns, crosses a dried-up ravine, and disappears into the gnarled undergrowth. Again Nehemiah considers the quiet. I, too, give pause, write down the stillness, I know this death knell. I know the sound of life's absence. Only Sonny's shuffle, only their feet on the dry ground give credence to any pool of promise.

Nehemiah thinks of asking Billy, "Why has it come to this?" But his mouth feels dusty, his throat dry. They are walking out the daylight. They are vanishing into what was once green fern, wildflowers. And in this barrenness, as they search, listen for Sonny, hope for Trice, moving along in the airless void, they are casting their faith, their hopes on Kate's words. Trice will be all right. Trice has angels. And they are hoping all of this with an intensity that you don't yet feel. They sense that the three of them are not alone traversing this ground.

The battle begins. (Now, here is where you will ask me to explain the unexplainable. Here is where you will ask me for the thread of logic that connects all rational human thought. Here is where I look at you and say, "Watch. From where you are, it's all that you can do.") There is the crawling of sticks, the flight of wings, the sound of footsteps in the trees, the howl of a dog, the scurrying of things unseen, the ugly whip of clouds rising over the dried earth. It is an unnatural looming and swelling black air, a darkness whose passion is to eat the light. Now there is the sound of cutting, of whipping fast and light. And as Billy and Nehemiah watch helplessly, the black swells and rises, moves toward them, lowers itself. And believe me when I tell you this, the blackness looks into their faces, searches out their hearts, looks for open doors. And suddenly is pulled back, then swells again.

The dark bears down upon them, the wind threatening a great and terrible devouring. They believe that they almost see teeth bared. That the teeth are swords, and the swords themselves spit venom. And now, as the brothers stand shoulder-to-shoulder, their greatest weapon is this, that they will not turn. They will not run. They will not back down. They stand determined, eyes watering in the wind, looking into the faceless apparition that could be worse than death itself. Later, Nehemiah and Billy both will tell you that they could have sworn they heard a rooster crow in the midst of this madness. That they heard it loud and clear.

The wind tosses around small limbs, scrambles the dirt on the ground, causes Sonny Boy to shake his head, circle back, cower at Billy's feet. That's when Nehemiah catches a glimpse, only the briefest of a glimpse of red fur, and he grabs Billy's arm. Their mouths are moving but their words are swallowed back. Nehemiah places his mouth against Billy's ear, is trying to repeat what came. For a moment I sense them separating, going in different directions, and am relieved, even I, to see the better choice made when Billy follows Nehemiah. And now the man from the capitol, who has known strategically what to do for nearly a decade, relies instead on the gift inside of him. The one that has been dormant but not erased.

Nehemiah follows the flash of a red tail until he makes out where he knew it was going all along, the cave. The fox turns at the cave's entrance and looks at Nehemiah. It is the last time that he will ever see it, this particular creature of consequence. One time it called for him to forget a place. This time, it calls for him to remember. And he does. If Trice's dream was a vague awakening, the fox's eyes are an electrifying challenge. They say, *Remember, Nehemiah. Remember who you are.*

There is a flash of light. Not one that Billy sees, or Sonny Boy, but it is a flash that jolts Nehemiah's memory. And Nehemiah is ten again. He is holding tight to Trice's hand, breathing in the wild smell of her hair and listening to Billy's voice from the darkness saying, "Careful, careful, we're almost there." And from beyond his voice, out there where there isn't anything that they can see, there is a growing growl. Their knees and hands tremble. Their mouths go dry as they cling to one another and descend lower and lower into that cavity.

Twila had looked up at the clock just then, realized the distance of the time that separated her from the children, realized where they'd gone, and could feel them in her soul as they moved farther along the rocks, the ridged edge. She stepped out on the porch, the screen door slamming behind her, her hands in her apron pockets, full of faith and believing, and stood there looking across the field and into the beyond. There she is now and almost now, on the porch with her prayers, and me summoned at once to receive them. I step into the cave's core. Nehemiah, Trice, and Billy reach the bottom of the wet cave. And something begins to reveal itself. I move before it and lift my wings full-force. Light spills out from beneath in a great feathered fury. It spills into Billy's big heart, is captured in Trice's hair and cast over Nehemiah like a mantel, where it will remain forever. And over on the porch where Twila stands, peace falls. A peace beyond reason but one she easily understands. She pulls her hands from her pockets and goes back in the house, busying herself with dinner. Waiting for the children to come home.

Nehemiah is remembering this now. *Remembering.* And for just a moment he looks my way, but it's only a fleeting feeling. A really true feeling.

And as Billy aims the shotgun at the fox, as Sonny Boy howls, Nehemiah pulls the silver thread from his pocket. And the silver turns to water in his palm. Nehemiah looks up and calls for the rain. And immediately the rain pours down. It is a watershed. Billy wipes his eyes with the back of his left hand. Nehemiah reaches over and places his hand on the shotgun barrel, lowering it for his brother. He motions to Billy to follow him, and the wind subsides. The rain is eating the wind, forcing it underground. The rain is keeping them alive.

Nehemiah has remembered his way. And his way now leads them to Trice. They travel through the rain, echoing the footprints of the fox. Then they step inside the entrance to the cave. This is a cave they know. This is a place they have come before. In the twilight years of their past. The childhood days of their youth. The delightful days when they believed in impossibilities. And in treasure.

The rain still falls without but inside there is cavernous silence. The temperature has dropped twenty degrees and they can hear the clear sound of their boot steps on the rock floor, hear the dog's shuffling paws, his nose now touching the ground, inhaling deeply. He is smelling, familiar.

Nehemiah drops the bag, bends to one knee, unzips it, and takes out their old helmets. He passes one to Billy.

"Nehemiah ... " Billy puts on the helmet, trying to find his voice. He begins again, "There's a battle going on out there."

"Let's go get her, Billy." Nehemiah puts on his helmet, turns on the light, and focuses the beam into the cave. "The battle will wait."

They follow what to others would be blind madness. Cool caverns that turn and twist and disappear. Places so small even children would find it difficult to squeeze through. Remarkable, magical places that open into rooms the size of cathedrals. Secret rooms that rain gold drops.

Once there were three young souls who mapped out every trail, memorizing the paths before them and behind them. They were meticulous in their work. Serious in their discoveries. Silent with their secrets.

"You know what's missing, Billy?"

"Yeah, the sound of water."

The underground rivers, their much-celebrated waters in these dark places, are missing.

Suddenly, Sonny Boy howls, runs ahead of them. He turns to the right and through a small opening in the wall. They bend, shuffle, rise up into the larger room, following the howling that reverberates off the dry rock. They follow him with the beams of their lights, pick up the pace of their steps. Just ahead lies an almost discernable form. A form who turns out to be their Trice. They find her eyes closed and motionless beneath an outcropping of rock, an interior shelf, wearing the same clothes she had on last night.

Nehemiah bends down, lowers his ear to her mouth, feels her warm breath. In her hand is her note paper from their conversation, the lines and circles forming a wild diagram around the word *TIME.* Nehemiah pulls the paper from her hand, refolds the edges, and places it in his shirt pocket. He lifts her from the floor, while Billy cautiously looks around. Nehemiah could tell him something but he doesn't. Not yet. He could tell him that as long as the rain falls outside they are still safe.

They retrace their steps, walking out from the cave's entrance and into the rain. Now the wind is gone. Only a soft rain that follows them as they retrace their steps until they reach Old Blue. Billy opens the door for Nehemiah, who climbs up inside, holding Trice across his lap and in his arms. Once settled, he pulls off the helmet, drops it to the floor. Sonny Boy jumps in back as Billy starts the truck. He has driven away before he realizes the rain stops at the road. He looks back to see this anomaly, this rain with jurisdiction, but there is no rain. No rain anywhere. He looks over at Nehemiah, who is brushing the dirt from Trice's face. A dry, dirt-caked face. He runs a hand across his chest, his clothes now dry with the exception of wet rings beneath his arms.

"You want to explain this to me?" Billy asks. But Nehemiah just says, "Not now, let's get her home first."

Without a second thought, Billy knows where home means. He turns the truck east and drives past Magnolia, makes a silent note to call Kate and Magnus and Blister as soon as he walks in the door. He will simply say that she's all right. He will simply say that she is sleeping. But he's not sure that's the case. He's not sure of anything but the fact that his brother is finally back. Finally home again. And from the way he is holding Trice, there's a chance he might just stay.

Saturday Night, 7:44 P.M.

Nehemiah places Trice in his mother's bed. He carefully takes off her shoes and pulls the quilt up over her. Before he leaves, he searches the cover of the quilt, looks for gold, any pockets of forgotten dust, but there is nothing but the faded fabric.

Nehemiah joins Billy where he finds him on the porch. He imagines that before he will be able to get some much-needed rest, he might have some explaining to do. That's something he'd like to put off for another eight or ten or twelve hours, and if his brother will let him, he'll do just that.

"She still asleep?"

"Yeah."

"Don't seem natural."

"It's not, but she'll be all right."

"How do you know that? For certain, I mean. Just how do you know that?"

"Momma's bed happens to be good medicine. Don't ask me why or how, because those things I don't know. I just know it is what it is."

"You want to talk about what happened out there today? Or what happened out here last night?" he says, pointing toward the tree. "Or maybe what happened at Kate's with that clock, or how about we jump to after the tree and the clock to some dang thing breathing in my face that I can't see . . . "

"You know, Billy, I do. I really do. But right now, my eyes feel fried. I'm thinking just a few hours would do me better than good." He parks in the rocking chair on Billy's right, but they are too tired to even rock. They just sit flat and heavy. Unmoving.

"So you were right about that fox."

"The one you tried to shoot."

"If I'd've tried, he'd be shot."

"Not that fox."

"Now, see here, that's what I want to talk to you about, as in, how do you *know*?"

"That fox made me remember. That's the most of it. Made me remember, but you know, Billy, I'd like to rest. Just to have a moment to catch my breath. And if we can talk tomorrow . . . "

"No sir, no sir, Brother. I'm as whipped as you are but you got a few minutes to catch your breath and then do some explaining. You know, enough weird is enough. What about all that slithering, crawling, blowing attack out there? Huh? What was that? And what about all that rain and then, bam, bam, just like that I'm dry again? Huh?" Billy means it. All the way through. And he means it so much that he hasn't even heard Nehemiah whisper, "Hell," or seen when he closes his eyes and says, "Wasn't rain." And Billy means it when he stands up and walks across the porch, still saying, "Huh? Huh?" and walks down the steps and out into the yard.

What I know that Billy doesn't is that there is space now for a small pause from their battle. For the moment, Nehemiah has remembered who he is. And with that knowing, his soul can sigh with satisfaction. Tonight the smell in the air is pure spring. The magnolia tree on the side of the house, the one you can't see from just where you're sitting, has its first flower quietly opening. It's the one at the very top of the tree, so very far out of reach. Tonight the dark scent of death is not hiding on the backside of the petals. Just calm. A supernatural curve of peace. And if Twila's old bed is good medicine for Trice, it's the peace on the porch that reaches out to Nehemiah and settles over him just like his momma's quilt.

Peace will find even Billy when he stops considering over and over again the day's circumstances. When he walks a few steps out into the yard, stopping to listen to the insects, to look up at the sky, searching for the moon. For the first time in so many years, here he is with Nehemiah on the porch and that blond cotton-top Trice, after so much scare and worry, tucked a stone's throw away in his momma's bed. It's the peace of their closeness that reaches him as he bends down and scratches Sonny's ear and tells him, "That's okay, boy, you done just fine today. Just fine." When he rises and turns around, he finds Nehemiah fast asleep in the rocking chair. Billy starts to wake him, shake a shoulder and ask him again about the night, but decides not to. Instead he turns back and takes his place beside his brother so that, side-by-side, they may ride out the night together. Whatever it may bring.

─◦ *Sunday Morning* ◦─

It is Trice who wakes first, wanders through the house, and eventually opens the screen door to discover Nehemiah and Billy where we left them, recovering the sleep sacrificed in the last forty-eight hours. She carefully closes the screen door, pulls her jean jacket tighter about her in the morning chill and tiptoes out in her sock feet to sit on the top porch step, her back against the railing. She thinks of the absence of cats and wonders about Magnus, but it's a passing wonder.

Right now over on Magnolia, Magnus is holding court with the cats. She is fussing with them about Trice's disappearance. About the fact that *she hasn't showed up at the door, not even called her since she went off into the night. And all the worrying, all the stomach-tied-up-in-knots minutes, not worth a thing to Trice. All the . . .*

And Magnus stops and catches her breath, as tears well up in her eyes, pour down her cheeks, because it's not the fussing or the hurt feelings that pull her up short, it's the knowing that without Trice, she would have turned to dust years ago. Without the life of Trice, she didn't have a hope. Never did and never will. She wipes her eyes, says, "You understand, don't you, General?" The cat appears to slightly nod his head and blink as if to say, "Of course, Magnus. I've know that all along."

The sun is not fully up, the world still in the delicious stage of opening. It's Trice's favorite time of day. She is Shibboleth's miracle. Their baby from the Well. And although Kate said she'd found her so she rightfully belonged to her, no one would allow it. Oh yes, they nodded their heads. They said, "Of course, of course." But Shibboleth adopted Trice that day, even while she was still in Kate's arms. You can hold the baby all you want, they could have said, but she is ours. All of ours. And that never changed. Not in the way they watched her grow. Not in the way they claimed her. Whether it was Blister as he used to be, or the Gettys (with twelve children of their own), or least of all Magnus, whom Trice visited regularly in spite of Kate's frustration. It seemed Trice had no favorites. No belonging to a person, but instead belonging to a people. With the slightest of exceptions: she had belonged the most to Billy and Nehemiah. Or at least had belonged to the gang that the three of them had formed. And sitting here on their front porch watching them sleeping, Trice was back in the gang. And in the middle of such, the gang was back together. *Triumphant*, she thinks. But it's not the three of them that she is referring to. That word is directed at the sleeping face of Nehemiah. She wants to say "Thank you," to brush the hair back from his eyes and to ask him how he found her. But then she knows he won't be able to answer that any more than she could tell him this: that she knew all along, in the recesses of her mind, in her vague, waterless memories of *lost*, that she would be *found*. And that he would be the *finder*.

Nehemiah opens his eyes and sees her quietly watching him, her knees drawn up to her chest, her arms wrapped around them, her chin resting on her arms.

"How are you?" These are his first words.

"Okay," she says.

From the Gallas' place, a rooster is crowing. Close enough to be real morning, far enough to echo last night's storm.

He moves to the porch stair, sits down on the front porch step with her. "We're caught up in something, Trice."

"Yes, we are."

"Do you know what just yet?"

"I know we have some backing up to do. Something about recovering history."

"Should we wake the sleeping bear?"

"Bear's awake. Just resting my eyes and waiting for you two to say something that makes sense." Billy keeps his bear eyes closed.

"Maybe the two of you could tell me, truly, what's been happening since I've been gone?" Nehemiah looks at both of them. "You know what's going on is too ... " and he thinks but it is Trice that fills in the word.

"Powerful," she says and stands to stretch her legs.

"Yes, too powerful to be something that happened overnight." He cups his chin in his hand, elbow on his knee, and stares off into the distance.

Trice looks hard at Nehemiah and notices for the first time this morning that he is home again in a different way. An old way. Why, for a second he looked all of ten again. She'd seen that same pose in that same place. Top stair. Him staring off across the yard and the open field beyond.

"When did the water start to disappear?"

Billy rolls it over, thinking, but Trice doesn't miss a beat; she says, "The day that you left town." Then she leans out over the railing looking down the road. "Who could that be at this hour?" Trice stands up and looks hard into the dawning light. A trail of dust a mile long is flying out behind a car, which, as it comes into focus, is a '92 Buick, and behind the wheel is Kate in all her glory. She wheels into the front yard, cutting a sharp right, brakes at the last minute, and throws the car into park. She gets out, still moving at the speed of light.

"Y'all just gonna set there or can you give me a hand unloading what I got? Seems to me a person gets up at dark to make you breakfast and carts it all the way over here to you, the least you can do is help unload." But already her hands are full. Full, I tell you, of sacks holding biscuits and bowls of gravy, and a dozen scrambled eggs, and a ration of bacon, and some fried fruit tarts just for a taste of sweet. "Oh never mind, y'all move like molasses, it'll be cold for sure if I wait on any of you. Get out of my way." And with that, still talking, she has stepped over them and is tearing down the hall and into the kitchen before anyone has barely made a move. Isn't she something? Don't you just love her? God does. This much I know to be true.

They will smile and shake their heads and be so very thankful for Kate, for the substance of her being, for her unchanging predictability. They will wander like small children to the kitchen, where they'll be scolded for not washing and sent to clean up. They'll grow younger by the minute as she makes a pot of coffee and gets down her sister's plates, sets out her sister's cups and tells them not to take a bite until someone has asked the blessing, and that someone she'll appoint. That's her job. On occasion, when she is in a hurry, she will ask the blessing herself. But this morning, she looks seriously at Nehemiah and tells, not asks, him to bless the food. The word *rusty* comes to mind, but Nehemiah pulls out an age-old prayer of health and blessing and good fortune and thankfulness. And with a round of amens, they begin to eat.

They will be full and fatter when Kate gets up and refills their coffee cups (she doesn't care for other people working in the kitchen). Then she will settle down and say, "Let's have it. Where were you, Trice, and how'd you get there?"

Trice leans back in her chair with her scrubbed face, picks up her coffee cup, and says, "The only part I can tell you is the part that I remember."

"That seems like a good place to start." Billy is impatient, has been waiting for this information all night.

Nehemiah spins the lazy Susan, keeping his eyes locked on the centerpiece until Kate tells him to stop. He does.

Trice leans back in her chair, standing it on its hind legs, slightly rocking back and forth. Normally, Kate would correct her, tell her to set that chair down right before she wears out the legs, but as long as Trice is talking, she's quiet, except for the parts where she says, "Go on." The sun's rays come streaming through the kitchen window, a golden light of consecration settling on the heads of the four of them. They go on unaware of what I see, but I have no doubt they feel the healing warmth.

"Strange things happened last night," Trice is saying, "Not just strange later but strange to begin with, when Billy came to get me and . . . "

Billy interrupts her, "That was two nights ago."

"Then Nehemiah was here, and we all started talking. Just sitting around the table talking. Me just listening mostly. Nehemiah did most of the talking, about what all has happened to him— well, maybe more aptly put, around him—since he came home. I guess you saw the oak tree out front. Well, that's one of the things. The oak tree being attacked." And this is where Trice is the only one who gets the word right, understands the fact about the tree.

Kate nods her understanding, "Lot of history in an oak tree."

"But more than that, it was the talking. And I was taking notes. Just scribbling really, but somewhere in those scribbling, those doodles, there was something trying to surface in the back of my mind the whole time. My notes . . . " Trice begins to search her pockets, front and back, jeans and jacket.

Nehemiah pulls the worn piece of paper from his pocket, passes it across the table.

"Like I was saying, I was writing everything down, listening to the words and the way that some of them would jump out at me like they were heavier than the others. Like this one," and she points to the word *TIME* in large, bold letters where she has re-traced it over and over. "And I knew right away that time and memory were linked together so I drew that link in."

Now you would think that people would be hurrying Trice along, trying to get her to get to the place where she stepped off the world and out of sight. But not at least two of these. They know that Trice has a purpose and a place, and that now she is the one holding court. She is the one who has the closest indication of where they're going to from here. And what you can see in Trice, all the way from there if you look, is that she is fearless. Fearless in the way that there is the absolute absence of fear, not a place where it is locked away, not a place where it is hidden, covered, and rubbed over, but completely missing. But then what else would you expect from a child from the Well?

"There was something about this," she traces the lines again with her bare finger, following the crosses and dashes and angles, "something about this that made me wonder. And when Ne-hemiah and Billy dropped me off, I sat there at the kitchen table staring at the paper. The biggest thing was the feeling that we," she stops, looks up at Nehemiah and Billy, "and I mean the three of us, had been at this place before."

Nehemiah nods his head. It's something he already understands. They are backtracking.

"And right after that realization, I had a creeping feeling about the two of you. That you were headed into serious trouble."

"You are right about that, Trice, 'cause we sure did run into trouble."

"Let her finish, Billy," Kate says.

"And I felt like I needed to warn you both. Felt like I somehow had to get help to you. But I didn't know how. I stepped out on the porch, stood, and listened for a while. Thought I'd call you at home, but you didn't go home and I knew that too. Just knew it. Then I was looking at the moon, it almost being full, and I admit I got lost in the moon for a while. And when I remembered what I was doing, what I was thinking, the picture was in my hand. The map of last night."

Nehemiah jerks his head up. He has been listening all along, but now he is listening *intently*.

"And I knew I had to get out of where I was and get help to where it needed to be."

"Tell it, Trice, tell it. Tell how you walked all the way from Magnus's house, all the way that I cannot understand down to the springs to find us. And you went down there and either passed us or we passed you on the road after the funky light saved us."

Nehemiah says, "Billy, you don't even use the word *funky*. Matter of fact, nobody does."

"Like I said, that funky light saved us. And then you just went sound to sleep right down there where we couldn't breathe. Where we couldn't breathe, you hear me?" Trice's eyes are growing wider as Billy keeps talking. "How come you could sleep down there where we couldn't even breathe?" Billy is at his limit on strange.

"Billy, Trice can't answer that because she didn't even know where we found her until just now." He turns and looks at her. "Did you, Trice?"

She looks at Nehemiah but doesn't voice an answer, just shakes her head no.

"Billy, you are wanting a lot of simple answers that you are not going to get, at least not yet. Look, Trice, it's okay. Just tell us what you do know."

"I told him to let her tell it, but he has never been able to let Trice have her own way with things. Never." Kate has a tender, sore spot where Trice is concerned. Doesn't like anybody messing with her. Doesn't like Billy being short with her, which is just his way, but his way makes no difference to her. Nice is nice.

"I remember knowing you were carrying me, Nehemiah. I knew that, and when I knew that, I knew everything was going to be all right. Then I woke up in your momma's bed. And that there had been a long walking dream, and that somewhere in between the dream and the walking, you would be the one to fill in the spaces. I remember a dream, Nehemiah, of you holding a silver thread, and the thread turned into a liquid, and the liquid turned into a fire, but you were never burned."

"Well, that helps a lot." Billy's barrel chest is breathing heavy. It is a hard thing for him, getting thrust into a world he doesn't understand. Having to fight an enemy where even his bare hands are worthless.

"Children, children." Kate stands up, puts her hands on her lower back and rubs. "Trice, let me see that paper you keep pointing at." Kate holds the paper out before her at arm's length, then noses her glasses up and brings it closer to her eyes. "Well, now, ain't that just something special." She passes it back to Trice. "Looks just like the one you drew about twenty years ago. Just about identical." And she is moving herself around the table, picking up dishes and stacking them in the sink. "Trice, you want a ride over to Magnus's house? Looks to me like you could use a shower." She is spectacles down again, peering at Trice over the rims. "Or get your clothes and get your butt back over to the house with me where you belong."

Trice drapes an arm over Kate's, leans a head over on her shoulder. "Wish I could, but like I told you, Kate, Magnus is my assignment."

"Whatever you say, Trice. Personally, I don't know why Magnus would be anybody's assignment. Not unless it was a punishment."

"You got that right," Billy says but that's from the whole dog feud.

"Seems if a person was raised in a place, they'd live in that place instead of living somewhere they ought not to that has got to be diseased with all the fur flying ... " And this rolling force is making her way out of the kitchen, down the hall, and out the door. Before they can thank her for breakfast (they have been a bit slow on their toes and tongues this morning), she has gotten into the Buick, fired it up, and now already the dirt is trembling, preparing for her takeoff as she revs the engine and backs up faster than most people can move forward. Kate is a force of nature. She was created to be that way.

Trice is hanging on the porch railing, watching the dust of Kate's departure fan out like a rooster tail until it eventually trails off into the air. Except for the full stomachs and the rumble in the ground, you'd never know that she had been there.

Nehemiah has followed Trice out to the porch, where in just a few moments we discover them sitting on the top stair, both facing in the same direction, out past the oak tree and into the open field beyond. If they had had their way about it, they would have still been there when Magnus called screaming for Trice's whereabouts and when was she going to come home with pockets full of explanations (and get her chores done). They'd still be there later, when Kate called them up and asked them to come down and sit with her after she closed up. They'd sit all day and do much of nothing. Which is an interesting thing, considering that Nehemiah would sit through another business day not taking care of business. It's interesting the way that he can casually lean over and ask Trice without looking at her, "You remember anything about a fox, a red fox? Did you happen to see one?"

And Trice will think about it, but she'll eventually say, "No, seems like I'd remember something like that." And after she is quiet awhile, she'll add, "Matter of fact, I'm sure I would. Don't see many red foxes around here anymore. Matter of fact, closer to never."

"Just thought I'd ask."

"Yeah. Well, guess I could ask you how'd you find me, specially down there."

"We ... " and Nehemiah stops. "You know it really doesn't matter how. Just matters that you're here. That you're back."

"Do you think I could've walked that far?"

"Could've. You grew up walking everywhere. Still walk everywhere. I guess your legs can carry you where you need to go."

"You know none of us have been down there in years."

And somewhere in the word *years* Nehemiah will remember how many years they lived at the dark, green springs. Remember all the sunlight filtering through the trees. Remember Trice standing on the bank and then diving in, her full form visible through the green water. And then him diving in after her and kissing her right there under the water, in the middle of the magic of summer, her face rising to the surface, her breathing in the warm air, the sun resting there on their heads as their feet and arms continued treading water. And Nehemiah remembers being mesmerized. Not only by Trice but by the pure, simple goodness of the sun and the water, the reflection of the trees making it look like he and Trice were swimming in green leaves. And this will trigger the knowledge that all of that was a long time ago. And that will trigger the memory of where he has been and the fact that not once has he called his office.

"What day is it, Trice?"

Trice looks at him and shrugs her shoulders. She is the last person to be concerned with the day of the week. Particularly now. Right now the day of the week is the last thing on her mind.

And then Nehemiah doesn't even get up to check his calendar, check his watch, make a call or attempt to make one. At least not yet. That will come later, when he sits down, determined to decipher exactly how many days he's been gone and clear his mind to think about what to do next.

He looks up at Trice, and he is so glad to be sitting on that old porch with her close enough that he could reach out to touch her if he chose to.

"Why didn't you ever come see me?"

Trice looks up at Nehemiah with a slight smile, has been half-expecting, half-hoping for this question. "You never invited me, Nehemiah. It's just that simple."

"I'm sorry."

"If it helps, I didn't take it personal."

"It helps." He runs his right hand over the rough hair on his chin. "I didn't invite anyone. Not even Billy." Then he reaches out his hand, "Let me see your note paper again, Trice."

She passes him the paper, which is getting more worn as the day goes on. "What did you say this looked like?"

"I didn't. Kate said something about a map."

"No, Kate said, like one from a long time ago or some such thing. You said a map."

"Well, when you look at it, it does kind of look like a map." Trice takes it from him, turns it counterclockwise, holds it at arm's length. "See, just like a treasure map."

Then there is what some people might consider déjà vu, that wonderful sense of repeating, reissuing words and then reliving their immediate results. But this isn't one of those feelings. It is a true copy of a moment, one slice of time superimposed over another, like laying a traced copy of a photo over the original. They both call Billy's name, are standing up, calling him to them and simultaneously rising to find him.

Billy has stayed inside. He has been watching something. He has been wondering if it is an old thing or if it is a new thing. He isn't certain yet of which one, but he is certain of this: Trice sees into the other side of Nehemiah. It's a side that Billy is far removed from. And he knows it. He can stand right in front of the things this brother knows and can't touch that world. It's the same as being with him in the capitol building in Washington. Billy might be standing there but he's not touching down, not touching that particular part of the earth. Nehemiah has spaces that Billy can't reach. But he sees who can. And there is something that he has silently known about his brother all his life: that there has been a deep, separate aloneness. Like a rock formed from a different world. Something indigenous to another place and indifferent to all of its surroundings, and he has seen him hurt because of it. Has seen him try to force himself to change, to fit a different mold, to erase the parameters of his identity. Now Billy sees that Trice knows Nehemiah's thoughts before he forms the words. *That* he can understand. What has surprised him, caused him to pause, is the recognition that Nehemiah feels Trice's feeling without her stumbling explanations.

Nehemiah and Trice are communicating with one another in ways that he does not understand, but he understands that it is happening. This is what sets him to contemplating the night of the fire, of Trice's call, of Nehemiah and Billy getting her and driving out there because who else would bother in the middle of the night on the whim of a dream. But now, looking at that fateful night through the lens of time, he thinks maybe he was just along for the ride. Trice's dream and Nehemiah's, what would you call that—faith? A magic moment? The flash of Blister in Nehemiah's arms. The flash of Trice in Nehemiah's arms.

Both times, in the rain.

With all the occurrences, with all the waves of incredulous things that have come crashing into the small, simple world of Shibboleth, he knows that the line of communication between Nehemiah and Trice is critically important. One big seesaw with one of them on one end, one on the other, and the essence of Shibboleth balanced in-between. It takes a smart man to recognize revelation when it comes. And it just so happens, Billy is a very smart man.

Now his name is being called, repeatedly, insistently. Billy meets Nehemiah and Trice at the screen door. They stand looking at each other through the screen. "Look, Billy, look," Trice holds the paper out in front of him, "tell us what you see."

"Well, Trice, let me get out there, for goodness sake. What I see is you standing behind the door." He opens the door as she takes a step backward, still holding the paper arm's length away from her toward Billy. "I'll be. It's our treasure map."

"Not exactly, but yes," Nehemiah says. "Somehow, it's a copy of our map."

And now there are three heads, as Trice sits down in the rocking chair with her head bent forward. Nehemiah and Billy's faces frame her shoulders, left and right, as they look over the words, angles, and dots. She turns it, ever so slowly, around and around, tightening their focus with every turn.

For just a moment, we could have been Twila's eyes from twenty years ago. Looking out from behind the screen door, catching these three involved in some serious business, their heads bent forward in grave consideration, as if the good of the world depended on their calculations. And if we were Twila twenty years ago, we would smile and shake our head, wipe our floured hands on that worn white apron, and go back to work. But we're not Twila and we're not smiling.

That was just for practice. That was the before. This is the now.

Sunday, 11:07 A.M.

Nehemiah drives up to the little, white wooden church. It sits on a green hill in Shibboleth. Just enough of a hill so that you have to feel gravity as you approach the doors. It is the sun in the planetary existence of Shibboleth. All the revolutions of its communal life travel annually around its calendar year. It is the fabric that makes up an entire town's collective memory. A memory of ritual that anchors them to the substance of their lives. Birth announcements and calls for prayer. Hugs and hellos. Warm bodies against warm bodies. Same familiar faces and families, year after year, layered upon one another. The same songs sung for every occasion. Same trembling, scratchy voices. Same melodious baritones and sopranos. A cacophony of can-sings and can't-sings all joined together. Elderly women in flowered polyester with tiny steps, being ushered carefully, slowly, to their pews as if at any moment they might break. Old men dozing off during the sermon, but shaking the pastor's hand at the end and saying, "Mighty fine, Pastor, mighty fine." And always the flux of babies growing into children, of children growing into brides and grooms. The perpetual twirl that makes room for the celebration of one more breathing brand new soul. Or the grieving over the loss of the last one. A collective town having dinner on the ground and knowing one another's histories and heartbreaks.

Nehemiah, Billy, and Trice had made it to church this morning with not much more than small talk. Trice was in the backseat, having sworn that Billy needed to be up front because he was too big, but the truth was she just needed some distance. She needed a moment to pause, and to catch her breath. To be able to look down at herself in her new dress without feeling self-conscious. But every time she had looked up, Nehemiah was looking at her in the rearview mirror.

It was Magnus who had picked out Trice's dress for her. Magnus who had told Nehemiah and Billy to "Sit down on the porch and I'll fix you some coffee while Trice gets herself dressed." Then, once they were out of her hair, she'd gone through Trice's messy closet and pulled that dress out of the back with the tags still hanging on it. It was the one she had ordered from J.C. Penney for Trice's birthday two whole years ago and the girl telling her all the time she didn't have any place to wear such a thing.

Magnus had laid it across the bed and was both thankful and surprised that when Trice walked in her old robe, looking a little tired but scrubbed rosy, she hadn't even argued about it. Had actually said, "Thanks, Magnus," like it was the first time she'd laid eyes on the dress. Like it was her birthday all over again.

Nehemiah and Billy had sat outside rocking and counting cats. "I bet she's got fifty," Billy had said. Sitting there in that rocker he had looked odd in his church clothes and tie. His clothes didn't fit and normally he didn't dress up so much but this time he'd put on his one good suit. Perhaps to not shame his brother who was, once again, dressed to perfection. Billy's one good suit was the last suit he'd bought for a funeral twelve years ago and that's just because no matter how much he sucked in all his body parts, the suit he'd worn to his momma's funeral just hadn't fit anymore. He had taken it off, looked at it long and hard, then took it over to Tommy Patchard's momma for her boy. He knew they didn't have much of nothing.

So Billy sat, looking tightly shoved into an outdated suit, and Nehemiah sat looking like the cover of a magazine. The cats didn't want any part of Billy because he always smelled doggy to them. But Nehemiah, oh yes, Nehemiah they had designs on.

They had wanted to rub and twirl against those smooth, dry-cleaned pants legs. Smear their multicolored hair along the toes of his polished shoes. They had even offered him a purr but the purr came with furr, and this kept Nehemiah constantly moving, twitching to keep them at bay. Then Trice had stepped through the porch door. She had reminded him of the day in southern regions where a person steps outside and realizes the azaleas and dogwoods have bloomed. All of them. Overnight. Although a part of you knows that isn't possible. It's just that one single day you look, really *look*, and there they are in all the fullness of their glory. And just like that, Nehemiah had been caught off-guard by the glory of Trice. And a little speechless. So much so, so obviously, that it had been Billy who had finally broken the silence by slamming his hands down on the chair arms and saying, "Finally! Let's go." Then they had all gotten into Nehemiah's rented Malibu. The same Malibu that he had forgotten about. Had forgotten it was parked right there on the side of the house.

Just this morning, Nehemiah had been determined that tomorrow, Monday morning sharp, he would take care of some serious business. That tomorrow he would get to the bottom of this thing, and get back to where he belonged. He had told himself these things in the mirror while shaving, and I had laughed when I heard this. I then looked into the pages of history yet to come and saw troubling twists ahead and looked back at the reflection of the man in the mirror, hoping so very much that he would make the right choices. It's a wonder he could drive at all.

Going to church had been Trice's idea. While they were still pouring over their copycat treasure map, she had quietly said, "Maybe we should all be going to church." And there had been no discussion and no argument. Only Nehemiah saying, "We should get dressed then," and he and Billy getting up and going to do just that. Just as if Twila had said, "Boys, get ready for church." The only thing missing was their "Yes, ma'ams" as their footsteps headed in the direction of Sunday.

Nehemiah, Trice, and Billy enter the church and sit up front next to Kate. They are wearing their Sunday best. They sit in their assigned pew with whispers to their backs, and Kate plumped up with enough pride to bust wide open. This is a regular affair for Trice, a seldom affair for Billy, and, of late, a never affair for Nehemiah. This is almost exactly the way it used to be. Only back then it would have been like this: Twila would have been beaming from one end of the pew, and her sister Kate Ann beaming from the other. They were the spiritual bookends that held Nehemiah, Billy, and Trice firm in their positions.

Trice's blond hair would have been curled very carefully with Kate daring the humidity to fuzz it up until after dinnertime. At least, she had figured, the child could look like a lady on Sunday. The rest of the week if Trice wanted to run wild with Nehemiah and Billy, well, that wasn't Kate's first choice, but it wasn't her last either. Her last would have been not having Trice at all. Miracle babies make you believe in magic. Miracle babies get spoiled rotten.

Twila would have slicked down Nehemiah and Billy's hair. Both of them would have been sitting there with wet heads. But their hair would dry before the end of the service and begin curling up on the ends just like their daddy's had. Kate would be so caught up in surveying everyone's hair that she would lose her singing place and have to find the verse and line in the hymnal again. Kate would have been thinking about how Twila hadn't looked too good. A husband passing can take the wind out of you. She should know. Had known all these years. Now suddenly, there they both were manless as can be. With children. Well, the Good Lord would provide. Somehow. He always had.

But that was almost thirty years ago and right now, this minute, what Kate is trying to remember is what she needs to know most. *Did I leave that oven on 350 or turn it down to 250? If I left it turned up, that roast is going to be cooked to pieces and tough on top and not fittin' to eat.* She hates not to have the roast. But if it's too tough, they'll just have to make do with chicken and dumplings and baby limas and cornbread and blackberry cobbler.

Kate Ann looks over at Twila's empty seat. It has stayed empty now for almost thirteen years. But that's still her space as far as Kate is concerned. The family has sat in the same spot for, well, all of their lives. The church was built when Kate Ann was but a baby. When Kate comes to church with Trice, she makes certain nobody sits in Billy's space or his momma's. Or for that matter that renegade Nehemiah's. And now, on this strange Sunday morning, here they are again. All buffed and shining. *Nehemiah's hair looks just right,* Kate is surmising. *He really is a fine-looking young man,* she thinks. Then she looks at Billy. And Billy's hair . . . *Lord!* Kate interrupts her busy mind with a prayer, *Lord, send Billy a good wife because—well just look at him.* She continues her survey with a critical eye. *And now would you look at that? Trice looks unusually bloomy. That's just the way she looks, bloomy. Her hair, even though it doesn't look tame, looks just this side of wild and that's an improvement. She's wearing a dress that is just a little more, well there you go again, bloomy. Where'd she get that? I haven't seen that on her. And she is sitting very, very still. And that's unusual.*

The fact is, Trice is very bloomy, as Kate puts it. And very still. And, she is staring straight ahead and not singing very loud and that's another sign of something but Kate isn't sure what. Not yet anyway. But it'll come to her. She knows it will. She looks over at Trice again, and down at her dress. *Flowers, flowers everywhere. Just like a . . .* and she pauses and leans over and looks hard at Trice, *like a wedding!*

It was in this church that Nehemiah's mother had married his father. Here at a later date, that they had carried William Daniel forward in their arms and dedicated him before the congregation. And two and a half years later, they walked forward once again with a new baby in their arms. Nehemiah looks around at the old walls, the same ones he grew up in and hasn't seen for years, and tries to picture this. Tries to capture this image of a Sunday morning family with four squares. But before he can squint hard enough to try to remember his father's large hands, feel one of them vaguely on his shoulder, the hand is replaced by the gentleness of Twila's or the surety of Kate's. His memories latch onto the curves and rest there. In the curves. Not so bad a place to be.

There is general upswelling good mood inside the church. There is the feeling of something sliding into place. There are people leaning and whispering at seeing those heads up front in their assigned seats after all these years. There are a few *"What-do-you-know's?"* and some *"I-told-you-so's,"* flying around.

Wheezer is in the back in his usual place, trying to huff and puff out the song. He stands with his knobbed-up knuckles grasping the back of the pew in front of him. Blister stays in back too. Keeps the angry side of his face turned towards the wall. Children have never been afraid of Blister, but he thinks they are. He thinks the scar alongside the left of his face, his pulled-down eye, and the skin puckered at his throat will frighten the pants off them. Because it does him. Over the years he has learned to approach people right side first, with his head turned slightly to the left.

Magnus is not in church this morning on account of the fact that she had her feelings hurt twenty-four months, seven days, six hours, three minutes, and counting, *ago.* She hasn't been back since. She is rocking on the front porch, singing "When we gather at the river" at the top of her lungs and slamming her feet to the porch

floor with every rock and pushing off again, hard. The cats have all
run under the porch or up the trees, but there is no escaping the
strength of her voice. It can carry for miles, and miles, and miles.
Right now, she is hoping it will carry right through the doors of
the church and up that aisle, straight up Kate Ann's spine. *It would
serve her right for telling me that I cannot sit in Twila's place. Twila has been
dead for over twelve years and she sure doesn't care if I sit on the pew next to
Trice but Kate sure does. Kate wants Trice all to herself. Always has. But it just
ain't ever never gonna be that way.* Magnus slams her feet hard and prays,
*God forgive Kate for being so pigheaded so she won't go to hell forever and ever.
Amen.* Then she adds as an afterthought, *'Course a short trip through
might do her some good.* Then she resumes her singing. Just when the
cats thought they were getting a break.

Pastor Brown is finishing the last stanza of today's opening
hymn. He is seventy-two years old and looks every year of it. But
he still looks it in a saintly way. In a white-haired, blue eyes, lanky-
tall kind of way. He looks like he could live forever and not be the
worse for it. And all the people that know him, wish this could be
true. He adjusts his glasses and looks out across the pulpit at the
faces of his congregation. He's seen a hundred faces born and a
hundred faces die, baptizing them in and burying them out. He is
the caretaker of what is natural in Shibboleth. He is Shepherd to
the flock. Watcher of the sheep. All faces should be equal to him,
he thinks. But they're not. Some are more precious to him. Some
more dear. And now he is watching one of those faces. One that
got away. The boy that slipped through his fingers. The one that
he knew needed comfort when comfort wouldn't come. When he
couldn't give what he didn't have.

Lately, he has been questioning his destiny. Not as a pastor, he
knows full well that he's been called. But he has been questioning
the decisions of destiny that he has made during the process of his

journey. He is questioning his motives and his might-have-been's. He is supposing that if he had been more honest, just a little more open, that potentially even the ultimate outcome of Twila's illness. *Well*, he thinks now, *wondering won't set the record straight or change a thing*. He is thinking about how he let fear get in his way and let it have its day. He can almost see her sitting there, full of brown-eyed faith, and remember how when he'd make a joke he'd check to see if that dimple was waiting on her cheek. If he had won her smile— even from a distance. Twila Trust. A simple woman, a widowed woman. A faith-filled woman. If only he'd stepped up and con- fessed his feelings then *maybe*, but then, there he was wondering again. And all the maybe's in the world wouldn't bring her back. Or keep Nehemiah in his place.

All his *maybe's* in the lonely evenings where he sits and reads his Bible, or simply holds it and doesn't read at all. Where he doesn't dare think the words *love* or *loss*, but he feels them in the marrow of his bones. He feels the empty echo of lost possibility. And he is ashamed that with all that he is (and he is a lot) that he was not man enough to express himself. Too afraid of what people might think, of what people might say. And the chance that he had to make a difference when a difference could be made—in at least four lives including his—had slipped away.

Twila used to tell him stories about Nehemiah. Stories about his *gift*, as she would call it. And years later, she was proved right when Nehemiah had walked out of that fire unscathed, carrying John Robert to safety. And she would look to him for guidance, for understanding, of the things that were different about Ne- hemiah. At church dinners and celebrations, she'd look to him for company, and for conversation. Maybe more. But he would only smile and nod his head; he was so fearful of his mouth. So fearful of his heart.

Now with Nehemiah here, actually *here* in Shibboleth, actually here in *church*, he hopes he might rectify a portion of what he missed. He thinks that perhaps God and Twila both have ordered him a second chance. A method of making his amends. Of setting that boy, no, that *man*, he thinks, as he looks out across the congregation once again, a chance to set that *man* on his path again. And maybe that will stop what is eating them, all of them, from the inside out.

Suddenly Pastor Brown is very serious. His serious looks like this. Like a man who has been carrying a lonely weight. The pastor's sermon today was going to be on the loving kindness of God. On the mercy of divine grace and of a love that is offered when no love is deserved. About how God loves people in spite of themselves. And about how human beings are to follow suit. To love without barriers. Without hoops for people to jump through. Without bells for them to ring. A wonderful message, but today calls for something different, something made to order. And the pastor looks up, and forgoes his prepared sermon. Instead he decides to preach from the Old Testament.

"There was once a man named Nehemiah. Now you know about him, don't you? Sure you do." A few people edge to the front of their pews and lean forward. They nod their heads and pretend *their* Nehemiah isn't there sitting among them. That the pastor preaching from the Book of Nehemiah is *just a coincidence*. The pastor puts his hands in his pockets, steps down from the pulpit and walks the aisle, his voice rises as he walks forward, "He wasn't much of anything, didn't hold a grand position, certainly wasn't a priest." He turns and addresses Nehemiah from the front and center of the church. "He had a simple job, one of loyalty. He was cupbearer to the King," and the pastor says, "interesting," almost completely under his breath. "Just a cupbearer minding his own business, until his brother and a friend go to him and reveal that things weren't very good at home. And do you know that with all those people in the city, not one of them made a difference until Nehemiah left the King and came home."

Trice is listening but fighting the urge to pull her notes from her purse to study the curving, squiggling lines. She is certain that something crucial is hidden somewhere in the clue of its design. That surely, if she looks hard enough, she will find the "X" that marks the spot.

Nehemiah is listening to the message with one ear and thinking, *he's talking to me*, but one ear is all he can afford. The rest of him is thinking about the dark cloud at the springs. And the knowledge that he knows down in his soul that the dark cloud is spreading, breaking beyond whatever boundaries held it there. He is thinking about the presence of evil and the power of good and wondering just where has Pastor Brown been in the middle of all this. *Why hasn't he done something? And why haven't the people of Shibboleth even questioned how all the water could . . . how did Billy describe it . . .* "The water just left town." *And why does Trice look so fine in that dress that he almost forgets she is Trice and thinks about her as a . . . woman.* He glances over at the flowers and breathes in the smell of something tangibly sweet, and he doesn't know if the smell is perfume or simply the essence of Trice. And he isn't aware that his glance has turned into a stare until Trice turns and looks in his eyes and then neither one of them are listening to the sermon with even a smidgen of an ear.

"It wasn't *that* Nehemiah's destiny to be a cupbearer. It was his destiny to save his city and his people. To fight whatever opposition stood in his way." The pastor walks back up into the pulpit. He pauses and looks into the eyes of the parishioners, "Whether that opposition was man," and Pastor Brown leans over, and tries to lock his eyes on Nehemiah's "or beast." He takes a breath and steadies himself, hands on both sides of the pulpit's edge, "You're purpose may be to march into the unknown for heaven's purpose, or perhaps," and here the pastor looks at Kate, "only your neighbor's yard to say 'I'm sorry,'" He raises an eyebrow her way but Kate just nods and smiles, and looks around because she knows the pastor sure is preaching to a lot of people in here that need to hear this message. "But whatever it is, it's not your purpose that matters. It's God's purpose for your life." The pastor pauses, thinking of his own life, thinking of cause and effect and the unknown consequence of fear. "Be brave enough to cross that line, whatever it may be that separates you from your destiny." The pastor wants to add more, he wants to tell his whole story and how his heart feels today. He wants to say everything he wishes he had said thirty odd years ago. But he only drops his head and says a closing prayer and adds a hushed, "Amen."

And with that they will sing another song. And then Trice and Billy and Nehemiah will be at Kate's table eating Sunday dinner like they used to do with an assortment of odd ends and pieces of people with no full table to go home to. Widows and widowers. Young people drawn to Kate's tough embrace and forceful nature. Every loose Sunday soul with the exception of Magnus. When no one is looking, Kate will make her plates to go with an extra large helping of dessert (because she knows Magnus has a sweet tooth) and pack it off with Trice to take home to her. Kate Ann may have her standards but she is not without heart.

After the service, in the general sudden commotion of people being released from their seats, they try to make their way out. But people have come forward to shake Nehemiah's hand, to slap his back, to give him a wink and say, "You're finally home, boy, where you belong." And he tries, ever so diplomatically, to smile, to be polite, as he works his way to the door. People joke with Billy about the fact that, "The roof didn't cave in when you come in so I reckon you can come back next Sunday." Billy doesn't tell them that actually he likes coming to church (minus the suit). It's the absence of Twila that keeps him away, the empty space in the pew that breaks his heart every time he looks down at it. Even after all these years.

Nehemiah is shaking hands with Pastor Brown when the pastor says, "I need to see you, Nehemiah."

Nehemiah smiles, shakes his hand, has misunderstood him. Thinks he has said, "Good to see you."

"I need to see you," the pastor repeats, "Noon. Tomorrow. Here at the church."

"Yes, sir," is his simple answer.

Pastor Brown briefly glances over at Trice and Billy and before he releases Nehemiah's hand, leans in and says, "I prefer you come alone." Nehemiah gives him a quizzical look but simply nods, and the pastor releases him to reach out to the next person.

The three of them stand awkwardly in their Sunday best (although Nehemiah's *real* Sunday best would have looked like his wedding day to Shibboleth), and Kate Ann is already at the Buick, the door wide open and her yelling, "Trice! You gonna ride with me?"

She looks to Nehemiah and asks, "Are you coming?"

"Yes," he says, "but first I have to pay a visit."

Trice nods and turns to go. Billy just says, "You go on, Nehemiah. I'll wait here." And Billy hangs back saying so-longs to the milieu of southern Sunday worshippers with all their Sunday-dressed children, little recreated carbons of the past. They are running through and around the legs of their mommas, daddies, aunts, uncles, and grandparents. Little cousins and bigger cousins making a noisy mess and having such a good time they forget they are hungry, forget to ask, "When are we going to eat," because they know that they will soon enough. And if they ask aloud, that will be the official answer, "Soon enough." Right now, they are just happy to have cousins and to be free, out in the open, and the sunshine. Running off an hour and a half of sitting pinched between adults on hard wooden pews. (Except for Cassie Getty, who always brings her own seat cushion to church.)

Billy makes small talk while Nehemiah makes his way across the churchyard for a long overdue hello. He steps gingerly through the flowers, the flags, the tiny symbols of the past. Walks past names like Walker and Skipper and Getty until he reaches a spot in the back under a towering magnolia, one resting now in the dappled light beneath the shadow of shade and the light filtering its way between the leaves.

"Hello, Momma," he says, but that's as far as he gets. Now, mind you, as I write, as I listen, as I follow, I must insert this to inform you: Nehemiah knows his mother's spirit isn't in this spot of earth. That truly she doesn't rest eternally beside their father's marker. But this is his touchable place. The tangible, concrete, earthly place where he can reach out his hand and touch her name, conjure up her face. Nehemiah doesn't know what else to say except, "Hi, Momma" and "I miss you." He thinks about all the times he has needed her advice, all the times he's thought he'd just reach out and pick up the phone and call her, but then, how silly was that? How many times he'd wanted to call her from Washington and tell her something to make her proud. But she wasn't there and so the proud had nowhere to go. And the thought of not seeing her face again, not until some faraway place like paradise, had choked him until he thought he would die. So he didn't think about that anymore. Or, at least, tried not to.

Wrapped in the folds of today's "I miss you" is the memory of a heartbroken eighteen-year-old boy. One kneeling by a grave in the rain of midnight, refusing to leave his mother's side. Refusing to leave her alone in the dark. And, behind him, standing in the dark with his own broken heart was a brother refusing to leave Nehemiah alone. A brother who quietly felt the shift of responsibility settle on his shoulders and wondered, *How am I gonna look out for Nehemiah's gift with you gone, Momma. No one's here to tell him how to be. And he's not like me. I taught him to fish, and to hunt, and to fight, but I don't know how to teach him to go on being who he is because you were the only one knowed that.* And so they had spent the night with Billy weeping and Nehemiah wailing over a wet mound of fresh dirt that signified the end of a long, peaceful chapter in their lives. And the beginning of a different one.

One that would carry Nehemiah into the far reaches of a much different city where he was determined to evolve into a different man and never look back to the place where things had come undone. Where all his talents, his gifts, and his stories couldn't bring his momma back to life. Where he decided if he couldn't help her, he wouldn't help anybody. He was mad at himself—or mostly at God—he couldn't decide which. Maybe a lot of both. And, eventually, that anger had spilled over onto the entire town and every soul that dared to still breathe when the goodness of Twila had been ripped off the face of the earth.

If Nehemiah's arms could have reached down through the very earth that night, ripped open that casket, and pulled her out, he would have. Oh, yes, he would have. But then who, in the midst of the terror of grief, the aloneness of grief, wouldn't do the same?

Nehemiah is remembering this night as he stands by her grave. He is remembering his brother pulling him up the next morning saying, "Come on brother, we got to go home." And Nehemiah looking at him with eyes full of sorrow and shock, as Billy had added, "Momma would want us to go home."

And so they did, and there they found Kate and Trice and Magnus and Blister and he doesn't remember who else. People just there because being there was all they could do. And Nehemiah had washed his face, and Trice had come through the bathroom door, stood looking at him in the mirror until he'd turned, put his arms around her, and in the sweetest, quietest way, she'd whispered, "It'll be okay."

Nehemiah had thought all these years that he would be standing here sooner. But, surprisingly what he feels now—is that he is Twila's strength. As if it's rising up from the ground, from her very bones, and pouring into him. As if she is reaching out, telling him to go on with what he has to do. To carefully identify his priorities. "And Nehemiah, the true ones," she would often say, "are not always the ones that appear the most obvious." If there had ever been a time that he needed her sage words, he felt that time was now. Her understanding of the presence of things unseen. Her unshakable, unmovable faith.

Billy is waiting, leaning against the car when Nehemiah picks his way back through the concrete tombstones.

"Momma says, *hi.*" Nehemiah says, as he gets in the car.

"Is that a fact?" Billy closes his door.

"Yep." Nehemiah cranks the Malibu, revs the engine, and puts it in reverse, "And to tell you that you that you need to get a haircut."

Sunday Night, 9:33 P.M.

Nehemiah is pacing the perimeter of the house. Pacing in circles. Around and around. *Treasure maps indeed*, he is thinking. A wind is blowing from across town, whipping through the tops of the trees, bending them over. Lightning flashes, far away, still in the distance. An out-of-season lightning storm. *This is August weather,* he thinks. Everything is out of season. Everything is out of time. He is still trying, despite his best intentions, to put things together from the perspective of some leftover residual of logic. Just when I was thinking he had come so far, so fast, that there was still a chance.

"You should come inside. It's fixin' to storm." Billy is hanging over the porch railing.

"I know that," Nehemiah says, pacing by and passing Billy in front of the house. "That's part of the problem." Nehemiah points his arm up at the sky, "Does this look like a normal storm to you? Well, does it? Because it's not." Nehemiah has disappeared again around the back of the house. By the time he clears the corner, Billy is sitting in a rocking chair. "Does making those circles help?"

Nehemiah pauses long enough to say, "You know, it does. But not for long." He walks up the steps, sits beside Billy. The wind whips the trees, bends the tops over. The sound of it can be heard over into the next county and beyond.

They rock back and forth just as if the weather was still as pretty as it had been this Sunday morning. From one extreme to the next. From all flowers to all fury.

"You know something, Nehemiah?" Billy's drawl sometimes slows to a crawl. "Me and Trice went to Washington to get you for a reason. I guess you been here long enough to figure out the reason ain't bogus. What you ain't been here long enough to figure out is exactly what you're supposed to do, and I imagine that must burn your butt like a mound of fire ants. But you can pace in circles around this house all you want, the fire ants are still biting, and you're no more closer to the answer than when you first started out."

"Thank you very much, Brother, for that astute observation."

"You're welcome."

"What do you think we should be doing?"

Billy shakes his head, rubs his face, and stares off beyond the porch railing. "You know something, I don't know. I really don't. But the funny thing is, I think you do. And that you just don't know it yet."

"Maybe you're right. Maybe it'll just come to me when I'm not looking so hard."

"What's down there in the springs, Nehemiah? Do you know that much?"

Nehemiah sighs, or was that a groan that I just heard? "I know it's bad."

"Even I got that much figured out, and that only took one trip."

The oak tree shudders. They stop rocking, wait to see if another limb will be ripped away. Satisfied, they resume rocking.

"Here's the thing, Billy, this is what I need to know real bad. Why didn't you know something bad was down there before? Why didn't you get the feeling ... Well, how long has it been that the water's been disappearing?"

"For years. Only it was little by little. Not overnight, Nehemiah. You've been gone a long time. You know, you go down to the water, and the water's a little lower, only you don't notice because you go down to the water every day. Maybe it was even disappearing when we were kids and we didn't notice."

"No it wasn't. Trust me."

Billy laughs out loud. This is an old joke between them. Their last name had been a school joke and a topic of conversation since the day they were born. Some say their great grandfather chose it on his way to America to make himself sound, well, like a man of his word. But the only Trust man they ever knew was their father, Joshua, and what they knew was so very, very little.

"I do trust you, Brother. But you got to tell me about the fox, and about the rain. You got to reel me in."

So, as the brothers rock and talk, Nehemiah goes over once again about seeing the fox for the first time. And about seeing him the last time. Then he talks about the night that he walked into that burning house full of flames and walked out again untouched with Blister in his arms. The wind howls. The trees scream. Sonny Boy comes out from under the porch, leans against Billy's leg, submits to some serious head scratching. After all, they are a family. And when the storm comes upon them, even Sonny Boy figures they are better off if they stick together. Keep one another well within sight.

"Did you know, Nehemiah, when you went into that house, that we thought you'd killed yourself?"

Nehemiah thinks again of Trice's eyes when he walked out. "I did when I looked at Trice."

"We thought you were a dead man when you rushed in there, Nehemiah."

"I didn't see what you saw."

"I know that now. What I don't know is why."

"Some things, Billy, I really cannot explain."

"Yeah, I know that too."

Lightning flashes across the sky. Trice would tell you if she were here that lightning is sometimes friendly. Sometimes it is just plain fire.

The night that John Robert's house caught on fire, the blaze was started by lightning. That night had unveiled Nehemiah, scarred John Robert, and scared Trice and Billy so bad they were never the same. The lightning was one solitary bolt out of the sky. Caught a pine tree that was so dry the tree went up in flames like a huge match. Then the tree fell, crashing over into John Robert's roof. With him sleeping. Soundly. Or maybe, more correctly, passed out. He was known as a drinking man, and it had been a drinking night. Folks around Shibboleth, guessing what his condition might have been, had said him being alive at all was a miracle. Never mind his condition.

When the pine tree hit the roof, it caught nothing but the tar paper that John Robert had used, in a bit of drunken haze, to repair the last leak. The tar paper sucked on the fire like it was juice, and blew up. The rafters ignited and, little by smoky bit, the rest is history. Well, it's *that* history.

Nehemiah, Billy, and Trice didn't see any of this. Nehemiah answered a phone call from Trice in the middle of the night. She told him she had heard John Robert scream in her dream. Then she said, "Oh hurry. Please hurry," as if she were on fire herself. What she didn't know was that the pine tree had just caught fire at the point she woke up. Had just fallen over when she dialed their phone number.

And within minutes, the three of them had been tearing down the road in Old Blue, who was in his glory days of brand-newer. When they pulled up, what was done was almost finished. Go ahead. Ask me why Trice didn't wake up an hour before with a premonition about the tree. Wake up before lightning ever struck. Ask, but don't expect an answer. All answers come in the Sweet By and By. And we're not there yet.

But now we are at the part when Nehemiah and Billy can rock and recollect in the middle of this new storm. This storm made of funny, fast-cracking lightning. Odd shoots of lightning from odd sources. A crack from the sky. A bolt low over the field. No pattern they've ever seen, and they've see a lot. And the wind. And no rain.

We have come to the part of their remembrance where they will again carve out those countless slow-motion minutes. Count them out one by one by one.

"Then we were standing there with Trice yelling, 'Oh, God! Do something.' Over and over again. And me looking for a hose. Do you remember me looking for a hose, Nehemiah? Like that was gonna be able to do anything."

"No. I don't remember the hose." And he doesn't. And he doesn't remember Trice's screams. He remembers John Robert's. He always will. They were the screams of a man dying while he's still alive. And the screams of a man who knows it. "What I remember, Billy, is needing water. Needing a lot of water. Needing a miracle. And then when I looked up, there were those clouds," he pauses in wonder all over again, seeing the clouds all over again, "and then there was the rain. Rain like I'd never seen, the house being doused and turning to wet smoke and me running in to find John Robert keeled over. He was more of a shadow on the floor than a real man. Then there I was picking him up. You know the funny thing about that?"

"What?"

"Maybe I never told you this." He rocks a minute. "Or maybe I did, but looking back on it, even in the middle of all that madness, I didn't just snatch him up and run. You know, you think someone in that situation would snatch and run. But I didn't. It was like I was in slow motion. Picked him up as carefully as picking up a baby from a crib."

"And walked right out of that fire big as you please." Billy finishes for him. Finishes like he is watching it happening right now before his eyes. "Did you know there were pieces of his clothes still in flames when you walked out?"

"I remember Trice taking off her housecoat, and you taking it and wrapping it around him, taking him out of my arms. And then the most shocking thing, that was when I turned around, Billy, and you know what I saw."

"Yep. That house ate up in flames."

"That shocked me."

"Would shock anybody that experienced what you did."

"Still shocks me." Nehemiah's throat catches. "And you know I still can't explain it. Still can't."

"Maybe there's some things ain't meant to be explained." Billy points to the sky.

"You were the one that was wanting all the answers, Brother."

"Wanting answers and needing them are two different things." Nehemiah grins. Full face. Dimple in place. His brother Billy never fails to humor him. Or surprise him.

The wind whips the trees into a dancing frenzy. And in the middle of this storm Billy and Nehemiah are rocking. Recollecting. Funny how things can look on the surface. They seem as unaware, as unconcerned about the wind in the trees and the lightning cracking around them as you please. But there is not a second that the hairs on their arms have not been standing up, sensitive to the lightest touch. Not a second that they haven't been ready for anything at any moment. And yet they will talk until they are weary and tired of talking, and after all, they are still full of Kate's cooking from a noontime dinner.

Tonight they will rest well. Tonight, in an act of great defiance, in the middle of this storm, they will lie down and sleep. Full of peace. Pregnant with purpose.

—❧ Monday, 6:33 A.M. ❧—

The sound of metal crashing wakes Nehemiah. He opens his eyes, rolls over in his old bed. He crosses his arms behind his head and stares up at the ceiling, just the same way he had that night in Washington that seems like a hundred years ago. The crashing sound is now rolling, blowing across the backyard and off into the distance until it hits against a stand of trees. The picture of Nehemiah, Billy, and Trice smiles down at Nehemiah, and he smiles back. He looks around the walls at the old emblems of his boyhood. A wild menagerie of skins and photos and dreams of another kind of life. There is his collection of knives on a shelf, his shotgun in one corner, his fishing reels and rods in the other. A bronze metal that belonged to his father (Billy keeps the purple heart). And a six-foot rattlesnake skin nailed along one wall. His momma hadn't wanted it in the house, but when he was twelve he'd killed it and skinned it and at twelve it might as well've been a fire-breathing dragon. And that thought leads him back to where he is and what he's in the middle of.

"This is a boy's room," he says aloud, "and I'm not a boy anymore." He throws off his cover and reaches for his jeans.

In the kitchen he finds Billy awake, sitting at the table, waiting for the coffee to finish.

"Toolshed roof." Billy says, sleepily.

"Thought so." Nehemiah gets a cup down, stands arms folded next to their mother's old coffeepot. Billy never updates anything.

Nehemiah is staring at the percolator's top, watching the coffee shoot up into the crystal top and down again, as if he was looking into a crystal ball. "How long have I been here, Billy?"

Billy thinks for a while. "Why don't you let me wake up good before you ask me such questions."

"It should be simple to answer."

"Well, if it's so simple, you should know."

I'm thinking maybe they shouldn't either one of them talk any more until they've had their coffee.

Nehemiah looks out the kitchen window, where he can indeed see the toolshed roof blown clear across the open field where the garden used to be. Can see it in the distance leaning against the stand of trees. The sun isn't coming up today. The sky is getting lighter but the light isn't coming through.

"It's going to be dark now," he says, looking at the sky. There are no physical clouds, just a haze. A strange, sickly yellow haze.

Monday, 7:53 A.M.

Kate is cooking up a storm as usual, but she has started to notice that people aren't eating. Not as much. Not the same. But she doesn't know why. Everybody says everything's all right. Sitting in that pale yellowish light coming through the window, that's what they tell her to her face. "Everything's all right, Kate."

Even Catfish, who came by his nickname as honest as a man can by being able to put away more fish and food even as a child than a grown man could. Now even he nods his head, says the same thing, but he has piles of potatoes and eggs left on his plate and that's just unheard of. And when Cassie Getty eats only one biscuit, it leaves Kate speechless. Cassie can eat all the biscuits in the kitchen. *Is she on some kind of new diet?* Kate thinks. But then, *Cassie's not one to diet. She stays too busy with her cloning conspiracy for that. But come to think of it, she hasn't even mentioned cloning today.*

Now then, that puts Kate in a mind. She approaches Cassie's table with all the subtle gentleness of a bull.

"You on a diet?"

"Course not."

"What's the matter, then, with my biscuits?"

"Nothin' I know of."

"You didn't eat but one."

"Biscuits are all right." There's that word again, and Cassie says it with such a bland blankness in her face that it forces Kate back into the kitchen, makes her stand with spoons to her nose and tastes to her mouth.

Then she goes to the kitchen door again, stands there with her hands on her hips watching what isn't happening. Listening to what isn't being said. *Something is definitely not all right.*

Monday, 8:33 A.M.

A black Lincoln Town Car is making its slow, methodical way to the house of Nehemiah Trust. It is moving like a battleship through the seas, as if parting the winded trees in its wake. It slowly passes the graveyard on the right, the old one that is not as well kept, the one where the dead died before the time of living memories. They are now truly dust and ashes, no longer living even in the people who came after them. They are only a vapor. But the vapor contains seeds. Seeds that may just rise up and carry into tomorrow. We'll wait and see.

But the driver of the Town Car doesn't know this. The driver knows to drive. To seek. And to find. And Nehemiah is the only focus of this search. The search will end when Nehemiah takes his second cup of coffee out on the porch, wearing nothing but his jeans. And just you look, he's barefoot. Cutting a fine picture as the Lincoln swings into the driveway and parks. The front door slowly opens, and a black wingtip touches the ground.

Nehemiah recognized the car in the distance. He has no questions or doubts about this visitor. This is old stuff. He hadn't wanted to handle things this way, but now *things* are at his doorstep.

"Hi, Butch," Nehemiah says to the suit that is now steadily approaching the porch.

Butch doesn't speak until he walks up the steps, looks around at the house, down at Nehemiah's bare chest, down to his bare feet, where his eyes hang for a moment. "Hi, Nehemiah."

"Mike come with you?"

"Not this time. Told me to check on you. So here I am." He continues looking down at Nehemiah's toes, keeping a straight face. "I'm going to tell him that you're alive but shoeless and I don't know what that means."

Butch is a *special* employee of Senator Honeywell's. One that remains on the senator's private payroll. He is the son of an old army buddy of the senator. A buddy who passed away from complications from heart surgery, and keeping an eye on Butch was the only thing that he had asked Mike Honeywell to do for him. And this long before he was a senator. Now Butch keeps an eye on the senator. And draws a healthy paycheck for doing so. He's a former marine, although Butch would frown at *former*. The marines didn't rub off and it's obvious that he's enlisted in something. Obvious in his barrel chest and his steel spine. In his hair cut so short that you can see his scalp.

Butch surmises enough to see that Nehemiah is well. At least some type of well. Although he can't exactly tell what type of well that is. He turns, surveying the sky. He looks at the wind in the trees and tells Nehemiah without turning back around, "I thought the weather would be better here."

"Tell me, Butch, have you been driving all night?"

"No. Drove most of the way and stopped. Didn't want to surprise you at o'dark thirty. Came the last hundred miles this morning."

"When did the weather turn bad?"

Butch considers the weather, but not for long. "About fifty-six miles ago."

Nehemiah nods his head but doesn't comment. "Can I get you some coffee?"

"No, I'm fine." He reaches into his pocket, pulls out a cell phone, extends it to Nehemiah. "But you have a phone call to make."

"I know, I know, Butch." Nehemiah waves him back and away. "I had to know what was happening down here, what direction things were going to take, before I called. Otherwise," he twirls his hand in the air, copying a gesture of the senator's, "it would all be smoke and mirrors speculation. And you know how much Mike loves smoke and mirrors."

"Do you know what direction things are taking now, Nehemiah?"

"The direction. But not the destination."

Butch flips open the cell phone, begins to dial, "Well, at least *that* will give me something to report."

"Butch." Nehemiah squints against the yellow glare. "I just left a few days ago. Don't you think your being here is a little, well, premature?"

"You broke your pattern, Nehemiah."

"My pattern?"

"Senator Honeywell says you broke your pattern. No call. No checking in. Not like you." Butch begins to dial the number. "It's time to check in, Nehemiah."

"I still think this is just a little excessive." Nehemiah gets up and walks back into the house, passing Billy in the hall.

"Work show up?"

"Yep."

"I figured that would happen." Billy is buttoning his shirt as he walks out of the bedroom. "You cooking breakfast?"

"There's not enough food here to feed us and the man that just showed up."

Billy lifts the curtain, looks out the window at Butch on the porch.

"He looks like me."

"You know, he sure does. Only harder."

"I was gonna skip that part, Nehemiah."

Rudy Harris is stocking vegetables in the back of the Piggly Wiggly, but he isn't teasing Billy Shook's youngest daughter, Ellen, like he's done since she started cashiering a year ago. He begins breaking down boxes but doesn't think to turn on his radio and play it so loud that it blares through the doors and out into the front of the store. Today there will be no one yelling at Rudy, "Turn that fuss down!" Rudy isn't making a fuss. And the silence is so heavy it feels like Rudy will never make a fuss again. Not in all the remaining moments of Shibboleth. Moments that seem to be waiting to be emptied into an abyss that screams lost and gone and forgotten and buried forever.

Monday, 9:38 A.M.

Nehemiah and Billy have invited Butch to breakfast. Nehemiah tells Billy to go ahead without him. Tells Butch to follow Billy. And then Nehemiah goes to pick up his girl. This is what he has decided in the night during the storm. This is what he has decided lying in his room, looking at that picture from the past while listening to the toolshed roof roll across the yard. Trice is his girl. Always has been. It just took him awhile to remember. He is hoping she remembers the same thing.

He pulls into Magnus's yard in the Malibu, walks past the cats without shooing them, and knocks on the door. Then he paces, hands in jeans pockets. He looks like a man who has come a long way in a little bit of time. Still I want to whisper, *Hurry, hurry.*

Kate looks up and sees Billy and Butch walk in and pull up chairs at a table.

Hmmm. Not their usual booth, she thinks, and gets ready to take them coffee. Darla has quit on her. Just run off with the Little Debbie Cake delivery man. Some people called it eloping. No decent engagement time. No friends and family at the wedding. No reception. No party and no food. She knew what it was and called it what it was by its real name: running off. "She'll be running back," she says under her breath.

"Company?" Kate turns over the coffee cups, fills them from the pot in her hand without asking.

"Aunt Kate, this is Nehemiah's . . ." Billy doesn't have a clue what Butch is. "Butch, exactly what are you?"

"Butch Norris." He rises from his seat, almost standing at attention. "I work for Senator Honeywell."

"Well, Butch, you look like a man that can eat. And I like a man that can eat."

Kate turns and walks away.

"Nehemiah has gone to pick up Trice," Billy yells at her back.

The storm in Shibboleth is growing. The yellow sky pressing down, unrelenting. The wind, although not whipping as wickedly as the previous night, never pauses. And as the sky grows darker, Nehemiah paces on the porch where we left him. Trice walks up to other side of the screen door. Then she stands there watching him through the wire, but she doesn't move any closer.

"What, Nehemiah?"

"I think we should take care of . . ." and *business* is what he wants to say. He wants to point at the sky that he sees is getting darker. He wants to apologize for leaving and for not calling and to say thank you for being here, for not disappearing or, even worse, being here and not waiting.

For a man with a wonderful command of the English language, and capable of common phrases of hospitality in six others, "Thank you for waiting" is all he can manage.

"I always knew you'd come home." Trice folds her arms, book in hand, finger holding her place. She continues looking at him through the screen.

"Are you going to come out here?" He's wearing that dimple again. It's well defined. Trice finds it a hard thing to say no to. She opens the door and takes a small step forward, and with one short step she is out of the house and into Nehemiah's life in a new way.

Nehemiah reaches forward and pulls the book from her hand, looks at the title. *The History of Western Art.* "Is there anything you *don't* read?" He memorizes the marked page number from habit, and closes the cover. Trice fights the urge to walk on her toes.

"I have to be honest with you, home I'm not sure of." Nehemiah takes her hand, pulls her toward him, and looks in her eyes. "You, I am."

"Maybe I'm just your familiar, Nehemiah."

"That you are, Trice." He smiles her favorite smile. "You're *my* familiar."

And here Nehemiah kisses Trice. A kiss that seals something. Defines something. Closes a window. Opens a door. Shifts a path forward. I write down, *Two single lines of future melt into one path of now. And, it is* good.

By the time that Nehemiah and Trice have gotten in the car, have driven to the diner, the sky has turned from yellow to a shade of sly brown. A brown that has something up its sleeves.

When they walk through the front door, Kate is just beginning to ladle gravy, pull piping-hot biscuits out of the oven, platter up omelets, something she rarely makes, but she believes that Butch would like an omelet. She is carrying food to at least one table that she knows, or at least hopes, will still appreciate it. The world could come crumbling down around them, and she would be feeding people in the midst of it. She would just think, *Well if it's all gonna end this way, people should at least get one last good meal.* And she'd mean it.

And as she places the food on the table, she takes note that Nehemiah and Trice are holding hands as they come in. *'Bout time*, she thinks as she walks behind the register and rings up a few checks and collects money from people who aren't smiling. Says *good-bye* to people not talking.

"Good to see your shoes on, Nehemiah," Butch says as he methodically butters a biscuit. He seems to study the biscuit itself, squeeze the sides a bit, watch the butter run down the edges of his fingers. "Your aunt appears to love to cook."

"Pure magic, Butch," Nehemiah says as he sits down, introduces Trice, and Butch makes a mental note to add the word *woman* to his report.

There is an awkward silence. Butch eats and makes mental notes. Billy eats as if it were his last meal, and of late he has considered the strong possibility that any meal could be his last. He actually slows down a little. Savors his bites. Trice grows paler as she looks around wide-eyed at the remaining morning diners. She looks at Nehemiah and rubs her eyes with both hands, like a child just waking up. Kate refills the coffee and thinks, *Even these three are quiet today. And that one over there doesn't look like he speaks much unless he's spoken to anyway.*

Trice barely touches her food. She is watching the remaining people. Watching them intently. She is watching them fade away. She sees through their slow bodies as they walk to the cash register. She watches them growing thinner as they get in their cars, as they back out of the parking lot. She is watching their images disappear, and she is still watching long after they seem to melt right into the highway. She squeezes Nehemiah's hand, but he only takes it as a warm gesture. He squeezes back and smiles, takes another bite.

Eventually, when Nehemiah has finished eating and Billy has pushed his plate back and reached for his toothpick, she rises from the table. She goes to the window and stands looking out, looking up at the clouds, her arms wrapped around her.

In a little while, Nehemiah rises, walks up beside her and circles one arm around her shoulders. They have unrolled their agenda. They have nothing to hide. It is the type of open acceptance of public affection found during times of war. When men are going away. When there is no promise of their return. When moments are all that life is made up of anymore. And now, as they stand looking up at the sky, it appears to be growing darker by dimensions.

Butch seizes the opportunity to look at Billy and say, "Excuse me," as he retreats to the restroom to use his cell phone. Billy shifts his toothpick to the other side of his mouth, watching Nehemiah and Trice and thinking, *Well, now, they're finally on the same page.*

"Nehemiah, people are fading." Trice pulls away from the circle of his arm and turns to look at him. "They are fading as I look at them. Like the opposite of a picture coming into focus. Instead of focusing, they are fading away."

Nehemiah turns, looks across the diner. "Aunt Kate?"

"Fuzzy but not fading." She rubs her eyes again. "Maybe it's my eyes. Maybe I've been reading too much."

Nehemiah dismisses her stretch for an explanation. "Billy?"

"No." She shakes her head. "And not that man from Washington. Just everyone else." Trice looks down. When Nehemiah places his fingers beneath her chin, lifts her face to look at him, her eyes are filled with tears.

"And me?"

"You're fading the fastest of them all."

The eternal clock begins to chime. Now it is the three of them, Nehemiah, Trice, and Billy who look up.

"Your clock," Trice says, staring above the doorway.

"You can see it, too?"

"What does it mean, Nehemiah?"

Nehemiah shakes his head. "The only thing I know, Trice, is the clock showed up when I came back to town. No one saw it before then." He looks back at her as the chiming continues. "Not even you."

I wish I could tell her. I wish I could tell them all about the clock. About the time that they are passing through. Not the surface of time. Not the perimeters of time as man compartmentalizes it. But the essence of time. The heart and soul and embodiment of time. Of all the possibilities wrapped up in, and either reached or lost, in the borders of an atom-splitting moment.

"I have somewhere to be." Nehemiah looks back at Trice. "Wait for me?"

Trice steps up on her toes. "What's one more day going to matter?"

"Hey, Billy, tell Butch when he gets out of the bathroom and off that blasted phone to just tell Mike I'll call him just as soon as I'm able." And then he calls over his shoulder, "And keep Trice with you. At *all times.*" And he adds for good measure, "No matter what."

Trice sits down at the table, watches through the glass door as Nehemiah backs away. Keeps watching until he disappears out of sight.

"I see y'all finally got that thing worked out." Billy shuffles the toothpick to the side of his mouth with his tongue.

"Sure, now that everything is coming to an end." Her feet rise up on tiptoes under the table, but they stay locked that way. They don't dance.

"Better late than never, Trice."

Butch moves from the bathroom to the table in long, forceful strides. He looks pointedly around the diner. Outside the diner door. "Where did Nehemiah go?"

"He said to tell you that he'd ..." he stops midsentence. "What'd he say, Trice?"

"To tell you that he'd call Mike just as soon as he's able."

Butch sits down. A man trying to formulate a plan. He is out of place, thrust upon strange people he doesn't know, trying to report that Nehemiah is dressed strange and acting stranger. That he has stopped wearing shoes. Taken up with a woman. Not good signs that he will be back in the office the following day. Or even maybe the day after that.

The brown in the sky is getting darker. Becoming the color of cracked dirt. And it will stay that way until it pushes toward evening.

Billy looks out the glass at the sky, at the empty space where Nehemiah used to be. He moves the toothpick from side to side in his mouth. He's got an itchy feeling. Like bad on top of bad. Billy is pondering his brother leaving just now. *Maybe Nehemiah has said his good-bye's without saying them outright,* Billy is thinking. *Maybe he has left us all sitting right where we are and turned his back again on everything that belongs to him. And everything he doesn't want. Like last time. Was he angry? He didn't seem angry. Not with me. Not with Trice.* He glances over at her out of the corner of his eye. But Billy knows about Nehemiah's anger. And where that anger can take him. Of how it can take him away.

Billy always knew how to do the things that were important. Like fishing and hunting and even learning to drive a truck when he was only twelve. And this had made him Nehemiah's idol, and even with the curves giving him direction, he'd look to Billy and wait for his wink or the slight nod of his head that said, "Go on, Brother, it'll be just fine." No matter what, Billy's approval was paramount, and he'd had it at every crossroads. Except for one. And that was when Nehemiah had decided to leave town. Billy thinks now about the fight that day. It was a moment that changed the course of things. It was a crossroads. It was the only fight they had ever had, and it was a loud one. On Billy's part anyway. Nehemiah had turned white-faced, clenching and unclenching his fists repeatedly as Billy stomped around the house ranting and raving. Billy's anger was love unleashed. Nehemiah's was a seething river at flood stage. Backed up. With no outlet. And ready to wipe out everything that dared stand in his way.

Nehemiah had packed his bags and stood defiantly in front of Billy, saying, "You can either drive me or I'm hitching over to Birmingham and taking a Greyhound." And Billy, so lost now at being only a brother, not a mother or a father but only a brother, had simply shrugged his shoulders and gotten his keys. Not because he didn't care but because of how much he did. Nehemiah had made up his mind. The least he could do was spend the last few hours on the road with him. At least he'd have that much. Because down in his gut he'd known Nehemiah wasn't coming back. And right then, Billy lost his whole family. His days upon returning were spent wandering around the house, bumping into furniture, sitting at the kitchen table with his head laid down on his crossed arms. Crying.

Billy's heartbreak would have cut him wide open if it hadn't been for Trice. Leave it to that pain in the butt Trice to kick on the screen door one afternoon and yell, "Billy, get on out here. I got something for you and I ain't waiting all day." Whereupon Billy had rubbed his eyes, pulled himself up from the table, and gone on out to the porch, where Trice, not giving him time to think, had thrust a warm piece of flesh and fur in his hands.

"Now, he's just a little baby so you have to promise to take good care of him." Then she had shoved her hands in her back jeans pockets and stood there smiling like one of Magnus's cats.

The way Billy looks at it now, she had saved his life that day. Not physically, of course, 'cause he'd just gone on and on the way he was. Eating Kate's "poor, poor Billy" chicken. Looking pitiful everywhere he went. Folks shaking their heads and saying "Bless his heart" constantly behind his back. Nope. If it wasn't for Sonny Boy showing up that day, he'd have turned to dust inside. Simple as that.

Billy looks up at Trice's pale face. He sure doesn't understand the girl. Loves her like a sister, but doesn't understand her. Doesn't really understand why she hangs around Magnus or why she lives there when she could be over at Kate's without all that dang cat hair flying around. Doesn't understand why she didn't take that job in Birmingham teaching school. And for a long time he didn't understand why she didn't marry that Skipper boy who had been so crazy about her. But he knows now. Right now she is staring down at her notes that look like their old treasure map, and he doesn't know what to do with any of this mess. But he sure wishes Nehemiah and Trice would hurry up and figure it out. And he's wondering if Nehemiah just made a good show of things and then a quick getaway.

Kate walks past him and sticks a HELP WANTED sign in the window.

"What's for dinner, Aunt Kate?"

"Well, it looks like you're gonna sit here long enough to find out."

Butch asks one more time, "Where did Nehemiah go?"

"I told you, he didn't say," Billy tells him, "Did he say anything to you, Trice?"

Trice looks up at Butch and shakes her head, *no.* Then goes back to her paper.

Strange girl, thinks Butch. *Well, at least different. This whole place is different. I wonder if the senator has ever been here. Wonder if he really knows Nehemiah is from here. "Wait," he tells me. "Watch," he tells me. Well, I'm waiting. And I'm watching.*

"Well, Trice, how about you and me mosey on over to Zadok's so I can get a haircut," Billy says.

"I'll just wait here for you." Trice is intently preoccupied with the curves and lines on her paper.

"Nope. You can't." Billy reaches up and pulls the toothpick from his mouth. "Nehemiah said."

"All right, all right." She pushes back her chair, rises up from the table, but doesn't make it to the door before Kate has the back of her hand up against Trice's forehead.

"You feverish?"

"No, ma'am."

"I haven't seen you look so pale, Trice, since you had pneumonia. Billy, you keep an eye on her." She looks around the diner. "Now where'd your brother get off to?"

"Didn't say."

"Oh, he's a good one for disappearing without even saying good-bye. That's one thing I know. Might as well keep an eye peeled back on that boy because there is no telling. Matter of fact, I've got a mind to make a phone call or two and round him up." She stops, hand on hip, thinking. "Matter of fact, I got a mind to get in my car and go round him up, and I can do it, too." She aims this last statement toward Butch, who recognizes talent when he sees it. Has no doubt this woman can round up anything she wants. "But I guess since you're still sitting here, chances are he's still around."

"I hope so." Butch replies. But he decides right then and there, if Nehemiah isn't back within the hour, he's going to offer to take this woman for a ride. And she can drive. A man needs to recognize his resources when he sees them.

Monday, 11:47 A.M.

Nehemiah pulls up at the churchyard. The clouds have run together now so that the very heavens appear blocked, the sky pressing down close and hard to the ground. Nehemiah opens the car door and rubs his throat, remembering the choking, breathless feeling of his first night at the springs. I can see the parched look on his face, and the parched place trying to patch itself into his spirit. In the time that he has driven from the diner to the church he has indeed, as Trice has seen, been fading away. And he is becoming angrier by the moment. And now, with every mile and moment that he has drawn closer to this meeting, his soul has been moving in the opposite direction. It's a handful of second thoughts and self-direction that reaches for the church door. And it's a fugitive of faith that releases it, and without understanding why, begins to run in the opposite direction of his car, of Trice, and of Shibboleth. Out across the field of tombstones where there is nothing but death in his decision.

Inside Pastor Brown sits in a familiar pew. His sun-spotted hand rubs the worn wood. After all these years he is wondering what it feels like to sit here, year after year, watching him, listening to him. Waiting on him to make a move that is never made. And now he is waiting for his opportunity to be the help he couldn't be, or wouldn't be, so long ago.

There is a loud sucking sound around the window, one so powerful that the church's very foundation feels it. The pastor rises to his feet, and exclaims, "Not yet!" It's not a sorry hope, but a great command of a man of faith, shaken but not shattered, and I respond without a thought, without a plea, just instant accord. I spread out my wings, in their fullness from edge to edge, and hold up the corners of the roof.

The windows rattle and do not stop. They shiver and sigh as if they will relinquish their hold at any moment and cave in, and as the glass begins to crack around the edges of their panes, a moan is heard roaming just behind the windowsills. And beyond it, the sound of Nehemiah's cries reach the pastor's ears.

Pastor Brown strides purposefully through the pews. A man full of remorse, but also repentance. He knows the dimension of his dominion. Without hesitation, without fear, the pastor throws open the door and steps outside. A dark, transparent fog has moved in below the horizon, seeping up from the ground as if night has been turned upside down. As if the sky will meet the dirt and erase all of Shibboleth into oblivion once and for all. And although the dark remains, the moment the pastor steps outside with a level gaze, the wind is sucked back into itself, as if something is holding its breath. Pastor Brown begins to call Nehemiah's name loud and long.

Over at the barbershop, Zadok is trimming around the ears of Wiley Yinger, but the two aren't shooting the breeze like they usually do. They've run out of words, are just going through the motions. And neither of them finds it peculiar or awkward when Wiley stands, puts his ball cap back on his head, and walks out without paying. Soon, Wiley is a block away and Zadok has forgotten he was even there.

This is how Billy and Trice find him. Fuddled. Not at all himself. Not the outgoing "Howdy, neighbor." Or trying to tell the last joke he heard even though Zadok can't get a punch line right to save his life.

Billy sits down in the barber chair. Zadok stands behind the chair with a straight razor in his hand. He looks at the back of Billy's head as if he'd forgotten how to cut hair.

Trice sits down and begins flipping through an old copy of *Field and Stream*. Then she glances up at Zadok. Her eyes automatically go back to the page, but then she slowly raises them and *looks* at Zadok. "Hey, Billy, maybe we should come back later for your haircut." Trice is watching.

"Just a little off around the ears, Zadok . . ." Billy looks at Trice and scowls, "Maybe a little off the top."

"Billy, let's come back, *later*."

"Trice, can I just get a haircut? Can I? Everybody fusses at me and now that I'm finally here, you are ready to go."

"Get up out of that chair, Billy. Now."

Billy looks at Trice standing in front of him. Looks at the fury in her eyes, at her *I mean business* look, with her curls threatening to come undone. He turns to look at Zadok to try to understand Trice's behavior, but then he notices something peculiar, and the hair stands up on the ends of his arms and on the back of his neck. Zadok isn't there. Not really. Oh, the outward shell of the man is standing with a straight razor in his hand, looking back at Billy without much expression, but what is happening inside that shell, he couldn't tell you.

"Zadok, I think we're gonna put this off for just now."

Trice locks her hand on the crook of Billy's arm, and they back out of the door.

The wind whips around them as they step outside. The sidewalk the square and are peculiarly quiet. As they look around the streets, there is an absence of all life in Shibboleth. There is something, a whole lot of somethings, missing.

"What the hell was all that?" Billy is looking back over his shoulder, still staring at the ghostly apparition of Zadok looking blankly at him through the glass window.

"I'm not sure he knows who he is anymore. Or at least, right now he's not who he used to be." She puts her hands in the back pockets of her jeans, thumbs hanging out. "And he sure can't be trusted with a razor around your head."

"It's spreading, isn't it, Trice?"

"Not spreading so much as *erasing*. Like a horrible vacuum." They walk across the street, toward the square. Both of them are looking left and right over their shoulders. Behind them. Billy looks down the road, into the distance. No traffic. A complete and total lack of traffic. And while he is studying the distance of the empty highway leading out of town, they take a seat on the bench beneath the old Shibboleth Heritage Oak. And Trice sits for a moment, but for only a moment, because when she looks up into the branches of the oak tree she doesn't see the branches. She sees in pictures.

Now, I can't tell you exactly what happens in the next moments because they are things unheard and unspoken. They are the whisperings of life to life. But it is a type that is not so easily recognized. I can tell you that Billy is talking. Is saying something about how it's, "Definitely time to get something done." And more things like, "I never thought Shibboleth would come to this." And his conversational mutterings never seem to stop. But Trice doesn't appear to notice, and he doesn't appear to notice that she isn't responding.

Trice is listening to memories. Memories that have filtered up from that bench all of its life. Memories that have clung like moss to the branches of that Oak, have latched themselves on and refused to let go. Memories that were here long before the bench was built, back to the beginning of Shibboleth. And the memories are wrapped in the stories, and right now, strings of the stories are raining down on Trice from those branches in streams. Streams and strings of stories. And look closely, this is the part that you will love. Trice is raising her arms. Trice's hands are outstretched. Trice is capturing the memories and stories of young people sparking, and of old people telling stories, and of all people laughing and crying while they are told. She is capturing the voices of children on bicycles calling to one another, full of summer and full of joy, passing beneath the breadth of the Oak. Peddling through the shady shadows of its arms' reach.

Billy looks over and finally is able to hush. As he watches Trice, with arms stretched up and wide now, with her eyes closed, a smile flickering on her face, he knows that she is gathering something he can't see. *Now we begin,* he thinks, and he stands up to his full stature. On his guard. Protecting Trice. Just in case.

Pastor Brown has stopped calling Nehemiah. He knows now that Nehemiah won't, or can't, answer. He walks through the graveyard, stepping between the tombstones, some of them already unreadable in the shadows. The pastor continues to the edge of the adjacent woods and beyond. He circles through the brush and trees until he finds what he's looking for, a huddled shape beneath the trees. Nehemiah's back is leaning against the remains of an old lightning-struck pine tree. It is, and is not, the Nehemiah of your understanding. And I hate to see that it's come to this. I long to intercede and look to God, wait for a sign, a signal, but there is none. So I wait. And watch.

The two of them remain here like this. Nehemiah continues rocking, his arms locked around his knees, his teeth remain clenched, his words like daggers that escape between them. "I didn't want . . ." and the rest of the response is lost in his groaning.

The pastor crouches down beside him, speaking in a low, soft tone. "You've reached the place of your decision, Nehemiah." He points around him but he doesn't touch the wild, brown-eyed man. "Fight the will and the will fights you." Nehemiah covers his ears with his hands. "Kick against your purpose and it kicks you back." The pastor looks up at the dark sky, at the inky mist rising from the ground, and his voice drops to a whisper, "And there is no peace."

"I didn't want . . ." Nehemiah tries again and the pastor responds from some innate place of understanding because there aren't enough words being said to help him along.

"I know, you never wanted what was given to you. All that strange responsibility." The pastor stands and as he does so, both knees pop. He looks over his shoulders, half-expecting, half-hoping for divine intervention. At the least, not wanting any more inter-ference of the other kind. For a moment he wishes it was Trice standing here instead of him. Almost wills it to be so. But then he thinks of something, and slowly kneels down again. "Here's what's gonna happen. You're gonna lead and we're gonna follow. And if you lead us into this darkness, that's where we'll go. Right along with you. Me and Kate and Catfish and Magnus." He slowly stands again, thinks of his garden, just a patch of green and won-ders when was the last time that he *planted* something. *How odd*, he thinks, *I've lost track of the seasons*. He stares out through the woods, thinks he sees something moving. Then he remembers Nehemiah, remembers his reasoning. "Yep, we'll all follow. Cassie and Wheezer, Obie and Zadok, and Blister. Every last Skipper, Gallas, and Getty. Every last one of us in Shibboleth. We're going to fol-low you right into this," he brushes his hands against the black mist. "And of course that includes Billy and Trice," and he kneels down low enough to stare into the eyes that refuse to look back, "because your life is linked to our lives." A tree begins cracking near them, shaking and swaying. Then another. Then the trees begin to fall. "And we have no say in that matter. None whatso-ever. It's all a part of the plan." Pastor Brown looks at the trees closest to them. "So go ahead and fight who you are and we'll stand right here fighting with you." A tree crashes next to them so close a piece of bark flies off and cuts the pastor's face. He doesn't flinch but pulls his handkerchief from his pocket, swipes at the blood and looks at it, saying, "That is until nothing is left of us that you might recognize."

Nehemiah's shaking becomes less severe. His eyes begin to regain their focus, the pupils slowly getting smaller. Pastor Brown sits down next to him, and drapes his arm over Nehemiah's shoulder, something he has never done in all these years. "I should have talked to you a long time ago. I should have helped you way back when. This would have all been so much easier then." He waves a hand again at the air and the trees. "Or maybe it wouldn't have been at all."

Nehemiah tries to nod yes. The color starts to come back into his face. He doesn't want to be afraid. Hates the thought, really. And it's not the fear of what he is that has brought him to this point. It's the knowledge of what it will require of him. Or the suspicion of what he thinks it will take away. He's a man of acquired tastes. And he likes them. All of them. *Just what is it that God wants from me, anyway?* The shakes return and for a moment threaten to become violent. *I'm a good man,* he screams. But the scream is inside and no one responds. *And a good man should be good enough.* But then there is an echo of the pastor's words. "We'll all follow you. Every last one. Including Billy and Trice." And those names roll 'round and 'round. Billy and Trice, Billy and Trice, like a pair of dice rocking in and out of his reasoning.

"Trice?" Nehemiah is still speaking with shaking jaws.

"What about her?"

"She's not," the shaking starts again, harder and he waits until it dissipates. "She's not afraid of . . ." and he doesn't finish.

"Of what? The strangeness? It makes her a bit odd, I know. But Nehemiah, I've got news for you," Pastor Brown tries to steady the shaking shoulder while he watches the trees overhead, "Trice is not afraid of anything. Trice is perfectly content with being Trice."

And right now, under the Heritage Oak in the town square, this appears to be true. Trice is listening and gathering. There is a smile on her face, and in the midst of that smile, tears begin to stream from her eyes, roll down her cheeks, run onto her neck and down the front of her shirt. Billy stands with his arms crossed, no longer watching Trice but watching anything in her path, watching for anything that might interfere with what is happening. If I told you that five minutes had passed as they stood here, you would underestimate the magnitude of those moments. If I told you it's been all day, you'd shake your head and say, *No way.* I can tell you it is a time of transference. And, really, that's all time and no time at all.

Eventually, Trice lowers her chin, opens her eyes, and wiping her face, turns to Billy. He stands quietly watching her. "It's time to go get Nehemiah."

They consider for a moment the possibility of this as the wind and black mist whips about them. As if stepping off the island of the Oak is not a wise decision. As if they have found their anchor in the middle of the tempestuous surface of the city. Then simultaneously they put one foot down off the curb followed by the other.

"Let me drive, Billy," Trice says. And he lets her. When they are looking for something lost she usually gets behind the wheel. It helps her feel her way along while Billy keeps a lookout. Dogs, missing cats, one time Obie had a husband that went missing but he was never found. Billy looks at Trice's jaw, at the squint between her eyes. He's hoping their looking will have better results.

"Remember Obie's husband, Trice." They both stare into the diner windows out of habit as they drive past.

"Obie's husband didn't want to be found, Billy, simple as that." Trice cranks the window down in spite of the wind. And as she circles the block one more time, as the wind hits the side of the truck like an iron fist, Billy cast his thoughts out toward his brother just like bait on a line, and tries with all his might to mentally reel him in.

Old Blue passes Magnolia Street and farther down on the edge of town. It passes by the road to Billy's house, and he thinks to suggest they go check there but he figures Trice knows where they're headed but he asks her anyway for good measure, "You know where we're headed?"

"We're fixin' to find out if I do or I don't," she says. In a little while she turns and drives down the road to the church and they can spot the white Malibu in the distance. Trice pulls Old Blue up right next to the car but they don't get out. Not right away. A buzzard is watching, circling high up in the sky.

"Something don't feel right," Billy says.

"You've got that right, Billy." Trice rolls up the window and puts her hand on the silver door handle but she doesn't open it. "The church door's never left open like that."

"Not even in spring or summer." Billy looks over in the car, trying to see through the haze and into the windows, searching for any sign of Nehemiah.

"We better get started," and Trice opens up the door and puts her foot out in the mist that is strangely growing cold. "What is this stuff?"

Billy gets out and kicks his leg back and forth, "Something not natural—that's for sure," he says, and begins to look through the windows of the Malibu.

"He's not in there, Billy," Trice says and starts walking out to the side of the church and through the graveyard.

"What about the church?" Billy says walking towards the open door.

"He's not in there either." Trice keeps walking until she reaches Twila's grave where she stops, crouches down, and lays her hand on top of the cold marble.

The buzzard circles lower and lower in the sky until it lands on the highest branch of a scrub oak, the one just at the edge of the tombstones. It hops down to the next branch, and the next, until its eyes are in line with Trice's head as she bends over. The buzzard flaps its wings, arches its neck out. Trice and Billy don't see him, their minds are elsewhere.

Billy walks up behind her, his hands in his pocket, his head down, looking at the ground. "You talkin' to Momma?"

"No, Billy, I'm remembering." She stands to her feet, pushes her hair back from her face and the wild strands fall out across her shoulders. Trice walks off across the graveyard and into the edge of the woods, and Billy follows the blond outline of her hair into the inky darkness.

It's Nehemiah who sees Trice first. And Trice finding him and him finding himself seem to be interlocking pieces. His teeth stop chattering, and little by little, his shoulders stop shaking. The pastor looks up into Trice's clear, blue eyes, at Billy's wrinkled brows and shaggy hair, and he is so very, very thankful. Billy extends an arm and offers his hand, which the pastor receives with great appreciation and stands slowly to his feet.

Trice kneels down, places her hands on both sides of Nehemiah's face.

"I dreamt I was lost," he says, "and that you were the finder."

"Well, finder's keepers, Nehemiah." Trice looks into his eyes and he manages a smile, almost a dimpled smile, and says, "Amen."

And there, in that one last frozen place, not larger than a human eye, the pain and pleasure of Shibboleth find their way back into the heart of its man. I make notes and watch carefully as Nehemiah stops wresting with his purpose and makes a choice.

The frozen eye melts into liquid fire. That's my sign. I release a fresh wind from beneath my feathers. And with it, a renewal of hope, a focus on the business at hand.

"We need our map, Nehemiah." Trice says, squeezing Nehemiah's

arm, finding courage in the solid flesh. "We must find our map."
She and Billy help him to his feet but it's a mere gesture of kindness. His strength is returning by the second. His legs are solid.
Pastor Brown looks to the sky as if to speak to God, to confirm
something, but the sky doesn't look familiar.

"Trice, nobody has seen that map for years. There's no telling
what became of that thing." Nehemiah pushes a strand of hair
back from her face, wants to kiss her but doesn't. Not here. Not
now. Not with Billy standing there with Pastor Brown.

"Ya'll never told me you wanted that map." Billy is suppressing a
grin. And then it can't be contained anymore, and the grin spills
over on his face in spite of the surroundings.

"And what difference would that have made?" Trice asks.

"Because, I've known right where that map has been all of my
life." And now he begins to rock slightly back and forth on his
two, big feet. He feels that for the first time, he is the one that has
something wonderful and mysterious to offer. And he is absolutely
full of himself.

"And where would that be, Brother?" Nehemiah lets go of
Trice's hand, steps back and crosses his arms.

"Right where Momma put it."

Monday, 1:38 P.M.

Kate stands absently wiping her hands on her apron. She is looking out the window of the diner, facing toward the oak tree in the
center of the square. Right now there should be a late lunch crowd
and stragglers with nowhere better to go or nowhere they would

rather be than holding court at Kate's, just waiting for another re-fill on their coffee. Someone to shoot the breeze with. To talk with about all the important things happening in Shibboleth and across the nation. But right now, there are only Kate and Butch sitting solidly at the table.

Kate begins to speak to him without turning around. "You know, I think you can go ahead and get in that car and point it back towards Washington."

"Why is that?" Butch pushes back his on-the-house lunch plate. Kate had set it down in front of him, declaring, "I can't stand around with a kitchen full of food that is going to waste and at least one man left on the planet that can eat it."

"Look," Kate says, pointing at the sky that has started to change colors again. "I guess you can see there's a little some-thing going on that's a little unusual. Nehemiah can't go any-where until it's fixed." *That is, if he can fix it. If it's not already too late,* she thinks. What she also doesn't add is the fact that she was watching Nehemiah and the way that he was looking at Trice. From the looks of *that look,* he won't be leaving without Trice. And Trice won't be leaving the city that saved her. This much Kate believes to be true.

While Butch is trying to reach logical conclusions, Magnus is trying to make some kind of logic out of her situation on the other side of town. Watch her. She is standing by the phone in the living room. She is looking at the phone as if it was a peculiar ani-mal. She picks up the receiver again for the third time, holding it to her ear. There is no dial tone. "Hello?" she says, "Hello?" as if someone trapped on the other end of the line might have erased her connection. She looks over at General, who has splayed himself out on the back of the couch. "This isn't good," she says.

Magnus steps outside and looks at the sky rolling beyond the tree level and out across the open field. She has lived in Shibboleth now for almost sixty-four years (minus one) and she has never seen anything like this. "Have seen the Devil," she says to General, who she knows can hear her (and he is the only cat that truly listens), "but I ain't never seen anything like this business." And for just a moment, Magnus forgets who she is and where she's standing, as if something had just sucked it right out of her. But then her eyes latch onto her feet, and her feet are wearing her house shoes, and she manages one thought with one purpose, "I've got to change my shoes." And that thought pulls her to the surface, where she can survive.

"I have a job to do, ma'am." Butch tries the *ma'am* word on his tongue. He's heard it enough to know it's important, but he originates from Philly and it doesn't translate.

"Listen here." Kate turns around, pulls up a chair and sits down with a sigh. "Let me help you out. Your job description has changed. Senator Honeywell doesn't know that. He's not here to see this. And you can call on that little phone back and forth all you want to. He's still not going to understand anything that's not black and white at the moment. Even though he's a son of the South, he ain't never seen nothing like this."

"Don't underestimate him." Butch is quick to defend his employer.

"If I didn't think he was smart, I wouldn't have voted for him. So I don't think you need to tell me that." She runs her dishrag over the back of her neck. Closes her eyes. And sits there that way. Then she *stays* that way. It looks as if she has just shut down, like a toy that turned off without warning.

"Are you okay?" Butch leans forward, touches her arm lightly. Kate opens her eyes.

"You were talking about the senator," Butch says to prod her memory.

Kate gets up again. Looks out the window as if she is day-dreaming, and then she turns, sees Butch, and steps back a step. "How did you get in here?" she asks him as she moves toward the cash register. For the first time since Butch came to town, he's the one who is suddenly on guard. He stands quickly to his feet.

"You were telling me about the senator."

Kate's expression remains blank.

"I'm a friend of Nehemiah's," he says, trying to find some common ground, something to trigger the right response. She continues staring at him. "I came to check on him. See if he was all right."

"Mister, now I know you are full of lies. Nehemiah hasn't been here in over ten years."

Monday, 3:33 P.M.

The magnolias of Shibboleth are turning brown. The giant white flowers falling from the trees, most of them huge buds that have never opened. The leaves themselves seem to be crying out for water, curling at the edges. And yet, not so long ago it rained. But when it's this kind of dry, it takes a lot of rain to sustain life. A lot of water to make the rivers run. And with this kind of dry, the little bit of water that comes is eaten up by the air itself, never gets beneath that first epidermis layer of dirt. What the people of Shibboleth need right now is a good soaking. But the origin and manner of that, if it's to be at all, is still to be revealed.

Right now, I believe that particular crucial occurrence is related to the look riding on the three faces looking out over the hood of Old

Blue. I believe the end result is riding on the focus in the eyes of those faces. On the origin of its passionate intensity. I've seen that look before. But not in this world. I've seen it in places that reach beyond green streams and magnolia blossoms. I've seen that expression look over suns, reach between planets, beyond black holes, and stretch into what lies beyond eternity. But then, that story is from a different place in time. That story is mine.

Nehemiah, Trice, and Billy pour out of the doors of the truck like running water. They are dust on the wind, racing ahead of the storm, running with it right on their heels. Carrying, even yet, petals of possibilities. *Run,* I want to yell. *Run while there is at least a split atom of hope.* They are already inside the house, down the hall, in the kitchen, when they hear the chiming of the clock. They look above the sink where Twila's old clock is no more. It is now replaced with the clock without hands. The one that reaches into a different space and time and place. The three of them freeze, look at the clock until the chiming has stopped. Then Nehemiah and Trice look at Billy and say simultaneously, "Hurry."

He reaches his hand out and spins the lazy Susan once before he reaches into the center of it and removes an old flower vase that has stood there as long as any of them can remember. He removes a red plastic rose from the vase, then lifts it from the table and turns it over in his large hands, tapping it twice. An old rolled-up sheet falls into the palm of his hand.

They roll it out gently on the table and look down at the images, the lines and symbols they drew so long ago. The clock begins to chime again and as they look back, Nehemiah looks at the map and back at the clock face. The symbols are the same. He silently points to a triangle on the paper, then to a triangle on the clock. Trice says nothing. She keeps one hand on Nehemiah. On his arm, his shoulder, his back. It doesn't matter. *If I just keep touching him*, she thinks, *if he starts to disappear again, somehow, maybe I can hold onto him, pull him back. Or if all else fails, follow him into the nothing.*

"Now that I brought you two to the old map ... " Billy stops, turns a quizzical look up at the clock and back at the map. "Shouldn't this thing have turned to dust by now?"

"Well, if it should've, it didn't," Nehemiah says.

"Anyway, now that we have it," Billy switches his weight back and forth from one foot to the other, "could either one of you tell me what we're looking for?"

"We're looking for our way back, Brother." Nehemiah lays one hand on Billy's shoulder, traces a dotted path on the map with his finger. His finger stops at a dark smudged mark. A word that is barely readable, but there it is, still there after all these years. The word *TIME* printed out in a child's hand. "A way back to find what is being stolen."

"You get the bag, Brother," Billy says. "I'll get the batteries."

Monday, 4:16 P.M.

Over at City Hall, Trudy Getty looks up from her desk, where she is paging through the latest *People* magazine, but she isn't really interested in the people. Not in their clothes or their eccentricities. Right now, she isn't interested in anything. She flips the page with one tanned finger. Occasionally, Trudy drives all the way to Troy to get a suntan from a booth. Not too much of a tan, but just enough to make her look like she's been somewhere.

Trudy studies the styles and fashions of other places so she'll be prepared to fit in when the opportunity to leave arrives. She has decided to move to a big city, maybe Birmingham or even Atlanta, and to get a job as a receptionist at a law firm. It has to be a law firm, because that is the way that Trudy has imagined it since she was eight years old and learned all about lawyers from television. She is going to go to night school and become a real paralegal.

She has lots of plans, and those plans include being in the right place to meet the right husband because she will someday have a big house and throw elegant parties. During the winter they will be inside in the great room with the fireplace, and during the summer they will be out by the pool. For the summertime parties, she will hostess in her not-too-much-but-just-enough tan, wearing pastel colors made out of drapey fabrics. Because she doesn't know what she will wear in the wintertime, the summer parties are her favorites. She knows that she will serve large platters with cocktail shrimp, but that's as far as she has gotten with the food. Right now her husband doesn't have a face or a shape, but sometimes she picks out outfits for him to wear. Things that will coordinate with her dresses.

Trudy has a lot of well-thought- over and dreamed-about plans. But in the evening light of Shibboleth, in its closing hours, when the phone rings on her desk, she answers "Hello" instead of "Shibboleth City Hall." This is the most glamorous part of her job, the part that usually gives her the best practice for the time to come. But this afternoon there is no one nearby to notice how out of character this is for Trudy, and the person on the other end of the line simply says, "Wrong number" and hangs up. Trudy is left, phone still in hand, looking out the window, forgetting all about the paper-doll promises that she was hoping for, not even caring if they come to pass.

An exodus of sorts is beginning around the edges of Shibboleth. Carloads of Skippers, truckloads of Gettys, even walkers, out on the highways and byways. They don't know where they're going. They just know they are leaving. They aren't packing anything because they aren't moving away. It's as if the wind itself is picking them up and tossing them off toward the horizon. Off into the unknown corners of the world.

Those not wandering away are sitting unmoving on couches or chairs or porch steps. They don't know why they are sitting, but they can't think of any reason to get up. They can't think at all. They've lost their reference points. They're missing their landmarks, the ones in their souls that take them back to where they came from and point them toward tomorrow and the next hour. But now the next hour is lost on the people of Shibboleth. The next hour rests in the plan of three people retracing their steps, finding their way.

Obie has walked off and left her shop, back door standing wide open, and gotten in her car and started to drive. She is about to get lost trying to find her way home. She has forgotten where home is, and she will drive around and around the emptying town trying to find her way to anything that reminds her where to stop. Finally, she pulls back up to her own shop and, leaving her car running, gets out and walks through the back door without closing it behind her.

A country mile away, two big feet in two big, flat, ugly boots are walking steadily down Magnolia. One plodding step at a time. At the corner of Magnolia and Main, the boots stop, and Magnus looks to the right and to the left, spits between her fingers. She stands still, frozen solid in her tracks, then she turns all the way around and looks back down Magnolia. She begins walking forward, back down the road toward her house. Five steps later, she stops, turns around, spits again, and heads forward toward Main Street.

The stray dogs in Shibboleth have taken cover. They are hiding alone, or grouped together, under porches. Against back doors. Some dogs are scratching to get in, even the ones that know the answer will be no. The cats have hidden. The birds have roosted early but are deathly quiet. The sky has gone from the brown shade of dirt to an evening red. But it's not a sunset red. It's an unnatural red that pulses with a power that is unrelenting. And unholy.

Blister looks up at the sky. He is trying to *think*, trying to remember if he has seen this red before. It is knocking around vaguely somewhere inside him. *Seen this before,* he thinks. *But where?* Blister has managed to make himself move, to get himself in his truck. It takes a long time before he remembers that the key is in the ignition, that he was going someplace. *I am going to see someone,* he thinks. But he has forgotten who the someone is. "Maybe if I just keep driving, I will find them. Whoever they are," he says aloud. And then he slowly pulls away from his trailer.

Monday, 4:35 P.M.

Butch is watching Kate. Kate is watching Butch. They are at a standstill. She stands behind the cash register, pulls the phone from the cradle, and dials Dwayne's number. She has it memorized. *If she can't get the deputy,* she thinks, *if he's not already out this way, there will be no point in trying. Maybe I can call Zadok, he's close by. And to think, all the knives are in the kitchen and this gorilla is between me and the knives.* Kate is looking around for something else to use as a weapon when she spies the ballpoint pen and thinks, *If he gets close enough I'll put his eyes out.*

Monday, 4:55 P.M.

Magnus is counting her steps down Main Street. *One brown boot. Next brown boot. One brown boot. Next brown boot.* She has determined to focus her attention toward town. And the image of the Heritage Oak is in her mind. She is concentrating on the trunk, on the branches, on the leaves. The patterns coursing up through the wood. The green pulse of life behind the pattern. She fixes herself on this image so solidly that it draws her forward like the beam of a lighthouse drawing a shipwreck survivor through an empty darkness. *There's one hell of an undertow today,* she thinks. And takes another step forward.

Monday, 4:58 P.M.

Cassie Getty has watched her sister drive by on the road without even a nod or a wave. *Sister might be a clone by now,* she thinks. *That's just what a clone would do. Drive right on by like they don't even know their own sister.* She pulls out a suitcase left over from her trip to California in the fifties. All the way to the Pacific and back again. She had once thought about writing a book and naming it just that. *To the Pacific and Back Again.* But she didn't. She couldn't think of another line besides the title and that had slowed her down some. And she couldn't think of anything great to say about the experience except she had gone there and had come back. It looked like the end of the world to her, but nobody wanted to hear about that. She had been trying all of her life to warn people about the world ending one way or another, and it hadn't gotten her anything but ridicule. *Well,* she thinks, *any fool can look outside and tell this is the end. They don't need me for that today. Should've listened to me while they still had time. But a fool and his minutes will be parted right down the middle. Cut sideways and crossways. Minced moments till nothing is left. I tried to tell them,* she thinks, *but now it's too late.* Cassie Getty sits down in her rocker and waits for time to stop completely. She wonders what will be her last thought, or if there will even be one. If there will just be the sound of her rocker on the wood floor, the sound of back and forth, back and forth, finally replaced by the sound of nothing. Nothing at all.

Monday, 5:16 P.M.

Magnus has made her way to the square. She pauses long enough to spit through her fingers. She looks absently around the square and crosses the road to the oak tree. Once she reaches it, she lays one hand up against the trunk and says, "I'm here," as if she had struggled a million miles. "I finally made it." It is the oak tree she is addressing. Then she sits down on the bench, sticks her worn boots out in front of her, and waits.

Across the square behind the oak tree, Kate is looking out the window. She had been concentrating on Butch, who hasn't moved an inch in a very long time, but when she catches sight of Magnus walking through the square and plopping down at the oak tree, that sparks her thoughts in another direction. *I've got to tell her,* she says to herself. And without another word, she places the phone back in its cradle and walks out from behind the cash register and, still wearing her apron, out the front door.

Butch releases a deep breath he's been holding in and pulls out his cell phone. He presses one to speed-dial the senator's direct line, but instead of the sure and steady voice of the senator, a recording begins to say, "Due to circumstances beyond our control," and Butch hangs up. "Out of control all right." He walks over to the phone behind the counter and picks it up, but when he puts the phone to his ear, there is no dial tone. He taps the receiver button. No change. He hangs up the receiver, waits, and lifts the receiver and tries again. No change. He looks out the window at the blackening red and thinks, *The senator's not going to like this.* Then he looks out the window to make certain that Kate is not on the return and turns toward the kitchen, where he hopes to find another piece of chicken. And another piece of pie. Maybe two. And then he forgets the reason he came to Shibboleth in the first place.

Monday, 5:20 P.M.

If you could look at Shibboleth today from a hawk's eye, you might see some of the leftover patterns. But they have already begun to disappear. Gardens are unattended. Nothing has been watered. Nothing raked. Nothing broken, fixed, and put together again. Little by little, people have been drying up at the root. Death and dry rot running up the stems of their souls. They are not waving when they pass anymore. Babies are not being coddled but dismissed. Or overlooked altogether, as though no one really saw them. Stories are not being told. Laughter is not being heard. Wishes are not being made. The music of the life of the people of

Shibboleth has been sucked away. Most of them are as empty as locust shells now. Vaguely familiar shapes holding no substance.

Monday, 5:33 P.M.

"What are you doing out here?" Kate is standing over Magnus with her hands on her hips.

Magnus spits between the *V* of her fingers. "Danged if I know, Kate." She looks up at Kate and shades her eyes with her hand as if the sun were in her eyes. But there is no sun now. "What are you doing out here?"

Kate sits down next to her on the bench. "Danged if I know, Magnus."

And the two of them just sit. As if this were their ritual. As if they had sat on this bench through all the girlhood days and glory days and days gone by. And once upon a time, they did.

"It sure is quiet," Magnus says.

Kate offers her, "Yeah, looks like some kind of storm is coming."

"Have you seen this kind of storm before?" Magnus paws the dirt with one heel of her boot, then answers without waiting for Kate Ann to reply. "I have. I've seen it. It took me a while to remember where. Took me a lot of steps to remember when, but when I got here, when I laid my hands on that tree," she shoots her thumb over her shoulder at the oak, "it all came back to me. But it was funny, like looking through one of those glass-bottom boats I saw one time in Florida. You can't touch what you're seeing. And a part of you just wants to get out of the boat and not to drown." She spits again. "It's unnatural, that ride."

"What are you saying, Magnus?" Kate is shaking her head back and forth, trying to wake up. She is hearing Magnus's words from a long way off. The truth is, Kate isn't really certain if she is awake or dreaming that she and Magnus are whispering under the covers of a dream. Kate looks down at her hands, still flecked and sticky with flour dough. *Must not be a dream*, she thinks, *if my hands are this sticky.* "Go on."

"It was the night that Blister got burned." She turns and looks at Kate, reaches out and takes her sticky hands. "That night, I had a dream, and in the dream was this," she waves her hand at the dried-up town, the stores, and the fear breathing down on them from the air, "and I woke up afraid, Kate. Everybody was leaving town, and whether they go'ed or whether they stayed made no difference, they were all leaving for good."

Kate lets go with one hand and reaches out and pushes Magnus's gray hair back. *She's too young for all this gray hair,* she thinks. *Isn't she? Lord, how old are we now? When did this happen?*

"And this is what I knew," she has started to whisper. "If Blister died that night, we all died. And that makes no sense at all. What's an old drunk got to do with the end of the world, anyway?" And one tear slides down Magnus's worry-lined face.

"Blister's all right." And Kate looks around the square at the stores with no one in them. The open signs gleaming like lies from the windows. The old PURE station sign as dead as Randy Johnson since he passed away. Now everyone had to drive five whole miles out of town to the convenience store to get gas, and Kate didn't think there was anything convenient about it. "Can't even get gas downtown anymore." Kate has forgotten about Blister, barely remembers that Magnus is holding onto her hands.

"See here, Kate, Trice *saw* what was happening at the minute in *her* dream, but she was still living with you so I didn't know we were *both* dreaming. *Both* seeing. I was *seeing* what was happening today." She looks around like Kate at the neon in the windows, the open signs and open doors. And empty buildings. "This is what I saw. The empty streets and stores. The people all sucked away. It was just as horrible then as it is now. Only ... Blister was in my dream and he was all twisted up. Inside and out. And I kept saying, 'Get up, John,' and I called him John 'cause that's his name, of course. 'Get up!' Over and over I kept saying it, but the funny thing was that he wasn't down. He was standing empty-handed in front of me. Just standing there, and he kept saying, 'What do you want me to do, Magnus?' Then he'd shove those empty hands in front of my face and say, 'This is all I got.' And I would say to him again, 'Get up!' and that's all I ever said." She takes Kate's other hand, squeezes both of them hard. "That's the first time I ever told anybody about that dream. It has haunted me bad all these years. So bad sometimes I have a dream about the dream. And all I know is Blister was supposed to do something but dang me Kate if I know what it was. But I know this. It's the doggone reason he's still alive and if Blister doesn't figure it out ... " Magnus lets her voice trail off and her mouth fall open as Blister's red Chevy appears in the distance, approaching them like a torpedo from the past. And the clock slows down so much you can audibly hear it ticking. It is keeping time with their heartbeats.

Monday, 5:53 P.M.

Blister has driven now for hours. Driven up and down all the back roads of Shibboleth. And he still doesn't know who he's looking for or why, but he's certain that he needs to remember something because it's important. "Critical," he says aloud to no one listening but you and me.

He has driven to the east side of Shibboleth. He has driven to the west side of Shibboleth. He has driven downtown and is now circling the square. *Well look-a there. You don't see that anymore. Women just sitting under the oak tree.* He drives around the circle again. *Boy, they sure do look kinda familiar.* He slows down to a crawl and drives around a third time. And then his eyes lock with *the Mighty Magnus* and something explodes inside his brain. It is the past, present, and future all meeting in the same moment. And he knows what he has to do. And that he has to do it. And without further notice, he floors the Chevy, drives full speed on around the square and on down the road.

"He didn't even wave," Kate says. She would have waved, but Magnus had such a tight grip on her hands that she couldn't move one. "Just like he was a stranger to us."

"He's no stranger," Magnus says.

"Well, of course not. Everybody knows Blister."

"His name is John Elias Robert." She peels back seven layers of her skin as she reveals, "and he is the father of my baby."

Kate's head turns quickly toward the receding red truck. "I never would have guessed it." And then she says quietly, "John Robert is her daddy, then. All these years I wondered but I was afraid to ask."

"Who'd you think?"

Kate shrugs. "Maybe the old Debbie Cake salesman. They seem to be good at sweeping women off their feet."

"Kate Ann, does she ever ask about herself?" Magnus is crying now, but it's a silent cry. The tears stream down her face as she talks. She doesn't wipe them away. She doesn't let go of Kate's hands. "Don't she wonder about how she came to be in this world?"

Kate, her big blue eyes floating in saltwater, replies, "She asked when she was little. For no reason, because she had me and Phillip for momma and daddy. There weren't no reason for her to be asking. But she was eyeing me with those blue eyes."

"You know something funny? She's got those blue eyes like yours."

"Well, God's got a sense of humor, I reckon. But she kept eyeing me funny. I'd catch her out of the corner of my eye. Like she knew from the beginning I come by her in an extraordinary way. And she'd ask me every few months until I finally told her she was a gift from God. A bona fide miracle. That I raised her up from the wishing well."

"And she believed it." Magnus doesn't say it with a question mark in her voice. She says it with a smile.

"She's Trice. She believes in miracles, Magnus."

"That's 'cause she is one." Magnus finally releases Kate's hands, stretches both palms out and wipes her face flat.

"Well, she is to everybody that knows her." Kate straightens her apron, pushes the hair back from her eyes.

"And we don't ever need to tell her any different, Kate. Just let things go on being the way they are." But then she looks up at the sky and remembers the way things are. "Or maybe the way things used to be."

"We've kept that secret a long time, haven't we, Magnus?" Magnus nods. Kate looks up at the oak tree branches. "And just to think, it all started right here with us working out the details. Remember?" Magnus nods. "We were young."

"Not *so* young. Not me anyway. I was already an old maid—thirty-five and done for. You were a little younger. Young but already strong."

"I was married. Let's not forget that. Made it easier for me to be strong."

"I was so scared," Magnus says, and looks off somewhere over Kate's shoulder as if she could see the whole thing. The conversation on the bench. That long bus ride. That year away.

"You were scared back then. I've been scared ever since."

Magnus looks at her in surprise. "What have you got to be scared of? You don't look like you'd be scared of the devil."

Kate Ann looks over the empty streets again. "Scared of losing her, Magnus. All of her life, I've been scared of losing her."

"Me too," says Magnus, "losing her to you." And the two of them, tired and turning gray, somehow manage to cross that long, decayed, invisible bridge to one another. And to hold on.

Monday, 6:14 P.M.

Old Blue pulls up at the south entrance of the springs. This time they have left the shotgun at home. Shotguns won't make a bit of a difference in this fight. They could bring in grenade launchers, tanks, and troops to no avail. It's not that kind of battle.

Nehemiah looks up at the sky with Billy watching him. *Maybe he's gonna call down that rain. Maybe that will help us.* So he asks him. Figures it can't hurt.

"You gonna call down that invisible rain, Nehemiah?"

Nehemiah continues looking at the sky. "No, Billy," he says. "We're past that rain now. We need to hurry."

The three of them begin to walk through the rough sand pines, the scrub oaks and underbrush, occasionally a magnolia is to the left or right, and Trice notices that the blooms that should be just coming out, just exploding into white, are withered and brown.

The smell of sulfur grows stronger, and with every step their foot-steps crunch and crackle. It is the sound of dry, dry, dry. They are approaching the cave from a different entrance. They are trying to go in at a different level. Come up in a different room. They are trying to take a shortcut. But sometimes shortcuts are deceptively long and treacherous.

I look at Billy's stomach, at his shoulders. I am thinking it's not going to be a tight squeeze—it's going to be impossible. But they don't know this yet. They have forgotten that time's natural passing means growing up in more ways than one.

"Where's the wind, Nehemiah?" Billy asks. Trice keeps a hand on Nehemiah's hand, his arm, his jacket. She is holding on. And silent. She doesn't want to tell them now what she sees. And what she doesn't see.

"I can't tell you, Billy." Nehemiah shifts his pack.

"I don't understand this," Billy says, "and I don't like it, either. This is downright suspicious. Like if we were expecting the wind, we won't find it, so something else is gonna come up." Billy looks around and whispers under his breath, "Something else that's no good."

Nehemiah begins to contemplate Billy's *something else* with each step. Watching the ground, watching the trees, watching the sky. What he wants to say is, *Brother, I got a bad feeling. A curious feeling. One that says we're not gonna make it out of here alive.* And then he stops, pulls up short because what he sees is a different set of tracks. He looks down at his boots and they're a different pair of boots. As if the tracks and the footsteps belong to another man from a long time ago. In a jungle a long way away. And he realizes this feeling is not his feeling. It is his father's feeling. The second to the last feeling he would ever have as he walked straight into the middle of nothing but a heavy silence. A red sky. With no visible enemy. And with no return. His final words, "Get down!" were shouted just before an ambush of enemy fire opened up from all sides and land mines began to explode as men tried to take cover. And David Trust's final thoughts had not actually been complete thoughts at all. Only images. Images of the face of the woman he had always loved and the two small faces that would grow into men's faces without him. And any closing prayer he had that day was simply *Dear God*, and it was attached to those faces just before he laid down his life. He hung those two words on those faces, and then he died.

And in an inexplicable folding-over of time and fruit from one of the shortest prayers ever heard, Nehemiah says, *Get down!* but then he realizes he has said the words to himself. "Get down!" This time he forces the words over his lips as he reaches for Trice and pulls her down with him. It appears that finally, after so many years of being wrong, Cassie Getty has gotten something right. As far as Shibboleth is concerned, the end of the world has come.

Monday, 6:24 P.M.

Kate and Magnus are embracing. Right out there in public. Sitting right there, on the bench. Out in the open under that unrelenting black-red sky. Rocking one another back and forth. It's too bad that it had to come down to the end for this to happen. It would have been a glory for Zadok to see and point it out to the men in the barbershop. They would have all said, "I'll be" and "Would you look at that!" If Cassie Getty had been coming out of the beauty shop after her regular appointment, she would have just looked backward one time through the open door and shouted at the top of her lungs, "Hell has just froze over. Thought y'all would like to know." Ellen over at the Piggly Wiggly would have gotten on the intercom and called up Rudy from the back and said, "You just got to get up here and see this." But that isn't the case on this day. And in only seven seconds, a shock wave will roll down the street and knock Magnus and Kate back so hard that the bench they are sitting on will carve a permanent notch into the oak tree. It will hit them both as they cling to one another knowing that at least now they can stop worrying about their big secret. Because the big secret will die with them.

Blister has driven five miles farther, has spotted Old Blue pulled off on the side of the road. He is just beginning to turn around, to go back, to follow the path that he knows he needs to follow, when the shock wave catches the side of his truck with such fury that it lifts the truck as it's turning, lifts it up on two wheels and holds it there. The truck freezes with Blister's hands on the wheel, then it begins to slide toward the ditch. Then it begins to roll. Over and over on itself, as Blister thinks, *Just when I was fixin' to get something right.*

Monday, 6:25 P.M.

The waves that roll over Nehemiah and Trice and Billy's head are tangible. Can actually be seen with the naked eye. There is an electric current that pulses across the edges of their backs, and if they were to look up they would see them. But they are huddled as close to the ground as possible. And by force shoved against one another, and then against the tree line and unable to breathe. But the rolling continues beyond them, tilting trees, blowing rocks, and somewhere in the distance Billy hears the glass blown out of his windows and thinks about Sonny Boy alone at home and hopes that he's all right.

In a little while they will pull themselves to their feet. They will find that they can stand. And then they will discover that they can run, because, without any explanation, Nehemiah begins to run toward the southern entrance to the cave. He is not slowing down, he is not looking back. And without question, Trice and Billy run after him. Trice in a desperation to put her hand back on the body before her. Billy in determination to save his brother from becoming a sacrifice to something he can't see for a reason he doesn't understand.

Monday, 6:27 P.M.

Exploding glass causes Butch to freeze in the kitchen, where he has one finger in his mouth licking the remainder of the blackberries from the empty pie plate. He drops the pie plate to the kitchen counter and quickly pulls his gun from his shoulder holster and takes a step into the dining room. All the windows are blown out. Butch doesn't know exactly what he's doing here or where all the pie came from, but he does recognize a war zone when he sees one. He walks to the window, the glass crunching underneath his feet. He surveys the street. *There's no sign of the enemy. But there does appear to be a couple of wounded, and from this distance they look like old women.* He is trying to remember his mission because right now it evades him. And he would really like to know. *What are my orders? And whose side am I on?* Then, as he surveys the women struggling to their feet, he thinks, *Looks can be deceiving.* He takes aim at the shapes of Kate and Magnus as he steps through the empty door frame.

Monday, 6:29 P.M.

Nehemiah, Trice, and Billy are approaching the opening, but from a level distance there is nothing to see. This is the passage of their childhood. This is the passage where the world disappeared into mystery and possibility. And eventually into the place where they found the stuff that they were made of. But that was many years ago, and today some things have changed.

Nehemiah reaches the downward path before them, and Trice catches her breath as he descends the natural rock steps until he is out of sight. She pushes forward even harder, and by the time she arrives he is already below, leaning into the crevice doorway. Trice looks down and follows him, hurries down the steps, grabs his arm for reassurance. Billy arrives panting. He stops and puts his hands on his knees, breathing heavily.

Nehemiah, turning sideways, tries to push through the opening, but it's too tight. He pulls back out, removes his blue jean jacket and hands it to Trice. Then he finally realizes what I already know. He looks up at Billy standing above them looking down. Then he looks at Trice. Then they both look back at Billy.

"What is it?" Billy is still catching his breath in great, gaspy gulps. Billy needs to run more often, I am thinking. Bank fishing is a fine sport but not much exercise.

"Billy," Nehemiah is looking up, "we're bigger, a lot bigger now."

"And let me guess, I'm biggest of us." Billy stands up, crosses his arms over his chest, starts down into the hold. "Well, that settles it. I guess I'm the official lookout." He looks back over his shoulder, "Or I can go around, enter from the other side, and find you two."

"It's been a long time, Billy," Trice says. "I don't think you'd find us. The tunnels are too confusing." Years ago, they had used the sound of underground rivers coming up and disappearing again as their guides. A watery map of sound telling them where to turn or how far away they were from a room or a hallway. Now there would be no waterfalls to their right or streams to their left for guidance. Only darkness.

Another shock-wave blast rolls over their heads, shakes the ground, and throws them against the cave walls.

"You better go on now, Brother."

Nehemiah nods at him, wants to apologize for missing out on his life for so long. Wants to tell him all the things he's never said. Now he knows those are words that should have been said years ago. But years ago is gone. He simply says, "Be careful, Brother," as he turns and pushes himself through the opening so tight it scrapes the skin from his back and chest before he makes it through.

Trice reaches into their cave bag and tosses Billy his light helmet and a flashlight before she pushes the bag through to the other side. She turns and looks one last time at Billy, who, when all is said and the day is done, has been her best friend for the last twelve years.

"No matter what happens, Billy, I'll see you on the other side."

"If you beat me, Trice, you tell Momma and Daddy ... " and the bear breaks down but doesn't cry. But he can't say anything more.

"I'll tell them that you still need a haircut," she says, then she turns and disappears inside the cave.

Just inside, the temperature drops significantly. Nehemiah has strapped on his helmet and turned on the light, and is passing one to Trice. He shoulders the backpack, reaches for Trice's hand, and they begin to walk deeper into the darkness of the earth. And toward the presence of evil.

Monday, 6:41 P.M.

Butch is standing over the disheveled figures of Magnus and Kate. They are pulling up to their knees as they try their best to collect themselves, to remember where they are and what has happened. Then Kate looks up and sees the man with the gun, and she pokes Magnus in the side. Magnus takes her eyes off of her feet, where she is standing with one boot on and one boot off, and looks up at Butch.

"Do you know him?" she asks Kate.

"He looks familiar. She pulls the glasses down on her nose that have amazingly stayed on her face and looks over them at Butch. "I think he's a friend of Nehemiah's."

"If you ask me, he doesn't look like a very good friend," Magnus says, and she makes the motion of spitting through her fingers although she has actually swallowed her tobacco.

At the name of Nehemiah, Butch slowly lowers the gun. He looks around the town square. At the broken glass and the uprooted trees, as if he was a man waking up from a dream. Because he is. It is the same dream that has been stealing intentions and leaving people vulnerable to all manner of madness.

"We better get inside," he says to Kate and Magnus. He shoulders his gun and stretches out two hands to help the women to their feet, and the odd threesome walk, looking frequently over their shoulders until they feel safely inside.

Cassie Getty is lying on the floor where the rocker dumped her before tumbling onto her back. She rises to her knees and pushes it off. She sets the rocker back upright and goes to the window and looks out. The windowpanes shook with complaint but held fast to their form. Cassie squints through the panes and sees that the earth is still there. *So far,* she thinks. She decides she will go to the kitchen and get a snack. "I might need to keep my strength up," she says out loud as she pulls a box of graham crackers down from the shelf. She returns to the living room with her hand in the box and is standing there, just like that, when the next wave rocks the floor under her feet so that she looks as though she is dancing, trying to keep her balance. Suddenly Cassie wishes that she was not alone. A wish that has been a long time in coming.

Monday, 6:44 P.M.

Zadok was sitting in the back of his shop when the first shock wave hit and knocked out his glass storefront. He didn't pay much attention. Just kept sitting, staring at the walls like he had done for the previous hours of the day. Zadok was disappearing inside of himself, and when a thought came he would just let it go on by until he was back on empty. If there had been someone who had any intent of stealing, they could have easily walked right in and taken all the money in the register, if there had been any. For that matter, they could have taken the register. Zadok would still be sitting in the chair, his scissors hanging limply from his hand.

If Zadok had been able to stare through walls, he would have been looking into a mirror image of himself in Obie's salon. Right now she and Zadok are bookends staring through a cement wall. Finally, Obie reaches around behind her and turns on the hair dryer. She is hoping that it will drone out the noise inside her head, the same noise that has been bothering her all day.

Monday, 6:47 P.M.

Blister wakes up where he is lying, fallen against the passenger door. Blood is dripping from a cut on his hand, and he can feel blood running down one leg. He feels like all of his body parts have been dislocated and put back together the wrong way. He pulls himself as upright as he can get. "What do you know? I'm still alive," he says. Then he looks up toward the open door window above him and begins pulling himself upward by hanging onto the steering wheel.

Blister tries to push the door open and, when he fails, settles for pulling his body through the open window. He falls out toward the hood and rolls down the front, catches himself and falls to his feet. *I'm a regular action-adventure character. That's what I am,* he thinks.

Then he locates Billy's truck and starts walking in that general direction. He is staggering, but it's not from drink. It's from dizzy. Blister hasn't taken a drink for a very long time.

Monday, 6:59 P.M.

There is Pastor Brown. Right where he's been all afternoon and now into the darkest of nights that Shibboleth has seen. *No moon or stars tonight,* he thought. *We are being erased.* And there was a truth in his statement that I wish he had captured earlier. A truth that I wish he had conveyed to his sleepy, contented congregation. But the pastor has recognized the fullness of this truth an hour and a day and a decade too late. He missed the opening signs of the shifting of Shibboleth. They were so easy to overlook that they almost weren't even there. Subtlety is a favorite weapon of the enemy. And unless you look very closely, you might just believe he has mastered its maneuverings.

As the first shock wave rolled its way from the dried-up springs and across Shibboleth and down into the town square, Pastor Brown dropped to his knees and prayed very simply, "Forgive me." The remainder of his prayer was nothing but a silent heartache. But it was just as easily understood.

Monday, 7:14 P.M.

Nehemiah and Trice are walking deeper and deeper into the earth. They have gone as far as their feet remember. "Let me see our map, Trice," Nehemiah says, and waits for her to pull it from her pocket. He waits as she reaches into her rear pockets. As she reaches into her front pockets.

"Don't tell me," Nehemiah says, but Trice doesn't have to tell him anything. "I just had it, Nehemiah, when we ... " Then Trice stops because she can't remember where they were when she had it. She can't remember much of what happened before this very moment. Things are getting foggy inside her mind. And if Trice could see herself the way she sees everyone else, she would understand why. "We have to go back."

"There is no time left for turning back." Nehemiah looks down the corridor before him, tries to remember a thousand childhood trips. "Let's just move forward and see what happens. Maybe something will trigger our memory."

Trice wants to tell him that this is suicide, that moving forward in the darkness is insanity, but she doesn't. Their choices are so limited. So missing. So gone. She takes his arm and they move forward, following the beams of their headlamps down the long, dark corridor, with nothing but blind faith to guide them.

Monday, 7:23 P.M.

On the surface, Billy is tapping his fingers on his arm. He rocks slightly in the hole. Not like Nehemiah but back and forth on his feet. One foot to the other foot, the helmet swinging in his hand. Then he looks at his watch as if it mattered. Then he looks down. And what he sees causes his heart to beat twice as fast. It's a rolled-up sheet of yellowed paper. He bends and picks it up gently. He is hoping that Trice has burned the images into her brain, knows them like the back of her hand. *If she hasn't,* he is thinking, *they'll never make it out of there alive.* He takes one look into the cave's entrance, shoves an arm through and half of a shoulder, listening for sounds in the distance. Nothing. He shoves the map in his jeans pocket and crawls up out of the path's entrance. He is thinking that he will find them. He is hoping he will find them. Or he is determined that the last good thing he'll do is die trying.

Billy begins jogging back to Old Blue as fast as he can. He is singing as he goes in—a march tune, "No time like this time, no time like this time, and this time is all the time I need." And he doesn't stop when he reaches the truck. He is still chanting softly as he knocks the loose glass out of the window with the light helmet. He quickly picks up the largest pieces from the seat and tosses them to the ground and is engrossed in doing this, chanting and picking up glass, when a bloody hand taps him on the shoulder. That's when the chanting stops and the cussing begins.

Monday, 7:24 P.M.

Kate, Magnus, and Butch make their way back into the diner. Kate puts her hands on her hips and says, "Well, ain't this a mess."

Magnus just says, "Get me a broom." And the two of them set about cleaning up what's most obvious. They do this in spite of the night. In spite of air so thick a person almost can't breathe. They clean as though company was coming, as happy as two reunited friends can be when they are scratched up and shook up and in a state of shock. That is, until Kate discovers the empty pie plate. A pie that was most recently made. The one that explains her sticky hands. She holds up the tin, looks at it for a moment, and then nods to herself. She walks out of the kitchen, holds it up before Butch's face, and says, "You owe me some labor." And Butch, with the taste of berries on his tongue, says, "I guess I do."

He dutifully follows Kate to the kitchen with Magnus grinning at him every step of the way.

Cassie Getty has decided not to let the world come to an end. Not today anyway. It's a simple thought in her mind but a good one. She has decided that there are a few things still worth saving. She puts on her raincoat (although it doesn't look like rain) and gets her pocketbook (I guess she has decided to take it to heaven with her) and begins walking. I want to tell her she has a car. Want to tell her that the keys are right there in the side pocket of her purse where she always keeps them. But she doesn't seem to notice the car. She pulls the door closed behind her, takes out her keys, locks the front door, and puts them directly back where they were. Then she hooks the purse firmly inside her crooked arm, straightens her hat, and sets off walking down that dirt road with a determined look on her face. I am thinking this could take a while. It's a lot farther than a country mile.

Monday, 7:35 P.M.

Magnus continues sweeping. Continues picking up exploded glass. She goes to the kitchen, pulls the garbage can out into the center of the diner and sweeps up dustpan after dustpan, emptying them as she goes. She can hear Kate in the kitchen telling Butch what to do, and Butch doing it.

Magnus is thinking about her cats, particularly General, and about Trice. About the way that things almost work out, then sometimes do and sometimes don't. Then she starts sweeping again.

Monday, 7:36 P.M.

Nehemiah and Trice walk steadily forward and steadily deeper. They can see their breath, just visible now when they speak, which isn't normal. It shouldn't get this cold in their cave. It never has. "We should have turned by now," Nehemiah says.

"Which way?" Trice's teeth begin to chatter. Nehemiah puts his jacket over her shoulders.

"I don't know, actually. It just seems . . . " and he pauses, trying to get his bearings in a place where there are none. "Seems we should have turned one way or the other. We've been going forward a long time."

"We just don't remember yet, Nehemiah. This way is different." And Trice pauses, looks up at him quizzically. "Why are we going this way again?"

"Because you said to, Trice."

"No, I didn't."

"You did. You were looking at the map and said this way was the shortest. It's the way we always came in." Trice doesn't respond. "To get down to the treasure." Nehemiah pauses again. "Remember?"

"I'm not sure, Nehemiah, what I remember." Both of Trice's hands are in her hair. "And what I don't."

Nehemiah wants to hold her. Wants to kick himself for taking so long to get back to her. But the only way to remain with Trice is to end this thing that they're caught in and can't see. "We can remember, Trice, if we try. We know this cave better than anyone. You, me, and Billy. We could have found our way there with our eyes closed when we were kids. We had memorized our steps. We could count them out, right down to perfection." He squeezes her hand. "Now the two of us have to do this."

"Should we go back and count from the beginning?"

"No time, Trice. Just no time left." And now Nehemiah releases her hand, runs his fingers through his own hair, trying to think. Trying to find their way when all ways are lost. When the path is nothing but darkness with no light at the end. Only tunnel. And Nehemiah does something he hasn't done for a little while. Or maybe a long while. Depends on your frame of time. What does he pray, you ask? Well, what would you pray if everything you loved was passing away? If the key was somehow in your hand to turn the door to change? A change that would put a rock back in its rightful place? Make water spring from dry places? What if? Then *those* words you'll have to tell. Those you'll have to fill in here. And in the wonder of workings, perhaps it's *your* words that will light the way.

Monday, 7:44 P.M.

"Blister, I orta knock you down." Billy jumps back with a bloody imprint left on his shirt. "Are you trying to scare me to death?"

"I done been knocked down." Blister puts his hands on his knees, takes a deep breath. "And rolled over and over and over, I believe. You know," he looks up at Billy with the scar side raised up and looking angry. "You know, I think I've had enough of this foolishness."

"Blister, I've got to go," Billy is still pushing glass out of the seat of Old Blue. Then he turns back to Blister and says again, "I've got to go."

"Where's Trice?"

"In the cave. And in trouble."

"What kind of trouble?"

The ground beneath them shakes and rolls, threatening to cave in beneath their feet.

"Just pick your poison today, Blister. We got all kinds of trouble going on."

"She lost down in the cave?"

"Can't say that she's lost. Yet. She's with Nehemiah, and they both know that cave." He looks over his shoulder and in the distance back toward the opening in the ground. "Or they used to." Then he pulls out their map, which is looking more worn and vulnerable by the minute, "But they dropped the map, so now they're going by memory."

"It's gonna take more'n that to get them out again." Blister looks at the back of his hand and then wipes it on his jeans. "My memory's not been working too good today, Billy. Kinda comes and goes in a scary way." Blister looks up at a buzzard sitting on the lowest branch of an oak tree. He cocks his head sideways, trying to figure out the buzzard. Buzzards usually travel in packs or pairs. This one is alone. He turns his head and looks sideways at the buzzard with his better eye. The buzzard turns his head and looks sideways at Blister. Billy follows his stare.

"Don't worry, Blister. He's not gonna eat us while we're still standing."

Blister doesn't take his eyes away from the bird. "I wouldn't be so sure of that. Now listen here, Billy," he keeps his eyes locked in a dead stare with the buzzard, "we got to go get Trice. I got to tell her something before it's too late."

"Blister, I know you mean well, but I ain't got time to fool around." Billy's thinking Blister has never been one to run in a straight line. To cross from A to B without a delay. Or disaster.

"Listen here." He grabs Billy's arm and hangs on tight. "You think you know that cave? You don't know nothing, Billy. Ain't nobody spent more time down there than me."

"Oh really?" The ground swells and swallows again underneath their feet. "Since when is that?" They ride the ground like they are standing in a boat.

"Never mind all that. The truth is the truth." From nowhere a gust of wind whips the trees into a frenzy. The buzzard's feathers rise and fall. His wings flap once, twice, and are down again. The wind dies as suddenly as it came. But it leaves an old, dead smell clinging to the trees. The buzzard keeps his eyes on Blister and Billy, lifts his feet and moves a few steps down the branch closer to them.

"I grew up plundering in that cave. Never saw you around."

"Maybe it was before your time, boy. Did you ever think of that? Now come on." He starts off walking through the woods toward the southern entrance.

"I can't, Blister." Billy doesn't even have time to be modest. "I don't fit. I got to drive around and go in the other side."

"Well, what are we standing around here for?" He walks to the passenger side of the truck, pushing glass from the seat while saying, "Get in, then, and let's ride."

Billy pulls at his shirt collar. He is remembering the first night he and Nehemiah were down here. Remembers that awful feeling of choking. He looks at the buzzard one last time before he climbs into the truck. He cranks Old Blue, and the unlikely pair of Billy and Blister leave a trail of dry dust as Billy floors the pedal. They back out of the woods, take off down the road, passing by Blister's overturned truck in the process.

The long night will become one of the shortest of their lives if they don't pick up their pace. Their night will fall into an eternal darkness.

I lean forward and breathe on the back of the truck for good measure. Just a tiny breath. The buzzard is taken by surprise. Is blown sideways out of the tree, lands on the ground, staggering around shaking his head. A dazed predator not expecting a divine interruption.

Billy and Blister are stirring up a storm of their own as Old Blue leaves a dust trail a mile behind them. It will take them exactly twelve minutes thirty-one seconds to circumvent the roads and make their way back to the western edge of the springs. With Blister's limping it will take them seven minutes five seconds to cross through the woods to the cave's entrance. But they reach the entrance with dust in their mouths and determination in their eyes. Billy straps on his helmet, turns on the light. He hands the flashlight to Blister, who turns it on and then pulls Billy aside, makes him stop. "Listen here, if anything happens to me, anything peculiar, don't even slow down or turn back. You just keep on going. You understand?"

"Don't know what you're talking about, Blister." Billy turns his helmet forward in the darkness, takes off at a pace faster than he likes to walk. Normally. Right now he would like to run, but this is not a place for running. This is a place of surprising drop-offs. Of twists and turns and optical illusions in the limited light. Where the darkness can go on ahead of a man for a thousand feet. Or suddenly drop perilously thirty feet down into a cavernous room of rock. Billy knows just such a room. And, unknown to him, so does Blister. It is a room that requires a person to walk slowly on the backbone of the dragon to reach the bottom. And another room, like a cathedral full of sparkling light, light like angels' wings covering the ceiling. It is a place of mystery that goes on forever. Full of surprises. But there is only one surprise that Billy wants to find right now. That is Nehemiah and Trice, safe and in the treasure room of Time.

There is an animal groan that pulls Billy and Blister up short. "Did you hear that?" Blister shines the light up into Billy's face. "Blister, aim that thing down out of my eyes. Of course I heard it."

"What do you think it was?" He shines the light to the left and in front of them, but the sound seems to have no direction. It came from all around. "I think it is the whole earth complaining, Blister. I think it's saying it's thirsty. Parched to death." Billy pulls at his collar again. Tries to swallow. Wishes he'd thought to bring a canteen.

Monday, 7:58 P.M.

Nehemiah and Trice stop and listen to the sound as well. "Wind songs?" Trice asks.

"Can't be. No water. Wind songs come from the echoes of the water." He shines his helmet back and forth before them. "No water," he says again. And wishes he'd thought to fill the canteens before they left the house. The corridor before them is growing narrower and narrower, a throat closing them up inside. Nehemiah is trying his best, but he doesn't quite remember this part. He is trying to remember being seven. And seventeen. Trying to look with a different view, through an old pair of eyes. A different air hits Nehemiah's nose. An old, old but familiar smell.

"To the right, Trice." And they turn their headlamps to the right. There, just ahead of them, six feet wide, four feet high, is their crawl space.

"It's the Tiger's Mouth." Trice smiles in the dark. It's the first thing they've recognized. It belongs to them. It's the first thing that they had named. Named it for the way it curved up. For the cracks in the rocks that looked like whiskers on both sides. They had named every tunnel and curve. Every cavern and rain room. They all belong to them. At least once upon a time in their world. And hopefully, one more time, they will tonight.

They crawl in side by side, elbowing their way along. "Don't jump out too fast," Nehemiah warns her.

"It's okay. I remember."

They crawl over, and carefully, very carefully, slide their feet around to the edge. It's another reason Billy didn't need to come this way. The rock floor runs narrowly around the wall and immediately beyond their feet is a blackness that drops farther than they can measure. Nehemiah is wishing he had remembered to tie Trice to him, but it's too late. They edge their way along, holding onto the rock to their right. Carefully working their way deeper and deeper into the cave. They don't speak. Now they are counting steps. It will take fifty-seven steps to reach the first rain room. A rain room rains in all seasons. But not this one. Not now.

Monday, 8:01 P.M.

Billy and Blister have maneuvered their way through three tunnels and argued over which way to go on their fourth turn, with Billy finally relenting to Blister. Crawling for ten feet through a small, twisting, turning, cavernous tunnel that Billy could barely fit through. Now he is wishing he had brought some type of marker to help him find his way out again. That is if they would be a-getting out.

"You know, Blister, it's a wonder we didn't die in here when we were kids."

"Well, it still ain't too late for that." He keeps crawling but looks over his shoulder at the sound of Billy's breathing, "I know somebody that died in this cave."

"Who?" Billy has never heard this story. Is not sure that he would believe a story from Blister. But that doesn't mean he wouldn't want to hear it. He continues behind Blister, breathing heavily.

"Nobody you would know." Blister stops and turns to look back at Billy, shining the light in his direction. "And there is another person still in here, but I don't know who it is. Must have been before my time. But his bones are still stuck down in one of the crevices. Or they was last time I looked."

"Are you pulling my leg?"

"Not a piece of it."

They start crawling again. And speculating. "Could have been a Yankee soldier that got separated and tried to get out. Then got lost forever," Blister says, his voice taking on a singsong quality.

"Or a Reb that was sick and tired of fighting. Just decided to sit the war out," Billy offers. "Or an Indian."

They are occupying themselves. Distracting themselves from the unknown task ahead of them. Trying not to think about how Nehemiah and Trice are doing from the other side. Or how far they have to go.

Blister stops again, but only for a moment, then starts crawling again. "I don't think an Indian would have gotten stuck. Think he would have eaten the blind fish and stayed alive till he found his way out."

"Well, you couldn't pay me to eat those blind fish."

"I'd do it," Blister says with a certainty.

"You'd have to eat them raw unless you brought firewood and matches in with you."

"I'd eat 'em raw." Blister grins in the dark. "And lick my fingers."

"Some of 'em don't even have eyes."

"Then they won't see what's happening, will they?" Then Blister's voice grows dark, whispery, and serious. "Only to survive, Billy. Only to survive."

Monday, 8:12 P.M.

Kate, Magnus, and Butch have cleaned the glass up. The shock wave has left the windows wide open, as if they were sitting in a large covered patio. Normally the moon would be rising, but Pastor Brown was right. There is no moon. No stars. No natural dark. Only the dark red shadow of the sky, relentless in its suffocating gravity.

"Where do you think they are, Kate?" Magnus is sitting at the table. When she isn't talking, she is doing addition and multiplication problems in her head. She is trying to make her mind work.

"There, down there where it all started." She turns a coffee cup in circles, like Nehemiah. "But at least we know that they are together." She looks up and through the open space where the windows used to be. "Whatever happens."

"I was thinking, you and me could take your car and go out there." Magnus looks up at Kate.

"Go out where? To the springs? Right now?"

Magnus nods. She has a feeling. That's the only way she could describe it. One that she should be doing something besides just sitting here waiting. One that maybe, just maybe, there is something that she can do.

"We got about as much business being out there in those springs or down in that cave as a bat does in the noonday sun."

Kate waves her hand in front of her face, removing Magnus's eyes and the idea from in front of her face.

Then Magnus, seeing how she cannot drive, pulls out her secret weapon.

She looks nonchalantly out the window, takes a sip of her coffee, and says, "I bet they took off out there in such a hurry not a one of them took a bite to eat." She pauses, turns the coffee cup a revolution. "Probably not a thing to drink either."

Now, how long do you think it took this tiny tidbit of information to filter its way to Kate's weak spot? About as long as Magnus expected it would.

Kate pulls herself up tiredly from the table. She is so tired in her body. More so in her mind. She is still trying very hard to filter out the differences of what day it is. Trying to remember from moment to moment where they are traveling and why they are going there. And this is just in their conversations. The thought of driving off into this tangible evil presence, away from the place that gives her the greatest earthly comfort, is not one of her choice. It is one that overrides all her other instincts. And she's not sure that she can drive. She is feeling that unstable in her mind.

"I don't know, Magnus, what in the world you think we'll do when we get there." She pulls her glasses down to the edge of her nose. "But I am willing to try to do what I can." She turns and heads for the kitchen, whipping a dishrag over her shoulder. "You make a fresh pot of coffee, Magnus, and I'll pack up some food." She looks over at the table where Butch is sitting alone, contemplating his impossible circumstances. "I would be packing some mixed berry pie, but that won't be the case tonight."

"Yes, ma'am," Butch says. And it keeps him out of trouble.

Magnus has her head down in her hands. She is praying for something. I believe it is a miracle. It is a Mighty Magnus Miracle.

A prayer that has determined the end of a thing before it begins. Her first prayer was on the oak tree bench. A prayer of confused desperation. A prayer for the miracle of a plan. And so a plan was fashioned from the clay and breathed out that day. And Kate stepped into place. And her place embraced a life. And that life became a saving grace in Shibboleth.

Now Magnus prays while Kate wraps food in the kitchen. While she opens lids and pots, tries to conjure up food fit for a rescue. *But who is rescuing whom?* she wonders. And wonders if she should pack salt, a tablecloth. "This is not Sunday Dinner on the Ground," she says out loud. And Magnus yells, "What's that?" from the dining room.

The clouds outside seem to be drawing lower to the ground. They are becoming mist and fog.

"Is it time for dark?" Magnus asks.

"What's that?" Kate steps from the kitchen and looks at her, but both their questions rest on the edge of their lips. They have forgotten them. When they are together, near each other, or even touching hands, it is easier for them to remember.

The three of them, a very silent Butch, Magnus, and Kate, look out the open glass of the diner windows. They have forgotten why the glass is missing. Have forgotten the shock wave that peeled them back against their own skin. A dark ink mist rises to the window ledge, begins to pour into the diner and fall across the diner floor.

Magnus feels her mind tossed about, feels it coming into her and then leaving just as quickly, like a ribbon in the wind. She reaches inside with all her might and snatches her good sense and hangs onto it for dear life. Then she sets her mouth straight and stands up. "Butch, you get your car. Kate, whatever you packed is fine. We'll be going now." There is only the slightest hesitation as they comprehend and then comply. Kate plucks up a bag in the kitchen along with a thermos and walks to the front door, where Butch has walked outside and opened the back car door for the two of them. He sits alone in front. Driving forward as Magnus leans over the back seat giving him directions. He turns on the windshield wipers against the fog but it doesn't help. Not a bit. Through that dark, misty mind's eye, the same one that they are sharing, the old gas station PURE sign comes into view and catches both Kate and Magnus's attention. So much so that they turn their heads to stare as Butch drives past. So much so that they turn backwards in the seat and stare at the rusted sign until the encroaching darkness eats the word *PURE* one letter at a time. Then they turn around again. Slowly. They are thinking something and their somethings are the same.

Unknown to the trio cruising through the streets of Shibboleth in the Lincoln Town Car, Cassie Getty is walking just to their left. Through the brambles now tearing at her stockinged legs. Through the oak moss that in Cassie's mind has turned to snakes hanging from the trees. She talks to the snakes as she walks past them.

"You're not gonna bite me, you hear. I got business to tend to. Sure 'nuff end-of-the-world business. So hang all day if you want, but you keep your fangs pointed against the wind. Me and my flesh have decided not to die from a snake bite. Not today." She stops in her tracks, stares directly at a particular tree. "I'll turn to ashes first if I have to, right before your little forked eyes. Now you just try to take a bite out of that!"

She continues walking. The briars have ripped her hose, left bloody places along her shins. She's a flat-footed stomper, though, and she keeps up her pace, her purse hooked solidly in the crook of her arm.

I am watching the intricacies of an unfolding plan. There is that warrior Cassie Getty in the Garden of Snakes. There is Butch in his boat of compliance chauffeuring the Queens of the Kingdom safely to their doom. There is Blister, the absurdly brave court jester, partnered with Billy, a trustworthy and valiantly simple man, working to serve the Prince of the City, his brother Nehemiah, as he tries to fulfill his mission. And the fair-haired Trice. She's our weapon in disguise. But no one knows these positions yet. They are walking out the impetuses of their purposes without knowledge of the possibilities. Without the notion that they may not succeed. They have lost the terminology now of win or lose. All or nothing. They are in the deepest recesses of the valley of decision. Every move a significance. Every breath a salute to what will be or what will never be again. They are choosing this day. They are choosing. And the choices they make will have a residual effect that you will feel from where you are sitting. It's just that complicated. It's just that simple.

But look now, it continues. Billy and Blister are clearing the central cavern.

Monday, 8:59 P.M.

"Which way from here?" Billy has conceded to Blister the choice of the way to go. He will admit, without the map, without the water, without Nehemiah and Trice, he's become as blind as a bat. And missing the radar. This much he knows. What he doesn't know is this: Blister doesn't know, either. And he is thinking of the skeleton that he once encountered in this cave. Many years ago. Dried old bones. Time fried right there and stuck in between those rocks where some man had fallen, slipped in the dark. Never to get out again. And it was just one tiny footstep. Just an inch, maybe two, to the left when it should have been right, and there he went. Over and down. Hell's Jungle Blister had named it. He had found his way in from another door. A lower level. Had found his way in, found the strange contorted formations that cast grotesque shadows in every direction. Had felt the chill run up his spine as he searched for a way to climb up out of the cavern's bottom. And that's where, between the twisted, grotesque structures, he had found the bones. Still intact. The legs twisted and horribly broken. The face frozen in a grimace of pain. The arms splayed out. And then Blister had screamed. Long, hard, and loud. The strange echo from the cave walls had sounded like the screams of his long-dead companion. The screams of a dead man screaming while he's still alive. And from one who knows it. But for this man there was no rescue. Only a dying wish. One he is still waiting on to come to pass. Wishes never die.

"Don't step on him," John Robert says.

Billy stops walking. Freezes his feet in mid-step. "Don't step on who?" He has one foot frozen on the ball of his toes.

"Who?" John Robert shakes his head. He is trying to filter out the past but it won't work now. Time has melted, run together now in this spot. Two thousand years, one thousand years, one year, all running together.

"You said, 'Don't step on him.'" Billy shines the light around his feet, settles his heel to the ground.

"I did?" Blister shines the flashlight all around him. "This ain't Hell's Jungle." He looks up at Billy, shines the light under his own face so that Billy can see one eye and what's left of the other. "And he ain't here." He pauses for a moment, then adds, "unless he got up and walked off."

Billy has never been afraid of John Robert, but he wishes he'd shine that light somewhere else. In the cave, with the light shining up underneath his scarred, stretched skin, Blister looks like a dead man. But Billy doesn't say this. Billy turns around, talks while he keeps walking. "You need to help me think, Blister. We got to find them because they don't know where they are." And he's partially right. They don't know where they are.

Monday, 9:00 P.M.

I am watching Trice follow Nehemiah through tunnels. I am watching Nehemiah turn to follow Trice down old stairs carved out by time, down. The four of them are approaching the center from opposite directions. Trice and Nehemiah had entered from the short way, but now the short way is more treacherous. It is more tricky. Without the map, the short way has become the long way.

"Trice . . . " Nehemiah wants to say, Slow down. He wants to say, Be careful. And as he knows this contradicts their purpose, the ground swells beneath the rock, lets out a groan. A deep, long, lasting hungry groan.

"It's eating us alive," Trice says.

"What, Trice? What's eating us alive?"

"Don't you know by now, Nehemiah?" She turns to face Nehemiah, or almost face him, her light helmet turned slightly to the side so that her face is to the cavern wall, her eyes toward him. "Actually, I believe we both know what this is." And she stands with her eyes not on him but in him. In what's left of him that she can see. "It's that *thing*, the one we heard as kids. The one we convinced ourselves wasn't real."

"The thing we thought we saw." Nehemiah looks down into the distance.

"No, the thing we *saw*, Nehemiah. And it *saw us*. And it remembered."

"None of this was happening." He waves up and out toward Shibboleth. "All the fading and disappearing. There was water then. Water still for years."

"As long as we were watching . . . "

And Nehemiah finishes for her, "All it could do was growl. And try to take away—everything."

Trice reaches out to touch his face, but she is below him, cannot reach him from where she stands, and lets her hand drop. "Let's go on, Nehemiah. Let's go find what we came for." And she turns so quickly and retreats that he loses sight of her for a second. Can only see the beam of light ahead of her as she moves forward. The light appearing to grow dimmer with every step. And then the dimness fades to black. For the second time since Nehemiah came home, Trice disappears.

"Trice?" He falters on the steps, catches and rights himself, and calls out again. "Trice, where are you?" Then the whispered voice rises. "Trice! Answer me! Trice!" And the voice becomes a yell. And the yell is heard from a long, long way off.

"I can hear them." Billy says. "Listen." He puts his hand back toward Blister, who stands still and listens also. The sound of a voice carries. At first only the noise. The human voice sound. Then the recognition that it is Nehemiah and that he is calling. And then the unfortunate understanding that the call means he has lost something. Something precious. Something priceless. And from the pressure in the plaintive sound, that it's nowhere to be found.

"Sound don't carry like that down here."

"Must be a tunnel somewhere." Billy calls to his brother. Calls long and hard and moves toward the sound like a lighthouse in the dark. "A tunnel we didn't know about." And even with all the calls, with the twists and turns and crawl spaces, it will be almost an hour before Billy is standing breathless and sweating (even in the air that is cooler than it should be) before Nehemiah, who simply says, "She's gone."

Monday, 9:05 P.M.

Butch pulls the Lincoln up behind Billy's truck. As he opens the door and Kate and Magnus step out, the ground buckles beneath their feet, swells and then recedes, pulling at them. Butch has left his cell phone at the diner. And just in case anyone is left, in case anyone finds it, he has written a note. He has known men who went into jungles, into deserts, who knew they might never come out again. Today he has joined their company. He is on a one-way mission. He took a while to recognize it, but now he knows that for him, for all of them, there may be no tomorrow. He is thinking that at least if they die, he will be there to keep them from being afraid. He is marveling in the fact that, in the end, his final mission is one of mercy.

He reaches out to steady Kate with one arm, Magnus with the

other. They are carrying covered dishes, bags with paper plates and spoons and forks. A thermos with coffee and some cups. *What were they thinking?* He thinks of crazy things. His old schoolyard in PA. The boys down the block. His mother and father and three sisters. The nephews and nieces he hasn't seen since last Christmas. Or was it two Christmases ago? *I sure am a long way from home,* he thinks, and for a moment, but only the briefest moment, he thinks about turning and getting in the car, driving to Philly without stopping. Find someone he knows. For just a moment he wants to be with someone at the end who was there at the beginning.

Kate and Magnus try to walk across the rolling earth, stepping on pine needles as they make their way to the hole in the earth. The turkey buzzard is watching them. Has made its way across the dry ground. Has perched outside the cave's open passage and watches with great interest as they approach his tree. He is eyeing Kate specifically. Is so caught up in the flesh of her folds that he doesn't realize until much too late that Butch can reach the lowest limb. Or how unexpectedly fast Butch can be. He snatches the buzzard by the foot as they pass by. Snatches him just as the buzzard is slowly turning around, taking his aim. Butch grabs the huge bird by the foot, pulls him from the tree and swings him full force, slapping him hard against the tree trunk. Without a word he drops him to the ground and keeps walking. The stunned bird lays silent, temporarily breathless.

"Not his day, I reckon," Magnus says, never turning around. She keeps her boots determinedly moving forward.

I don't bother stifling a laugh, which no one but you and God can hear. Sometimes, in the midst of the darkest of situations, something funny is *still* funny.

Monday, 9:33 P.M.

Cassie Getty has found an old log and stopped to catch her breath. And to try to get her bearings. "It used to be right here," she says. "Or maybe," she looks off to her right, "back over there." She has been walking for hours now. She is hot and thirsty. And a little hungry. For a little while, she thinks about collard greens and cornbread. And about Kate's biscuits. Then she thinks about Kate some more, and that's what gets her back to her feet. Her bloody shins start off in a new direction. I'm thinking, as the ground lifts up beneath Cassie's feet and sucks them down again, that this may be her last chance to get this part right. I am thinking that it is intrinsically amazing how one life leads to another.

Monday, 9:35 P.M.

Blister leads the way to the steps that he's been both avoiding and searching for. I am watching the truth of this thought as he leans into the cavern wall to avoid falling and begins walking his way down the corridor, straight into Hell's Jungle. The only place in the cave where he'd ever been lost. The only place he'd thought that he'd never escape. A place he swore he'd never venture into again. But he's more than just along for the ride. Blister figures he has a debt to pay. And that his marker for payback has arrived. He shines his flashlight down the corridor into the cavern's bottom. There are the columns, and as he shines the light across them, he swears he sees something move between the twisted shapes. Something man-sized. Something strangely familiar. He stops in his tracks. *Just my eyes,* he thinks. *Just a shadow.*

"What is it?" Nehemiah asks before John Robert has time to move forward again.

"Nothing." He walks on, a little slower. "*Probably* nothing," he adds, emphasizing the *probably*.

Nehemiah is hoping in all of his flesh and bones that Blister knows exactly what he's doing. And that his doing is going to lead him directly to Trice. *How'd she fade into nothing like that?* he thinks. Then he says it aloud to Billy from behind him. "Billy, how'd Trice just disappear to nothing right in front of me? How could that happen?"

"Are you sure she disappeared?" Billy keeps walking. They are going down, getting lower. The air is getting colder. And colder. There is, oddly, a freezing breeze. Coming up from somewhere below them.

"What do you mean, am I sure? Of course I'm sure. I was looking right at her." Nehemiah stops, stands still, listens for any sounds of Trice, but all he hears is Blister and Billy's steps below him. His heart beating hard against his chest. His blood rushing through his veins faster and faster at the thought of Trice lost and alone. And then he resumes walking but slower. *I was looking right at her. Wasn't I?*

Monday, 9:36 P.M.

Kate and Magnus reach the cave's entrance with their one plastic flashlight. They are breathless, not accustomed to walking up steep hills in the dark. "We can't go on in there like this," Kate says, between short gulps of air. "We don't have enough light." She bends over and puts her hands on her knees.

"I don't reckon going in was ever our business." Magnus sits down on a rock just inside the cave's entrance. "I guess this is as close as we need to get."

"Well, need to or not, it's as close as we're going to get today." Kate carefully sets the plates down on the rock floor. "Whatever day it is anymore." She pulls up on the corners of her apron and fans herself with it. Then she stops and looks, perplexed, at Magnus. "What are we here for?"

"We're keeping a watch." Magnus says and spits without apology in the corner of the cave's floor.

"Are we sitting up with the dead?" Kate has lost her bearings, just like that. As if they were snatched out from under her.

"Not yet, Kate." Magnus says. "Not yet." And I'm thinking that in the end of days, the Mighty Magnus, as Blister calls her, has been mighty indeed. In the end, she has become fearless.

Monday, 9:38 P.M.

Nehemiah stops walking on the stone steps. *Something isn't right,* he thinks. There is a shifting beneath their feet. So hard the cave floor shakes. Almost tossing them off the edge. Now they have only fifteen feet to go, but it's a long and ragged fifteen feet. *She's not down here. Trice isn't here.* That's what Nehemiah is thinking as he throws his arms against the cave wall, trying to steady his legs. He is feeling Trice's absence like a vacuum. Feeling her blood grow colder with every step he takes. And without another word, he turns and starts back up the stairway.

Billy is no brother's fool. He immediately knows his brother is no longer close behind him. He's felt that absence for more than a decade. And now he feels it again. "Nehemiah?" When there is no answer forthcoming, he calls, "Brother?" but there is a hopeless, lost, and plaintive tone to his call. One that if you listen you can even hear from there. His headlamp searches the steps above him, but incredibly there is no sign of Nehemiah. "Momma, send some angels to watch over Brother, will you? He's all I got left."

"Who you talking to?" Blister turns back toward Billy. He is jumpy. Mighty jumpy. His skin is crawling all over him. Like it will jerk off his body and run off of its own accord. And if it could, it would.

"Talking to my momma."

"Oh" is all John Robert says. But he doesn't keep walking. He is too afraid. He's afraid of what's down there. And afraid of what isn't.

"Blister, go on." There is a pause because John Robert doesn't move. "We can't just stand here." And Billy's words come pouring out like prophecy because the next rumbling of the ground is solid tremor. It cracks the cave steps they were walking on. Shakes the foundation from beneath their feet. Causes what was solid only a moment before to come down. And still six feet from the bottom, Billy and Blister come tumbling down to the ground.

Nehemiah hears the caving in of the steps. The rocking throws him to the floor of the cave, but only for a moment before he is back on his hands and knees. He is on his feet again before the rumbling stops. Running before the ground is steady.

Cassie Getty is thrown to the ground. Her purse slips off her arm. It will take just a little while before she gets up. She stands and looks to the left and right until she spies her pocketbook. She picks it up and dusts it off with her dirty hands, hooks the vinyl strap back over the crook of her arm, and heads off in the same determined direction she was traveling before. She knows exactly what she has to do.

Butch has grabbed Magnus and Kate and pulled them together, pushing their heads down against his chest, their faces toward him. He has done this so quickly that they have had no room to protest. And they won't tell you so, but they are happy not to see what might be coming next. They both squeeze their eyes shut, tight as mothballs, and stay that way until the shifting and rumbling has completely stopped. Until Butch has gently released them, then resumed his pacing at the opening, as if nothing had happened. They look at his back, wordlessly. Then sit side by side on the cave floor, their backs against the wall. Silently praying for Nehemiah and Billy and Trice. But mostly for Trice. After all, she's their baby girl.

But another silent prayer is rising from the entrance of the cave. From a man on a mission who recognizes a mission when he sees one. Recognizes what weapon is required for that mission to be accomplished. And what he knows right now is that Nehemiah is on the most important mission of his life. And as it turns out, he hasn't been sent to check up on him. Or to bring him back. He's been sent to serve him. And the best he can do now is to guard the door. And pray like he's never prayed. To stretch his faith. To use a weapon he can't touch to aim at a target he cannot see. Because it's come down to this. Only prayer can help Nehemiah succeed on a mission Butch doesn't understand. Only prayer can bring him out alive. And a marine doesn't leave a man behind. Butch drops to his knees in the center of the cave's opening, and with his eyes wide open, looking beyond the space, he prays like a poet. Call it inspired. Call it desperation. Regardless of the source, these are the words that filter up from the cave's entrance and take flight. I write them down. "In darkness, be his eyes. In weakness, be his strength. In fear, be his faith."

Butch remains kneeling on those words with Nehemiah's face before him. And he determines that if he has to, he will remain this way until Nehemiah comes walking out. Or until there is nothing to walk out of, or into.

Magnus begins singing a song, first humming it under her breath, then the words come halting out. Magnus doesn't sing well. But she sings loud enough to make up for it. "Won't you come home, Bill Bailey? Won't you come home?" she sings. "I've cried the whole night long. I'll do the cooking, honey. I'll pay the rent. I know I done you wrong." Her words dissipate into humming.

"That's not a very nice song," Kate says. "You orta sing something better than that."

"Just popped up in my mind," Magnus says. "Ain't that a funny thing? I had forgot all about that song."

"Well, you orta forget it. It's not a very good one." Kate picks at her apron. "A woman's not supposed to pay the rent."

"Well, I guess not. But maybe she was trying to pay him back." Magnus spits again.

"What for?"

"Well, I don't know, but it says right there, I know I done you wrong. It musta been something."

"Musta been something bad if she was going to pay the rent," Kate says. Then she adds, "She musta been pretty desperate, if you ask me."

Magnus hums the song again for a moment. "It's nothing but a song, Kate. It don't really mean nothing."

"I guess not."

"But it's funny how things get stuck inside of you and come out at the strangest times." And Magnus is quiet for a while. Real quiet. Because what she is really thinking about, *who* she is really thinking about, is John Robert. About how she did him wrong. And about how, in her book, he did her wrong first. But now, twenty-nine years later, in the dying light of the world, things have taken on a different perspective. "Wrong is just wrong all the way around," she says.

And Kate adds, "Yeah, it is," even though she doesn't have a clue what Magnus is talking about.

Monday, 9:40 P.M.

The last shock wave caused a rupture in the wall between Obie's Salon and Zadok's Barbershop. Obie walks out of her front door and looks at the empty, dusty, dark streets. "It's not proper day or proper night," she says. Then she looks through Zadok's plate glass window, which, beyond comprehension, is still in place. He is still sitting as he was, in the barber chair, slumped down, staring at the wall. Or, more correctly, he is now staring at the crack running up the wall.

Obie opens the door and hollers at him, "Zadok!" He doesn't even bother turning his head. And Obie thinks he has had a stroke. Or maybe is sure enough sitting up frozen dead. "Zadok!" she yells again, this time louder, with more force. But Zadok doesn't move. She walks inside, approaches him carefully. Bends down and looks up into his face. Then she softly touches his arm and whispers, "Zadok?" with a question on her lips, and for the first time he moves, looks at her with the slightest comprehension.

"Zadok?" Obie talks softly now, like she is talking to a child.

"Get up, sugar," and she takes him by the hand, "we got to go." She helps him get up out of the chair and walks with him until they are both standing outside looking up and down the sidewalk. Obie has the compelling urge—to find people and to get them to church. She couldn't tell you anything beyond this right now. She couldn't give you a single recipe or piece of gossip if her life depended on it. She couldn't trim any bangs or comb out a curl. She turns to Zadok and explains the plan. "We are gonna walk around now and see if anybody needs our help." She pats his arm with her other hand. "And then we are going to church." Sometimes, in the forward course of humanity, without any explanation, a person just wakes up.

Monday, 9:55 P.M.

Nehemiah has circled back to the place where he lost Trice. He calls her name but there is no answer. He feels along the cave walls, without understanding, searching for something he knows must be there. A place where rock and reason hold no rhyme.

Then surprisingly a voice whispers, "I'm right here." But Nehemiah isn't certain whose voice he hears. "Trice?"

"I'm right here," the voice repeats, but it is a small voice. It is a voice that sounds so near and yet so very far away.

Then it calls him by name. "Nehemiah?" Then there is a long pause—it is a cavernous pause. It is a breath between dimensions. And the voice adds, "Give me your hand." And Nehemiah obeys what he cannot see. He stretches out his hand toward the voice in the dark. The air becomes colder still. So cold that Nehemiah begins to shake. He moves his light toward the sound and his light dims. "Not now!" he whispers to himself because goose bumps are rising on his flesh. Hair is standing up on the back of his neck. Something doesn't feel right. Even in the midst of all this madness, in the middle of the darkness and chaos, there is a river of peace that he can follow. But that river is not obvious. That river is not visible to the naked eye. And the light he so much wants right now, the external light to verify his steps, doesn't cooperate. That light grows dimmer and dimmer. He turns his helmet back and forth, searching for the substance of the voice. Searching for Trice. But the light grows dimmer, slowly fading, until it is completely gone. Now there is nothing but darkness. And a voice that continues calmly calling, "This way. Take my hand." Nehemiah wants so very much for the voice to be Trice. Wants it so much that his arm reaches blindly forward.

(How can I explain to you the chemistry of Nehemiah's *now*? Have you ever desired something so much, with all of your beating heart, that you reach for the wrong thing? Have you ever been deceptively tricked by the imposter into believing the false thing before the true thing appeared? I know you have. I've been watching you. But then, your story isn't over yet. I see time in your hourglass.)

"I'm right here," the voice repeats. "Right here." It is determined.

I will not paint the wrong picture. The wrong thing does not come uncloaked. The wrong thing comes with a hypnotic voice. A syrupy, seductive voice. One laced with sugary desire. Nehemiah takes a step forward. And another. But then he stops still in his tracks. And time moves forward as he listens, as he battles inside himself.

If you could see through the darkness hovering over him, you would see a man with closed eyes. A man who reaches out, touches his stomach with his palm, cocks his head to the side as if he is listening to another voice. One from somewhere deep inside of him. One more familiar than breath. One that is the Creator. (Just where do you think God has been in all of this?) Then Nehemiah's jaw clenches. And his expression changes, as he lowers his arm. An expression that says, "I don't think so. Not today." He takes a step back. And begins to move in the opposite direction. His back is against the cave wall, his eyes blind to everything but a treasure he is seeking. *And in that treasure, time will still be,* he tells himself. *And Trice will be well.*

"Over here," the voice repeats. It grows more forceful, slides its way along the rocks. And now, the voice is suddenly just at his ear. At his *ear*. Breathing heavy. "Don't you want me? Take me, I'm right here." The air has become frigid. And with every step Nehemiah takes, it becomes colder still. And more stale. With every determined step he takes, the breathing becomes less seductive and more voracious. Until its anger and frustration can no longer be hidden. Until the veil is lifted with a vengeance. The voice no longer whispers "follow"; it whispers "fear." The voice paints the past full of pain and regret. Paints the future so hopeless, so lost, it's as black as the hole it's hiding in. It shoots arrow words with one aim: to stop a man in his path. To call him back. Turn him around. It grows and shifts shape in the dark. Becomes a tangible presence panting dark breaths of sickness and disease. Words of death and destruction.

But Nehemiah is walking forward in the total blackness. Ignoring temptation. Ignoring torment. Continuing on his journey. One single, solitary step at a time. Just like you are.

Monday, 10:36 P.M.

Magnus is pacing the ground just inside the entrance of the cave. She turns suddenly and walks as far back as she can with squinting eyes. "I think I heard Trice." Magnus absently scratches her backside.

"Me too." Kate walks a little deeper into the solid blackness. "Do you think our ears are playing tricks?"

"No." Magnus listens again for a moment, "I think our minds are."

"I was wishing we could get on out of here." Kate throws her hands up over her head. "Just get up and go on home. All of us."

Magnus comes up behind Kate, puts an arm over her shoulder. "I think, right now, Kate," She turns her around where she can look at the shadow of her face, the whites of her eyes, "I think that we are better trying to remember what *was* while there is still some time for remembering."

Kate nods. And the two of them turn their hearts and heads toward the long, dusty road of their past. They start on the day at the oak tree.

This is what they see.

One old friend talking to another, although they are only thirty-something. One is wise but not so worldly. And the other is in a bad situation. And afraid. And alone. And there beneath the Shibboleth oak tree, the same tree that memorizes all the stories of its people, a plan is made. It is a plan of saving grace. It is a plan that is brought forth from both desperation and desire. And the two young old friends do the best they can to make some semblance of a life plan that they think will stand the test of time. Now they are sitting, graying, side-by-side and holding hands, just as they were so many years ago. And yet years ago was just a yesterday away. They are remembering. *Go ahead,* I whisper, *tell yourselves the story.* And they do. They skip the bus ride that Magnus took. They skip her year away. The one when she'd been called, or so they'd told everyone in town, to care for a distant dying aunt. That part they leave in the dirt of their remembering, like a lonely spot they skip over. A treacherous, lonely road for Magnus, a floor-pacing time for Kate. Caught in the months of the in-between. Both of them had said their prayers those long days and nights. They had said separate prayers, but unknowingly they were the same. They prayed for a healthy baby. Specifically, they prayed for a girl. And surprisingly, one with wings. They didn't know this at the time. Didn't know why they prayed that way, but now, now when they look at her, they realize that sometimes Trice's feet don't quite touch the ground. But this is the part that they skip over.

This is what they are remembering now. Kate is sitting on her bench at her wishing well. She is waiting and hoping. She is hoping that this part of the plan will go the way they had talked about. She is young and excited. A baby has been born. And it's meant to be hers to have and hold from this day forward. But there is no sign of Magnus. She is late. And Kate is getting nervous. She has begun to wring her hands a little. She has even pulled a coin out and dropped it in the well, making another wish. But it's really the same wish over and over again that she is making. Kate wants a baby. Kate wants a baby girl who will stand on a stool in the kitchen someday and make biscuits with her. Will sift the flour with the sifter, making little awkward cranking turns into the biscuit bowl. Will help her water flowers and learn their names one by one. Names like peony and dahlia, four o'clock and buttercup. One with silky, shiny hair for her to brush for church. One who will dress and be dainty in the ways Kate never was.

And from the tree line steps Magnus, worn, tired, with just a hint of bitter. But the bitter is only a weed now in the garden of her life. In due time, it will grow into a briar patch (much like the ones that Cassie Getty is navigating even now), and when that happens more and more each year, the way to Magnus, into her heart and life, will become so overgrown that only her cats will find their way to her unafraid. With the exception of one. One who does everything with a mind that seems to be elsewhere. One with wildly curly hair. One who loves to run barefoot even now. And could climb trees almost as fast as Nehemiah and faster than Billy ever could.

And it is this one now whom they see again as she once was. Brand new. Naked as the day she was born. Wrapped in the tiniest blanket. And Magnus, sure enough to the plan of saving grace, steps from the edge of the woods and walks toward Kate, placing the small bundle in her waiting arms. And she puts out her hand, one last time, toward the soundless child, but then quickly pulls it back and is gone, without a word of hello or good-bye. And now, in their remembering they know, their simple answer contained a poison. The unforeseen human element, as yet unknown. How were they to tell that this same Magnus, confused and all alone, would love this child with all her passion? And sit and watch her grow from two arm's lengths away. Full of regret at what could have been. And what would not be.

And yet Kate, sitting there that day, sitting with Magnus's pain in her arms, wept tears of joy. She did. It had been her greatest wish. Dropped right there down that well, her most passionate plea. "Breathe life into this dry womb," she'd cried. "Give me a child!" And her child had come, but on tiny, hidden strings. Ones that felt so tenuous that she had always felt that at any moment they might snap and she would lose the thing that she loved most. Her wish come true, her baby found.

And so a new life had stepped into Shibboleth, not trailing circumstance. Or disgrace. But wonder. And light. And love. And this life had walked the streets fearlessly. Covered by angels. Protected somehow by the city, which cherished its wish-come-true baby. And the strange woman on Magnolia growing old before her time with her cats and unkempt yard, growing stranger by the day. But this made no matter to the child, who drew nearer and dearer with each year. No matter at all. She fed the cats when she was five. Hung on the porch railing while Magnus rocked. Was so very unmoved by Magnus. By her angry approach to life. So she visited. And with each visit brought Magnus back a piece of her heart. Until one day she could almost be made whole. Almost. That's the day when Trice moved in.

Trice had been watching Magnus, had sensed something. And the day came that Trice had known what she had felt for years. And she summed it up like this. That love had no boundaries. That a person could have more than one mother and not lose anything in that translation. But she had never said a word.

And right now, Kate and Magnus are wondering about what I've already told you. They are wondering if Trice knew. They are beyond their game of tug-o'-war. Beyond their fear of losing her to one another. They only want to see her face again. *Even*, they silently tell themselves, *even if it is only one last time.*

Monday, 10:58 P.M.

Billy and Blister are making their way into the bowels of Hell's Jungle. Billy is wondering why they didn't follow Nehemiah. Why he didn't call to them. Why they didn't all go together. He is wondering, at the very least, why his brother would leave him without saying something, but right now all the wondering in the world will not change the fact that he is standing beneath the mammoth twisted shapes of rock and shadow. And it is not the shadows but Blister's twitchy behavior that has Billy nervous.

"What is it you see, Blister?" Billy turns his light to follow the trail of Blister's last jumpy reaction.

"I don't know." It's a shaky voice and getting shakier by the moment.

"So what is it that you think you see?" Oh, Billy is a smart man. He really is. In the way of alphabets and simple math. No convoluted equations.

Blister turns and looks directly at him in spite of the light in his eyes, so that Billy can see his one clear pupil dilate to a pinpoint. "I think I see me."

"You're right here with me, Blister."

"No, not me now." Blister looks back and forth between the rocks. "Me from the past." His voice drops down lower and years farther away. "Me from a long time ago."

Billy is quiet for a while. He is taking in the words and following them along their path. He is deciding where Blister is. In his mind. He knows that they've all been shifting, losing, and regaining mental ground. Memories come and gone. Good sense goes missing and then returns again. But not for long.

"Why did you bring me down here?" Billy puts his hand on Blister's shoulder. He jumps like a surprised cat.

Blister doesn't answer. Not at first anyway. Then he begins to speak. Billy thinks it's a riddle with no rhyme or reason.

"This is where something got started. A long, long time ago. And this is where something is supposed to end."

Billy doesn't like riddles. He wishes Trice were here. It's her specialty. She carries riddles around in her head forever. One time for three years. But she figured it out. "Trice, Trice," he says out loud, "where are you when I need you?" And there rises up a longing in Billy to see his fruity-tooty friend. That's what he called her in grade school, *Fruity-tooty Trice*. He had made it up to try to make her mad, but it didn't work. She just smiled at him like the joke was on him.

The ground rocks, and an amazing wind drives through the cave. It makes a music no one wants to hear. It blows so hard there is a sound of whistles and voices, and John Robert puts his hands over his ears and closes his eyes. Billy shines his helmet around the cave, bends his knees so that he doesn't lose his footing. John Robert falls to the ground and stays there, the wind circling over his head like the turkey buzzard from the tree.

"Leave me alone," he screams. But Billy reaches out and with one strong arm pulls him to his feet. The wind stops.

"Get up, Blister." His jaw has a determined new look to it. "Let's get this thing done." He points back to the empty chamber, through the formations of rock that water has left behind. "Let's get what you came down here for, and get to Nehemiah and Trice."

"Trice is here?" Blister wipes his wet mouth with the back of his hand.

"You knew that, Blister." Billy shakes him a little under his hand. Not roughly but the way a mother would wake a child. He wants desperately for Blister to snap out of it. He wants to get out of the wake of his walking dream. Wants to get to his brother. He has remembered the map. He has seen that piece of paper that he ignored so well for years. He wasn't a make-believe kind of boy. Didn't grow into a make-believe kind of man. But now he has seen it again in his mind. Just as if it were held before his eyes and not in his pocket. "Trice is why you came in here in the first place, remember?"

Blister just shakes his head. He can't remember but one thing: the shadow circling between the rocks, weaving in and out of the past and the present. The one that is calling him to finish what he came to do. To die. Once and for all.

"I am very, very afraid," Blister says with trembling lips.

"I know where they are," Billy says. He doesn't understand Blister's fear. Doesn't understand what he's running from but can't outrun. "I know where they are, Blister, and I need to get there." *Need* is what Billy says but *want* is the better word. He's known now for some time, just like he did that morning at the house, that it would take Nehemiah and Trice together, crucial pieces of the puzzle linked together, to save them from whatever this hole in time and space was. "If they don't find each other, we really won't make it out of here alive." This Billy says aloud, but he is really talking to himself.

"I never was, Billy." Blister turns and looks at him. "I don't think alive is any longer a ticket for me."

Billy looks at him hard. Sees what's written on his face. Sees what's caused his heart to grow pale and weak. "Get up, Blister, and stop shaking." Billy starts off into the dark, and Blister, jumpy and scared, looks to his right and to his left, but he follows quickly. Closely.

"You don't even know where you're going."

The lumbering bear answers without turning around. "I know I'm not standing still and that suits me fine."

"That's 'cause you're not the one supposed to die. I am!" The last words come out almost a shriek. Funny, Blister wasn't afraid when he came in. Wasn't afraid when his truck was circling the square, when he locked eyes with Magnus, and then knew suddenly what he had to do. But now, down in the depths of night, in the presence of the enemy of his past, he has become what he was a long time ago. Cowardly.

Billy turns abruptly, puts his light on Blister and doesn't look away, and then calls him by his name. The real one. "Listen here, John Robert. Sometimes death don't come easy. Sometimes it's full of pain. My daddy done it. And my momma done it. And it makes no never mind to me if I follow right behind them today or any other day." Billy has never been so growling gruff in all his life. "If you are meant to die today, you will. And if you aren't, you won't. And either way is fine. I have pulled you out of the burning gates of hell before, I reckon I can do it again."

"That weren't you." Blister shivers, settles down a bit. "It was your brother."

"Don't split fried hairs, Blister. Today I'm taking his place. Now get your scarred butt on up here and come face-to-face with whatever it is you're so afraid of."

Blister pauses for a minute, and he looks up at Billy, having regained some semblance of himself.

"Ain't you afraid of something?" He rocks back on his heels and puts his hands in his front pockets like they were walking next to the creek on a cool spring day. "Anything?"

"Yes, I am, but what, that ain't none of your business." And the wisdom of Billy prevails because he doesn't discuss his fears. Not here and not now. Not while the very thing, the only thing, that he fears might be taking place. And there doesn't seem to be much of anything he can do about it. Nehemiah might be leaving him to wrestle his years in this world alone. And life without his brother seems like no life at all.

Monday, 11:15 P.M.

Obie is making her way store by store through the broken glass—covered, empty streets. She has held fast to Zadok like a child. She has picked up Cassie's niece, Trudy, from City Hall, where she found her still sitting behind her desk staring out the window. She is walking now with Trudy locked in one hand and Zadok in the other. They are walking into the Piggly Wiggly and calling out for—she doesn't know the word for it—*survivors,* she thinks. *But survivors of what?* And she's not sure if or when Shibboleth is going down. But she knows it's under attack. She knows it's time to circle the wagons. Then she thinks of John Wayne and Rooster Cogburn, but all she sees is an eye patch and a horse. And the woman. *Who was that woman?* And for a little while she stops dead in her tracks just inside the Piggly Wiggly. Trudy is just as quiet as can be on one hand and Zadok quiet as he can be on the other. She can't remember the woman or what that movie was about. *An eye patch, a rifle, and something that had to be done. A horse and a eye patch. John Wayne was a big man. Katharine Hepburn was a skinny woman. That's it—Katharine Hepburn. Still don't know what they were doing, but it took the two of them. Lord, what am I doing in the tomatoes?* "Hello, anybody here?" She pulls at the hands of her compliant charges. "Come on, we got to go see people."

In a little while, Obie will find Dwayne in the storeroom and Ellen in the office all by herself, crying. No one else came to work today at the Piggly Wiggly. They have been left alone, and Obie gathers them up with words as smooth, as soothing, as water running over stones. She gathers them and talks to them, makes them link hands. Ellen's hand to Zadok, Zadok's hand to Dwayne, Dwayne's hand to Trudy. And then they are off again. Out the door and down the dark road with no moon or stars to light the way.

Monday, 11:23 P.M.

Blister is walking ahead of Billy, in between fleeting apparitions. Moving images that take on pictures of past pains. Serve to remind people of their failures. And remind them of their futures. But the futures painted here are all tainted with lies. There is a great web of woven deceit that sticks to men's minds and hearts, leaves them broken. Broken without a single injury to their bodies. Only their souls. Until finally they lay down and die as forgotten as they were told they were or would someday become.

"He's over here," Blister says. And Billy doesn't ask who. At this point, his mind is on his brother. His thoughts on his hope that Nehemiah will find Trice. That Trice will be alive. And that they will finish this.

"Look." Blister shines the light down on the cave floor. "Right here."

And Billy looks down but doesn't make a sound. His skin has toughened these last few days. He's traveled such a long way in such a little while. But his brows knit together and he does say, "Humph." What he sees is a man-sized skeleton. The clothes have rotted to nothing. Have been mice-eaten.

"He don't look like he died peaceful," Blister says. Then he adds, "Or happy."

Billy looks up to the ledge above him, where they had circled down. "He fell."

"I think he must've gone crazy." Blister looks around at Hell's Jungle, swears he sees a shadow dart between the rocks, one that is moving *toward* them. "Or maybe something killed him."

"Ain't nothing down here to kill him." Billy kneels down, looks closely and more carefully at the skeleton's bones.

"Oh, I wouldn't be so sure about that." Blister is looking over his shoulder. He's not afraid of the dead thing. It's that shadow that disturbs him. And when he sees it this time, he says, "Billy, something's down here." Then he pauses for a second, but not long, before he adds, "And it ain't good."

Nehemiah continues on a path intended to be full of dark despair. But what all the beasts of hell haven't counted on is that his aim is like an arrow. His purpose has been defined. And Nehemiah will not come down, will not rest, will not sleep, until this city, his city, has been rebuilt. Or, if all should crumble, the end of it will find him here, in these last moments, striving against all odds to stop the encroaching destruction, which would erase its people from the very heart of time.

And it is in this precise moment, as the breathing continues on his ear, so heavy and so tangible that a drop of saliva hits his shoulder, trickles down his shirt sleeve, and is absorbed into the cotton, where it slowly burns the threads—it is at this precise moment that Nehemiah first sees a light. Not a headlamp. Not a flashlight. An ethereal glow glimmering from below. He calls, "Trice," but it's really no more than a whisper. He steadily makes his way forward, toward that most unusual light.

"Trice?" Nehemiah calls again. And the breathing at his ear grows so heavy, so determined, that Nehemiah's eyes are looking through a misty fog. The light below becomes a vague, watery shape. The panting at his arm sleeve, the hideous beast of deception, drools a pool designed to drown. The shape shifts, moves in front of Nehemiah to block his way, but Nehemiah walks right through it. To the other side. The dark entity is surprised. At this bold, impetuous move, it howls to show its disapproval. The howl echoes down the cavern walls. Rocks its way along the interior of those age-worn shapes. Finds its way through cracks and crevices to the ears of those who are rooms of rock away.

Monday, 11:25 P.M.

Billy and Blister stop studying the skeletal death before them.

"What in the hell was that?" Blister says, his burnt eye screwed up so tight it's completely gone.

"I think," Billy stands up and looks behind them, wondering where his brother is, "that was hell itself, Blister." Then he gives Blister's shoulder a pat. "But don't worry." Billy wishes he could see through solid walls. "That only means that somehow maybe Nehemiah and Trice are winning." He turns, kneels, and puts his hand on the dead bones. "You know something about this thing you're not telling me?"

"Yeah." Blister looks back and forth again, dodging bat-like apparitions in the air. "I took his ring."

"Whose ring?"

"That man lying there. Or what's left of him. A long time ago." Blister jumps as if something had grabbed his shoulder. "It ain't nothing," he says aloud to calm himself.

"Long time ago what?"

"After he was dead, I took his ring."

"You know this man?" Billy tries to listen as another howl goes up. As the ground shakes beneath their feet. Blister's eyes, mostly the right one, search nervously back and forth for what he knows darn well is out there. Or, better still, right here. Right *here*. With a shaking fist he wipes nervous spit from the corner of his mouth.

"Billy, I got to go." Because all Blister knows right now is, *Go. Quick. Survive.* He takes a leaving step, but he doesn't watch exactly *where* he's going and his step leads him backward into the crouched-down Billy and, tumbling over him, he comes face-to-face with the skeletal remains of a faceless, nameless man. But a robbed man just the same.

Now the howling down the walls, growing more angry, more ve-
hement, pulls the strings of Blister's vocals like a puppet, and his
own wailing screams encircle him and Billy. They ride and blend
with the howling screams of the damned that wind their way
through the cavern. Wind their way to where Kate and Magnus
stand, hand-in-hand, remembering days gone by. To where Butch
has stationed himself upon his watch.

And beyond the confines of rock and dirt to the ground above.
Seeping up through the earth's very core, where the groaning
screams of man and manifestation cause Cassie Getty to fall to her
knees in the dark and whisper "Almost there" to no one but her own
unsteady heart.

The screams reach the ears of Obie's lost band as they climb the
small hill seeking sanctuary. They cause Ellen to begin to cry
again, and Obie says "Almost there" to comfort her, although
sweat begins to pour profusely through her own pores. The church
door is standing wide open, but it looks a thousand miles away instead of twenty feet. "Almost there," she says again. But every step
is weighted. Every step a battle.

Monday, 11:33 P.M.

"Do you reckon," Kate leans over on Magnus's shoulder, rests her
head there, "that they knew it would come to this when they were
little?"

"I reckon they did, Kate. I reckon they knew, and then they forgot it all again."

"Well, I sure hope they remember everything now they're supposed to." Kate looks down the cavern's dark opening, her eyes full of watery worry. "I sure do hope and pray they remember."

Magnus thinks about it for a minute. "Well, Kate, I'm thinking if Nehemiah hadn't remembered, he wouldn't have come home."

Kate nods her head yes, as she takes this in. Agrees with it wholeheartedly. "Then it's done," she says and pulls at her apron front, straightening it as if she's getting ready to serve dinner.

Magnus knows something that Kate seems to have forgotten. That sometimes the done doesn't look the way you expect it to. Sometimes the done requires a sacrifice. But there is no point in reminding her now. *Let the ending be its own story*, she says to herself. Then she thinks of Trice and all her stories, and smiles her sweetest smile. But no one but you and me and God can see.

Monday, 11:34 P.M.

"Shut up." Billy wants to cuss with all of his natural backwoods ability. Instead, he pulls Blister's screaming body up off the white bones by the back of his shirt collar. He is still screaming. "Shut up," Billy says again and stands Blister roughly on his feet. "Hush now. Just hush."

"Jesus, God Almighty," Blister says and reaches in his pocket for a cigarette even though he quit smoking over ten years ago. "Jesus, God Almighty," he says again, still patting his shirt pocket, and then feeling around in both pant pockets as if the apparition of the missing pack might suddenly appear from his desperate desire. He still carries his old Zippo, and he fishes it out of this pocket now, flips it open, strikes it, and watches it spark a blue flame. It's an old, familiar habit that makes him happy. He holds it up, shaking and grinning like a kid at Christmas. As if he had just discovered a new toy. As if his vocabulary had been diluted down to just one word, *Zippo,* and all his life can be contained in speaking those two syllables. "*Zippo!*" he says aloud to Billy and thrusts it forward, holding it up toward him. But then his screams break out fresh all over again. It's not the flame-flickering look on Billy's face that causes Blister to scream; it's what's standing right behind him.

Monday, 11:40 P.M.

Obie approaches the church door. With caution. She's never seen it standing wide open. All the normalcy of life, the routines and steady rollings, is missing. She holds tighter to her charges and pulls them, like a flock of geese in V formation, through the door.

Pastor Brown lies across the floor of the altar, at the foot of the cross. She thinks, *Maybe he is dead,* and isn't sure if she should bother calling. She doesn't want to upset Ellen again and make her start crying all over again. Instead, she decides to tell them to "sit down right here. That's right. Side-by-side," and carefully approaches the prostrate pastor. His head is turned to the right, his arms folded beneath him, his hands tightly clasped out of sight. She looks into his eyes, which are staring blankly beyond her, and thinks about poking them to see if they will blink. But she doesn't do it. Instead, she gets down on her hands and knees and whispers, "Pastor Brown, it's time to get up." When this doesn't work, she tries bribery. "Pastor, it's time to get up. It's time for *church*." She stresses the *church* so that it takes on special meaning. "Look here, if you get up right now I will quit smoking." Obie pauses, because no part of her wants to quit smoking. But then she reconsiders. She supposes right now they need Pastor Brown alive more than dead. *"I ain't gonna say it again, and at the count of three I'm going outside and lighting up."* Now, this is a bald-faced lie because Obie is out of cigarettes. But she thinks it might just be an "under-the-carpet-God-don't-mind-much-because-it's-for-a-good-reason lie."

"One," she says and pauses. She looks out at the frozen, pensive faces staring at her from the back pew. *They look like little lost children,* she thinks, *even Zadok.* "Two." She drags the *two* out long and teasing, like they are simply playing hide-and-seek and she is It. Then Obie looks back at the eyes, at the pastor, and sits back on her heels, her palms resting on the tops of her thighs. "You just ain't getting up no matter what I say, are you?" She places her hand on the pastor's back and lets it rest there.

Obie doesn't see where Pastor Brown is. Doesn't see what his eyes are watching. Doesn't know just how many miles he's traveled now for Nehemiah. Or that he won't be back until this is over. Or maybe he won't be back at all. He's somewhere deep, deep into it. And he'll stay that way until the very end.

Obie gets up off her knees, looks again at the faces holding hands like kindergartners on a field trip. She wishes, really wishes, that she could make good her threat and say "three" strong and loud and walk right out that door and light up. It's a curious thing to her why she's, well, alive, and everybody else seems to be if not dead, darn near like it. "Sleepwalkers," she says under her breath. And if Pastor Brown was in a place to respond, he'd add, "That's how all this trouble got started."

Below, Nehemiah is walking through the underworld of rock and cave to what he sees below. His eyes are so focused on the light below that he pays no attention to the howling shape that hovers over his every move. "Trice?" he says again with a question in his voice. He stops and bends down, hands on knees. Now he can see that the light is just inside the Treasure Room. The room is hard to recognize. *Even here the water is gone,* he thinks. In the days of their childhood, and long before, all the water had started here. Had bubbled up freely from beneath the rock and had filtered its way up to the people of Shibboleth.

Now Nehemiah sees beyond the absence of water. He sees that the light leading him is Trice. *Is* Trice. There is no Trice anymore. No form or fashion that he would recognize in another place. No arms or limbs or eyes. Simply light. Not glowing around her but from within her. And he moves closer toward it with every step.

Monday, 11:45 P.M.

Billy reaches out and grabs Blister by the shoulder because right now every fiber of his being, every pore, every bone is screaming of its own accord. Blister tries to point. To say, "Behind." But the word doesn't come from his mouth. It's frozen there. Billy turns, shines the light on the space behind him, the empty air.

"Blister, there is nothing there but your heebie-jeebies." He turns Blister to face the darkness as he shines his helmet back and forth to prove he's right. "Now straighten up and fly right."

"I *seen* him." Blister wails it. A child's cry more than a voice. He has left his courage on the surface of the world. Behind with his wrecked truck and aspirations of bravery. Somehow the past, *his past*, has met him here. As if it had been lying in wait for years. For the moment that his bravery would be needed. Counted on. And at this precise moment, his past has unleashed its attack. If allowed, the past can be a most formidable foe.

"Seen who?"

Blister points a shaky finger down at the skeletal ground. "That him, that's who."

"Look here, *that* him has gone on to be wherever he is."

"But I took his ring." Blister wipes the sweat from his forehead with the back of his hand. "I mean, after all, he was deader than a doornail, and it was just hanging there from his bony finger." Billy looks at him without saying anything. Blister purses his lower lip, thinking. Continues trying to explain, "It was gold so I knowed it was worth something." He looks back at the skeleton. "I think it might have been his wedding ring." And he pauses. Billy stands silent. Listening to the howling that is creeping its way through the walls. Then he listens to it closer, as John Robert continues his confession of the soul.

"It's not a good thing to take a man's wedding ring. I mean, just any other old kinda ring, maybe it's not so bad. Like a ring won in a poker game with a diamond stud, maybe that wouldn't be so bad to take from a man. But a dead man's wedding ring ... "

Billy turns around suddenly, shines his lamplight on the cavern walls to the left of them. Listens to the howling again with his ear cocked. "Not so good. Not so good at all. That's a widow's ring. 'Course I didn't know the widow. And with the looks of how long he'd been gone when I found him, well, you can imagine she was gone, but still ... " And Blister's mind filters off into a calmer state. He feels the beginning of a clean coming on. "You know what I did with that ring?" He waits. Billy doesn't respond. "Well, do you?" He pokes him lightly in the back.

"What?" Billy isn't really listening anymore. He is thinking.

"I sold it for liquor money. 'Course that was back in my drinking days, before all the trouble." He rubs the scarred side of his face. "Sold a dead man's widow's ring for a bottle. Ain't that something to be proud of?"

"No. I guess not."

Blister's shadowy past is dissipating. And the figure following him through the entrenched places of his heart and mind is fading.

"And you know something else I'm not too proud about?" Blister pauses. "I took all the coin money, too. Now, ain't that a lowdown desperate thing?"

Billy pauses from surveying the cavern walls and tries to place exactly how that wailing is reaching their ears so clearly when it shouldn't be. He hears Blister with one ear, but something catches his attention and he turns around again. "What coin money?"

"What coin money you think? Coin money from this cave we're standing in. Spent it all." Now the look on Billy's face changes so quickly, becomes so full of righteous wrath, that John Robert shrinks back some but keeps talking. He's a watershed of guilt now. A confession that can't be stopped. "Spent all of it. Just a little at a time." Billy's eyes appear to glow blue fire. Blister's voice drops lower. He speaks slower. "Just a dollar at a time."

The clock for Shibboleth has expired. The hands have come completely to a standstill. Only a reflection of Shibboleth remains. An image floating precariously on the surface of eternity.

Monday, 11:58 P.M.

Trice is standing in the Treasure Room. Normally, in the old days, before their time and beyond, a slight light would filter its way down here from the sky. More a memory of recent light than light itself. It would follow the path of dreams to their holding place. Trice finally pulls her eyes away from the cavern floor and looks up toward Nehemiah's voice.

"You took the coins from the cave?" Billy is so incredulous, so heavy with the importance of this, so ashamed of how time has gone by, how he has forgotten his duty, that he forgets to be angry. He isn't sure whom to be angry at.

Blister pulls himself up by the bootstraps. Pushes his chest out. He will not cower now in the face of truth in the telling. His apologies lie elsewhere. "I ain't proud of it, but I did it. Sure did. It's a sorry thing but what's done is done."

"Lord have mercy." Billy runs his hand across his helmet because he has forgotten that it was there and meant to run his hand through his hair. "We got to get to the Treasure Room. Quick." He turns around, surveys the wall again.

"What Treasure Room?" Blister shakes his arm. Asks again, "What Treasure Room?"

"The one where you stole the *money.*" He surveys John Robert again. "That wasn't just ordinary money. Didn't you know that?"

"Well, I guess not. And to tell you God's truth, I reckon if I had, it wouldn't have made a difference at the time."

"We've got to get there with a quickness, I tell you. This is not good. "

"Well, why didn't you say so? It's right through that tunnel." Blister points, but Billy doesn't follow him. "I'll show you," he says, but first he kneels down next to the skeleton. "Buddy, I owe your widow a ring. And I sure am sorry about that." Then he stands and strikes the Zippo, holding it out in front of him with his right hand and cupping it slightly with his left. "C'mon, Billy," he says, "I'll lead the way."

John "Blister" Robert has left the shadows of his past on the floor of Hell's Jungle. He won't be needing them anymore.

Cassie Getty pushes away the briars. Pulls at the overgrown vines covered in thorns. She has lost her raincoat and they rip and pull at her polyester shirt. Her heart begins to tremble, her lips to shake. She is so very tired. Ready to cry. She takes her pocketbook in her hand, and for a moment it looks like she will give up. Because for a moment she thinks about it. For a moment the shadow circling Nehemiah sends thoughts Cassie's way. They are thoughts that say, *No hope. There is no hope.* But Cassie remembers that if she has been born at the end of all days, there must be a reason for it. One greater than her sitting and crying in a briar patch. Alone and afraid. So she breaks out in a wavering song. It is the first song that comes to her mind. This is the song of Cassie Getty in the dark of her dimension: "Get up, get up you sleepy head. Wake up, wake up the sun is red. Live, laugh, love, and be happy . . . " The voice filters through the moonless night, as she wanders singing her way.

Monday, 11:59 P.M.

Nehemiah steps into the Treasure Room alongside Trice. He is wondering what part of her to touch. How to hold onto something made of light. Then he feels her hand on his face, and he closes his eyes and thanks God for the life of Trice. When she speaks, her voice is melodious, but the words cut through him like a knife. "The treasure is gone."

"Gone?"

"All of it. Years of it." Trice looks down again. She still wears her headlamp, but it isn't necessary. It is the light inside of Trice that shines now. And Nehemiah looks down with her. Where once there had been years and years and years of coins, years of hopes and wishes, there is nothing but bone-dry rock.

The wailing howl begins to shift. The shape begins to grow darker. Begins to materialize.

"We were the protectors, Nehemiah," she says with the innocent honesty of a child. "And we failed."

The shape begins to laugh. It is not a human laugh. It is something I hope your ears have never heard. Something I hope they never will. It is a laugh fueled by pain. And loss. And ending. The ground shifts, threatening. A sulfurous wind blows. The laughter increases in intensity until it is spitting in the face of what once was. And what was meant to be. And what is gone.

Obie shifts her attention away from the pastor and walks to the back of the church, where she closes the door. She turns around and approaches Zadok and Rudy, Ellen and Trudy. Then she gets in the pew in front of them, turned backwards facing them. She climbs up on her knees with her elbows resting on the pew and begins to tell them a story. It is a story of earth dirt people who had once upon a time almost come to the end of their days. When time stood still and then began to go away. When a great thief had surfaced and stolen what once belonged to them while they were sleeping. "But the people didn't ever give up faith. Not all of it, anyway." Obie looks over at the prostrate pastor. "Nope, they kept right on believing. Right up until the very end." And as much as she tried to tell a lighthearted tale, it came back to her in one word, *Believe*. And finally, she let her story rest there.

Billy and Blister are making a posthaste escape. They are moving as fast as their bodies can carry them toward the small round room that once held majesty and miracles. That once held the soft whispered wishes clasped tight in baby hands. Those hands so new or hands so old—all are babies' hands in the end. All wishing with the heart of a child, with the faith of a child, for dreams to come true. For the passage of time to take its intended course. For hearts to be healed and mended. Wishing. Believing. And then tossing in a coin of mystery and faith that the Well would hold safe and sound underground until the time came for them to bloom. A hundred years of wishes. A thousand wishes worn and carried in heart pockets. From generation to generation. A thousand wishes stolen and spent. A dry hole where dreams were once born and hoped for.

The laughter of the beast grows in magnitude. A rocky, dry sound.

Blister stops in his tracks, his Zippo still before him. "I think I caused this," he says to Billy without turning around.

"We all caused this." Billy lays a hand on his shoulder from behind. "Keep moving, Blister."

"But we don't have the money to put back when we get there."

"It's not about the money, Blister." Billy's voice softens. "It never was."

They are closer now. Have come up through an interior passage that Billy never knew existed. A shortcut from front to middle. A walk through Hell to the other side.

And they enter the room at a lower level. They step to the entrance of the Treasure Room, close enough to see inside. But what they see is not of any familiar form or fashion.

Nehemiah reaches for the light. And as he and Trice embrace, the shadowy shape of the beast begins to pull itself into this earthly realm.

A blasphemous stench rises in my nostrils.

This is what Billy and Blister see. The dark wings of a dog-like creature. A snarling, dripping mouth. Red eyes like coals that laugh at them as the earth trembles. As, somewhere above and near the entrance, Kate and Magnus hold one another in an increasingly tight embrace that means good-bye. As Obie spins the story of *Once Upon a Time in Shibboleth*, within sacred walls. As the pastor lies prostrate in prayer, seeing the same thing Billy and Blister see, just as if he were there. He is watching the beast have its moment in time. And he is so close to them that he begins to shake with cold. If Obie would turn and look at his nostrils, she would notice that the pastor is breathing frigid air.

The Midnight Hour

One clawed foot, and then another steps down. The shape rises on hind legs, a black wing whipping so close to their faces that they momentarily lose their breath. And yet it brings even colder air, until they are so cold they feel that they are blue.

I am unimpressed. But then, I am watching everything. I am watching, even now, as all the variations of the future line up before me. Even as the cave walls begin to crumble. As the threat of the death of all Shibboleth begins to rumble, I look beyond the veil of now into the time when the well-worn wishes of a people's hopes fell easily through the earth, through rock and dirt and time, to rest protected in their Treasure Room. A room that was once guarded by small bodies with big believing hearts. One that is guarded still. Look and see.

The guardians are embracing. And in that embrace there is faith. And in that faith, there is a future. The seeds of destinies have been unleashed. The gold of purpose, the light of passion take their stand. They are of one mind. Of one heart. And the Presence is personified.

The beast stops laughing. Slowly turns around. It is confused. For it is only now, in the final hour, that this messenger of the Thief has realized what is taking place. And it takes one giant step forward to stop it. To slice through the thing that Nehemiah and Trice have become. But before it can reach them, Blister leaps without thinking through the air, grabs onto the slimy surface at just the point where the wings hook into the back. And here, in this close proximity where there is no human air, he bites down onto something inhuman until it screams with pain. It's not the bite that inflicts hurt but the courage of it that sinks so deep. It is a man's heart that has been long in the dark, a man who has stepped forward for unselfish gain, that causes the pain. It's Blister's bravery that sears the beast.

The dark wings flap back and forth. Rage spills from its gut. The walls shake and threaten here to swallow Trice and Nehemiah and Billy and all of Shibboleth. All of them once and for all.

Billy reaches into his right pocket and pulls out his hunting knife. He calmly opens it and with one last look at that strange unified apparition, one-half his brother and one-half his friend, he turns to face the beast head on, face-to-face. The wings writhe and flap wildly and knock his helmet from his head, but he doesn't need the helmet light to guide him anymore. He follows the smell burning in his nostrils and leaps into the darkness with one intent. To give Nehemiah and Trice just a little more time.

Miles away, in the midnight hour of their existence, Sonny Boy lets out a long and mournful wail.

Cassie Getty pulls the thorny vines away from the stones. The skin on her hands is torn, and they are snagged and bleeding. If only Obie could see Cassie's hair now. It is truly the worse for wear. She clears the opening to the well that is so overgrown and hard to find. Even Kate's listening bench is covered now. "Lord, how'd I ever find it?" she asks and looks down into the darkness she knows is waiting but cannot see. She pulls herself up with both hands but she doesn't quite make it before she falls back again. She tries one more time and is up, with a little help from an unseen hand. (Sometimes destiny needs a holy push. It's called *colaboring*.) "Well now," she says, trying to straighten her hair, brush it from her eyes, "I made it this far." And straddling the well, with one leg in and one leg out, Cassie struggles to keep her balance as she opens up her purse. She doesn't realize that the very pits of hell are trying to swallow up Shibboleth one great clawing bite at a time. The earth rumbles. And with her purse open on her lap, with both her hands opening up her change purse, there is one great shake from below and Cassie tumbles over the side and into the darkness. Where once there was water that was cold and clear to drink.

Billy can feel black breath on his face. And he can feel the blade of his knife penetrate something. But what would you call that something? And how does a weapon from one world fight a manifestation from another? What I can tell you is this: it is Billy's heart and his intention in the fight that matters most. The fact that he has embraced his purpose, remembered his position. And he isn't the only one.

There are walls going up around Shibboleth. Individuals are laying spiritual bricks. Each fighting with unusual weapons. Courage and compassion. Remembrances and recollections. Prayer and persistence.

Cassie Getty has worked long and hard through this endless night, in this final hour, to reach her destination. John Robert became the man he was meant to be when he took hold of the slimy-ridged back of a winged blackness, determined to protect his daughter if he had to ride through the gates of hell to do it. To protect them all. Butch, a man of action, is holding his prayerful position. And Magnus and Kate are weaving songs in the keys of forgive and forgiven. And another, most wondrous thing has occurred. Nehemiah and Trice have become their essence. And now those interlocking destinies have joined the passion and purpose of Nehemiah and Trice.

Nehemiah is extending his hand out toward the empty spot where the treasure once was held. He is calling something forth. The Treasure Room has become a new force. The light that emanates from it needs no other power than itself. The light pours out of the space of that rock. The light is cutting back the shadows. And it is growing still. As Nehemiah and Trice believe the same thoughts, see the same vision, there is a new sound from above them. It hasn't even yet begun, but it is the sound of soft, metallic rain. A sound of wishes being found. Wishes upon wishes for an entire town. And wrapped up inside of each wish is a seed of hope that one day, one hour, one moment soon, the wishes will come true. Nehemiah and Trice can hear it. And so can you.

Cassie Getty is hanging by a rope. She has both of her short legs wrapped around the old water bucket. She is bruised and scarred. She looks up above her, where before she would have seen millions of stars, but now nothing. Just nothing. Her arms are wrapped around the bucket rope and her bottom's on the bucket's edge. If she were any larger than her five-foot frame, any wider in the hips, she'd be long gone, she figures. As it is, she has just enough backside to cushion the rim. But she thinks she may have dislocated something. A whole lot of somethings. Cassie's pocket-book has fallen to the rock far below, but still clutched tight in her left hand is her change purse. Carefully, with a shaking right hand, she reaches farther around the rope, opens the tiny bag, and pulls out a quarter. She holds it firmly in her right hand, closes her eyes, and wishes that this darkness will not prevail. Then she drops the coin below. And takes out another.

When all the wishing has been done, when all the coins of Cassie Getty have rained down below, her wishes count up to twelve. There has been one for their deliverance, for the city of Shibboleth to be saved. And another that it would never be blind-sided again. And a special wish for the Heritage Oak in the square, that it and all that it holds would survive the storms of time. Cassie says aloud, "Let the stories never die."

A special coin is dropped for all the children, for their inno-cence to be protected and treasured another thousand years. An-other for the church, that what stands inside the people would be stronger than the building's walls. One for fertile ground to grow good greens and all manner of other living things. And another for relationships (such a funny thing for Cassie to wish for), that the lonely would find comfort, that the angry would forgive and be forgiven. For the purposes of man to align themselves with the purposes of God. For the stars to be set right this night in the heavens (and as she drops the coin she wonders, is it really night?). The rope begins to sway, Cassie begins to turn. "For the sinners," she says. And raining down another coin, she says, "For the saints, of which I ain't." And then one last coin remains. One last coin is clasped tight inside Cassie's palm. It's her special secret treasure. It's a gold coin from her grandmother. Passed down from one lifespan into the next. Then Cassie makes a final wish as the bucket sways, as the earth below her trembles, as the stone walls of the well begin to crumble. "Let the river run," she says, "let the waters spring forth in dry, dry places." And she opens up her fist and the last coin falls down and out of sight.

It's then that I hear the beginning of the music. Not as you would first imagine. It is music that defies description. Music made up of overlapping voices from ages past and voices from the ages yet to come. They are singing a song that is made up of life. Of all of its pleasure and, yes, even its pain. Made up of every nuance and new child. The ages are singing. And their song finds its way into the cave, down the long corridor below the dried-up surface of the well and into the Treasure Room. And then, most majestically, the gold of Cassie Getty's final wish falls directly into Nehemiah's outstretched, expecting hand.

This is the one that he grasps as he turns to face the beast.

Billy is cutting with his knife, but with every slash of the blade the stench grows deeper. As if the innermost parts of the monster were more vile than its external apparition. John Robert is using his fists and his fingers, trying to work his way up the back so he can ram the sockets of those fiery orbs. There is a loud wail as the walls and floor shake. Yet, at the same time, the light inside that treasure room grows so wild, so powerful, it casts a net over the struggle. The light catches the beast off-guard. Forces it to close its eyes, to stagger slightly on its clawed feet. The light grows until it fills the cavern room. It lights all the dark, secret passages in. And all the secret ways out.

The beast screams, and its teeth show the stains of the hopes and dreams it has eaten. Devoured quickly before they could grow. Dreams plucked from the bravest hearts, faith ripped right from their bones. And it has left behind its greatest poison: dreamlessness. But then, this beast is the dream stealer. And without a dream, without a vision, ahhh yes—but you know the rest now, don't you? You've been watching it happen all along the way.

Nehemiah steps forward into the cavern's open room, toward the writhing, shaking shapes. The screams are deafening. They are from another dimension. And there is a yell that outweighs all the others. It is a warrior's cry as Nehemiah runs forward and climbs up without a pause until he is standing on Billy's shoulders. Billy grabs his brother's ankles to hold him steady, as Nehemiah comes face-to-face with the nemesis of Shibboleth. Trice steps out of the smaller room, and the light becomes so bright that Billy and Blister close their eyes even as they keep their stand. But Trice looks up at Nehemiah with a peace that is beyond description. Beyond understanding. Trice is already in another place. And part of that place is in Trice. And when Nehemiah looks down, all he can see is light. But he knows somewhere in that light is his love. And in truth, if he ever had to take a picture to remember Trice in all her earthly glory, this is the glory that he would choose. Trice filled with the Mystery.

Nehemiah turns and shoves that gold coin of sacrifice into the beast's gaping mouth. And as he does so, I hear these words: "Let there be light." But they are not spoken by Billy or John Robert. Not by Nehemiah or Trice. The words have come rolling in from another place. They are words that have never died. They echo through the cavern's walls and reverberate with explosive force. And in the middle of a roaring scream, the beast turns to dust. And the dust dissipates to nothing.

John Robert, Billy, and Nehemiah come crashing to the floor. Trice moves quickly to John Robert's side, bends over him as he tries to say, "So sorry. So very sorry." But those words are never uttered, as Trice lays her hand along his face. And suddenly John Robert feels like the new man that he is. Inside and out.

Now the light itself has multiplied. The cathedral rocks show multicolors, the sands of time having captured color. They are like stardust. Like fire from a night sky, resting in repose. What once was a den of death is now transfigured. And oh, how the lights are dancing! Glowing sapphire blue and yellow gold. Ruby red and amber. Green and amethyst. As if the rocks were celebrating freedom. Then there comes a new song. Rising from the ground. From all around. Perhaps it is only I who hear it. Or perhaps you hear it, too. It is a song that has been a long time in the coming. The rocks cry out. And the song reverberates, finds its way, winds its way, up to the surface and into the hearts of the citizens of Shibboleth. Who, finally, after all these years, one by one, begin to wake up. And to remember.

— Tuesday Morning —

Light falling and light hovering. There is light in the darkest corners of the cavern. Light where light has never been. Light that is not a reflection of light but the very essence, the presence of light itself.

Billy and John Robert are stirring, sitting up from where they fell. But then they fall back to silent sitting. To awed, hushed silence, as the images, the shapes, move and sing. As the shapes of Nehemiah and Trice become more distinguishable. As they begin returning as close to their old selves as they will ever be. And the light dances out from around them all.

Nehemiah and Trice hold hands and walk back inside the Treasure Room. They are traveling from a place between dimensions, between where time stands still and where time is not. And they are counting with all thankfulness the new hopes and dreams of Cassie Getty. They gather up the fallen coins and place them on the pedestal of the rock.

The dark night is cast off. Behold, the new day has come.

John Robert gets to his feet a different man, the one he was intended to become. He walks a few steps and extends a hand to Billy, who has been watching the lights dance across the cave's ceiling. Billy looks up into John Robert's face, but he doesn't get up. And he doesn't speak. Ahh yes. Beholding a miracle is a breathless thing.

This is how it happened and is happening still with Kate and Magnus. Kate and Magnus help one another to their feet, their

bones and flesh so bent into one another they have molded together. Now they are trying to separate, to get the feeling in their
feet back. To find new footing.

Butch closes his eyes, feels the release of battle spreading across
his face. *It's going to be a good day*, he thinks. *A very, very good day.*

"Well, I reckon they're gonna be hungry." Kate brushes off her
apron. "But everything sure is cold."

"I don't think," Magnus rubs her lower back, looks down and
sees that her boots are missing and wonders when she took them
off, "that they're gonna care." But she is still staring at her feet. "I
wouldn't even have died with my boots on," she says. And then,
without any explanation, Magnus begins to laugh.

At first it is a chuckle in her belly. But then the chuckle escapes
her lips, and when Kate hears it, it triggers something in her that is
closest to a giggle. But it doesn't stop there. There is a rippling of
laughter. But then the ripple becomes a rapid. And it overtakes
them and pulls them under. Butch turns around with a quirk in his
brow, a question mark on his forehead. But the laughter hits him
full in the face, because by now Kate is saying "Oh my" with her
hands on her knees and Magnus, with her head thrown back in
laughter, loses ten years from her face. They are laughing tears of
joy. And that belly-busting joy is very contagious. Butch begins
laughing with them. And he cannot stop. Even when he tries.

Cassie Getty's empty change purse falls from her hand as she
clings to the swaying rope. She wants to adjust her tired butt on
the rim of the bucket. It's cutting into her flesh and cutting off cir-
culation, but she is careful not to move. The crumbling walls have
stopped crumbling. And the rope slowly stops its swaying, coming
to a full stop as the first light of morning travels down the circle of
the well. "Lord have mercy!" Cassie says, and for the first time she
begins to cry for help.

Now there are two new sounds inside the cave walls. One is the distant reverberating cry of someone from far above. It is filtering its lonely way down through the wishing well, where Trice hears and looks up, with her head cocked to one side, listening intently.

"Cassie Getty is in the well," she says to Nehemiah. But she doesn't fully understand how she knows that is Cassie specifically. Knows this without question. But as time starts again in a new direction, the gifts of Trice will begin to surface just like the water bubbling up at her feet. Cool streams are springing forth from the dry places. And the water is as clear as glass.

Nehemiah, Trice, Billy, and John Robert make their way out of the cave's cathedral room. But first they turn back at the tunnel leading out, take one last look at the moving lights that appear to be alive. And they take one last look at the saving graces of Cassie Getty's hopeful wishes, cast like new seeds down the well, reflecting light where they've been captured and collected, and left on the Treasure Room pedestal rock.

The laughter has barely paused when the four of them make their way into the waiting arms of Kate and Magnus. There is a loud, rambunctious commotion. There are cries of celebration. There are tears of joy. And tears of relief.

Nehemiah sees Butch at the cave's entrance and releases Kate to shake his hand. No words need to be said. They have fought the good fight. And they have won.

Magnus walks toward John Robert, raises a trembling hand to touch his cheek, and runs her fingers across his eye. It isn't until he stands looking into the mirrored eyes of Magnus that he realizes that the same power which destroyed a dark force has made him whole again. In a new way.

Their reunion is short. There is a very important thing left to do and that is get to Cassie Getty from the well. So the party makes its way, cold chicken and biscuits in hand, out of the cave and across the wet, sandy ground, into the welcomed return of the sun.

The water gets deeper and deeper by the second. Kate has her dress and apron pulled up high above her knees. She and Magnus have linked arms, and they will in many ways stay this way for the remainder of their days. Billy, John Robert, and Butch walk behind them, trying not to laugh at the sight before them and then laughing anyway. Nehemiah leads Trice by the hand across the rocks just above the water's surface. But she doesn't think this is necessary. Her heart is so light, so free, she feels they could all walk on water. That, for just a little while, it would be possible today.

Each of them in their own turn, in separate ways, is more alive than they've ever been.

There's a promise waiting as they cross the waters. There's a promise.

The Sweet By and By

Nehemiah returned to Washington right away. He was making good his promise to his friend, the senator. After all, it was election year. But this time he brought back with him his new bride, Trice. This was their changing season. To every life, one must come.

For the most part, Trice spent her days reading in the cool, calm space of their brownstone. Sometimes, so far away from home and in such a different place, she wondered if any of it had really happened at all. But recently, one morning while making the bed, she ran her hand along the side where Nehemiah sleeps, and it came away with gold dust as fine as sifted flour. Later she showed her hand to Nehemiah, but there was nothing there. He had kissed her palm and said, "It's okay. I know. I see that light in you from time to time. Sometimes when you're sleeping, I look over and it's there." They have gifts, the two of them. Ones they still don't fully understand. But in due time they will. Right now they know the simple things. That they are together as they've always been and will be. And that today they are going home. To Shibboleth, where they will let their roots grow deeper.

And if you should ever wonder about that big marine, you can find him still in Washington. He traveled back with two fresh pies from Kate riding on the seat beside him. The blackberry one he ate entirely before he ever made it home. Some people say he has a different disposition. He goes home to Philadelphia on regular occasions, and very often he is heard laughing. For no apparent reason.

Most of Cassie Getty's briar cuts have healed, but her legs will never look the same. She has taken to wearing pants these days. And she's a little uncertain now about her cloning theory. Just a little. She is thinking if she had fallen down that well and things had not worked out, maybe if she'd had a clone she could have gone on the same but in a different way. Then she shakes her head and says aloud beneath the dryer, "That's just selfish cloning. That's what that is." When she looks up, she sees Obie staring at her with raised eyebrows. She raises her voice another octave and says, "Well, it's the truth. Just face it. We are all supposed to die sometime." But Cassie Getty, that good soldier, will not die for many, many years to come.

Trudy Getty, Cassie's niece, has gone to Birmingham and is studying to be a paralegal. She writes letters home about the city and everything it has. And, much to her surprise, what it doesn't have. She misses everyone in Shibboleth an awful lot.

On some occasions, Magnus goes over to the diner to help Kate out because it looks like Darla is never coming back. In the cool of the evening, John Robert comes to visit Magnus. They sit rocking on the porch. He is patient with Magnus and affectionate with the cats. Sometimes they talk about the way things might have been. But only for a little while. "All in all," Magnus says, "we are blessed." And John Robert adds, "Beyond measure." And they say this without knowing that Nehemiah and Trice will soon have a child. Thereafter, maybe three. I see babies on their knees.

The story of John Robert's face is something the town of Shibboleth will paint for years to come. They will paint a picture of a miracle. And the miracle looks like this: there was a man who lost himself but in the end was found.

The diner has new glass in all its windows, new curtains, and new paint. The menu has nothing new, but there is still healing in those piled-up plates. And Kate guards the gates of souls with warm comfort all around.

Pastor Brown has been preaching with new passion. Even his most hushed sermons possess an intensity that pulls people to their pew edge. They are listening.

Obie's still stepping out back to smoke, but she has switched to lights. And God knows, she is *trying* to cut down. She keeps an eye on things downtown. And she has moved up to the seventh pew on Sundays instead of sitting in the back.

Billy spends many hours driving the back roads with Sonny Boy or simply sitting at the diner. He feels that he is missing something, but what it is he doesn't know. He is contemplating opening up the PURE gas station. Something about that sign bothers him, its unlit darkness pulling strangely at his heart. "Guess a man needs something to do," he says, looking at the sign through the diner window.

Kate says, "You need more than that," but Billy doesn't answer or ask her "What's that?" He is deep in thought. Right now they are alone. And it is fairly quiet, but not for long. Kate is cooking up a storm. Tonight there is to be a party. Nehemiah and Trice are coming home. And as I look into that future, only one path lies before them. It is as clear as the spring's running water. Very soon, Nehemiah will run for mayor and by unanimous vote will become all that Shibboleth once embraced. And so much more. Far into his future, well into old age, he will tell great stories of battles fought and battles won with man, and fish and hell beyond.

All things considered, everything downtown appears to be back to the normal flow. But there really is no *normal* anymore. A warm breeze suddenly passes through this afternoon. It is a breeze that brings an air thick with perfume, a perfume that is peculiar in origin. And with the perfume comes the Presence.

Business comes abruptly to a stop. Zadok steps outside the barbershop onto the sidewalk. Obie and Donna Allen are already there. They are followed out by their customers, including Cassie Getty, whose hair is not quite dry. Cassie says it smells "like something from another world." But she doesn't say this in her usual tone. She whispers it. Ellen and Rudy and the customers at the Piggly Wiggly join them across the square. And Kate, batter spoon still in hand, steps outside the diner. Billy is right behind her. And the people of Shibboleth look across the square at one another, and they nod and smile. And then they look to the Heritage Oak tree. At the span of its branches and all that they hold. And they remember.

The light of twilight slowly fades as evening begins to envelop the city. It is a gentle evening, with the first glimmer of stars shining through the trees. The sky is still pink on the horizon, where the sun just lay down behind the hills. And there is a scent of celebration on the air. Celebration like the city hasn't seen in a hundred years.

Cars and cars from miles around have packed Kate's parking lot to overflowing. They fill up the square and beyond, all up and down the road. There are people everywhere. And there are pots and food like you have never seen. Kate keeps serving and counting heads, counting plates, wondering how it is that what's in the pots won't diminish. I simply smile. Angels like a party. Sometimes we help facilitate.

The diner doors have been propped open, front and back, to circulate the air. And now the party spills over into the parking lot. Sonny Boy is delighted. As far as he's concerned, the party is for him.

Nehemiah and Trice are holding court together. They are telling stories that take the two of them. Borrowing and adding lines back and forth, here and there. John Skipper, Rudy's uncle, has brought his guitar and is playing from his truck bed just outside the door. And then Billy Shook pulls out his harmonica and joins in. But it's when Ellen opens up her fiddle case and pulls out her bow that the party begins. It's the fiddle that catches the ear of Magnus, and in a flash she hikes up her skirt and begins to buckdance. Then Zadok joins in, and no one even knew Zadok could dance like that. Look how high his legs can go! Look how fast that Magnus can click her feet in those big shoes. And there is Pastor Brown and even Wheezer keeping time. They are dancing out the story of their deliverance. They are dancing out their delight. And above their music I recognize the sound of whistling.

And it is during this dancing, in the middle of such mania, that a strange truck slowly pulls into Shibboleth. A truck piled as high as it is wide. With a rocking chair on the very top and all manner of things beneath. It parks on the side of the road, just off on the dirt to the south of the diner. The driver's door opens, and a small, round woman climbs out. Sonny Boy stands, tail wagging, ready for attention, as the woman approaches the diner door.

She stops, speaks soft words over Sonny and makes a friend for life. She walks through the open door and looks around. Kate is pushing wet hair back from her face. She is hot, and she is tired, and she is happy. A very freckled hand reaches out and takes the HELP WANTED sign down from the diner window. The woman smiles across the crowded room at Kate. Then she points to the sign, and Kate nods and waves her over to her. But not before she has noticed something. That Billy has sat up a little straighter. That Billy is rising to his feet, making his way toward them.

"Hi, I'm Kallie," she says with a rich, rolling accent. And puts out her hand. "And I've come home to Alabama." Kate takes her hand, round and firm, looks her in the eye, and smiles. And as Kallie reaches up and removes her hat and shakes out her hair, Kate turns her around and introduces her to her nephew. Billy runs his fingers through his newly manicured hair. And smiles. Yes, it is a great and historical party. A celebration that will wear long into the evening until, overflowing with happiness, the people will find their way back to their homes. Full of the good life and all that it contains this night.

All is quiet, all is still when God takes his evening walk through Shibboleth. His hands are in his pockets, and he is whistling a new tune. The tune is carried up on the wind, into the night, where it settles on the hearts of all the people as they lie sleeping. It is a different song. Something ages old and yet just now created.

The song brings old, dormant dreams to life again. It plants new dreams as yet unknown. And the old dreams and the new dreams will spring forth with great power and great fruition. Because the dream and the people will no longer be separate. The dream and the people will be one. And the dream will be the song that is played out through their living lives. Listen. It is a mesmerizing song, full of possibility and of purpose. Full of purity and of passion. It is the song of Shibboleth.

It is a song of peace.

The *Everlasting* End

—∾ *Acknowledgments* ∾—

The Messenger of Magnolia Street was written in solitude. Some of these people protected the silence of that season. Some prayed for its completion. Some read the work in progress and fed me comments from time to time. Some fed me food and conversation so I wouldn't get lost in the alone. And some of them bore the fruit forward that it might find its way into your hearts, into your lives.

Here they are. I applaud them every one.

Mom, thank you for teaching me to love the world of written words and for introducing me to sacred space. Dad, the work continues without you but never without your memory by my side. Sister, without you, without us, I couldn't have written Nehemiah and Billy. They exist because we do. Cousin Deb, what a great adventure we are. Thank you for that late night magic when Messenger was discovered. Mother Nancy and the Hicks clan, your honest support means more than you realize. Sylvia Odenwald, you made these words shine and kept me moving forward. Marcia Pitts, you loved these words from their very inception, and fanned the wind beneath my wings. Shirley Holland, Anna Gee, Susan Benson, and Linda Sheffield Dykes, your prayers encircled me by day and by night. Look here, the blessing of your secret labors. Dorothy Padron, you are my unexpected angel in disguise. Fran Oppenheimer, I hope someday to possess your humor and your glorious, giving heart. Jill Grinberg, your savvy and passion continue to shape my life. Renee Sedliar, you invited me to the dance and kept me in perfect time. You bless my boots off, you do. Michael Maudlin, your guiding wisdom continues to shape this story by wonderful design. The team of HarperSanFrancisco, for every unique, incredible gift you've invested in this novel, a thousand good cheers. Owen Hicks, what can I say, my love, but thank you for everything and for always. And for you, dear reader, for embracing *The Messenger of Magnolia Street*, cast forward now on the shores of time.